Tan Lines

by
Bob Adamov

Packard Island Publishing

*Bill,
Enjoy this Presidential adventure! My best,
Bob [signature] 4/30/11*

Other *Emerson Moore* Adventures by Bob Adamov

Rainbow's End	Released October 2002
Pierce the Veil	Released May 2004
When Rainbows Walk	Released June 2005
Promised Land	Released July 2006
The Other Side of Hell	Released June 2008

Next **Emerson Moore** Adventure: *Sanduste*

ISBN: 0-9786184-2-4
978-0-9786184-2-1

Library of Congress Number: 2010924892

Cover art by Red Incorporated
Cover photo by Bob Adamov

Submit all requests for reprinting to:
BookMasters, Inc.
PO Box 388
Ashland, Ohio 78735

Published in the United States by:
Packard Island Publishing, Wooster, Ohio

www.bookmasters.com
www.packardislandpublishing.com
www.BobAdamov.com

First Edition – June 2010

Printed in the United States

Acknowledgements

For technical assistance, I'd like to express my appreciation to John Herrick Jr., former Assistant White House Deputy Press Secretary; Dr. Jeff Reutter, Director - Ohio Sea Grant College Program, F.T. Stone Laboratory, The Ohio State University; Matthew Richmond with the Navy SEALs, Captain Pat Thompson of the Sandusky tug, *Jesse*; David Noble of the Noble Foundation; JD Owen, former sniper and a Put-in-Bay singer; John Hageman, The Ohio State University's Stone Lab Co-Manager; and Chief Warrant Officer Jay Franklin of the U.S. Coast Guard Station at Marblehead. Special thanks go to my long-time friends for their coaching – Bill Market at the Miller Ferry and Dale McKee at Island Transportation.

I also would like to extend my appreciation to Put-in-Bay's Tim Niese, who owns the world's longest underwater bar, Splash, for sponsoring the "book cover girl contest" in the novel. And a special thank you to cover girl winner, Lauren Decoeur! It was one of the most interesting events that I've had to judge!

I'd like to thank my team of editors: Hank Inman of Goldfinch Communications, David Noble, Jackie Buchwalter, Cathy Adamov, Sam Adamov, Bob Adamov Jr., and the one and only Joe Weinstein.

I'd like to acknowledge Bruce Kenfield and Wayne Valero, who run the Clive Cussler Collector's Society and introduced me to my hero, Clive Cussler. And a special thank you to Cris Kohl from Seawolf Communications and Great Lakes shipwreck hunter Dave Trotter for your role in linking me to Clive Cussler. I'd be remiss if I didn't acknowledge gregarious Ralph Wilbanks, discoverer of the Confederate submarine, *The Hunley*.

Dedication

This book is dedicated to my beautiful, loving and caring sweetheart of a wife, Cathy, and to my mother, Anne Adamov, who has been the consummate inspiration to me to reach for the stars. I'd also like to dedicate this book to Uncle Mike and Aunt Jo Janick in Harrodsburg, Kentucky, who have been enjoying this writing adventure with me almost as much as I have.

Donations

The **Stone Lab** will receive a portion of the proceeds from the sale of this book.

If you would like to help with the restoration of **Cooke Castle,** please send your donation to:

Cooke Castle Restoration
The Ohio State University
1314 Kinnear Road
Columbus, Ohio 43212

If you'd like to support the **Stone Lab's Sustaining Fund,** which is used for equipment purchases to support courses and research at the Lab, please mail your donations to:

Stone Lab Sustaining Fund
The Ohio State University
1314 Kinnear Road
Columbus, Ohio 43212

Checks should be made payable to OSU. Donors can also donate to these funds on line at http://stonelab.osu.edu/fosl/give/

For more information, check these sites:

www.ohioseagrant.osu.edu
www.MillerFerry.com
www.cusslersociety.com
www.Put-in-Bay.com

They that wait upon the Lord shall renew their strength; they shall mount up with wings as eagles; they shall run, and not be weary; and they shall walk, and not faint. – Isaiah 40:31

Lake Erie Islands

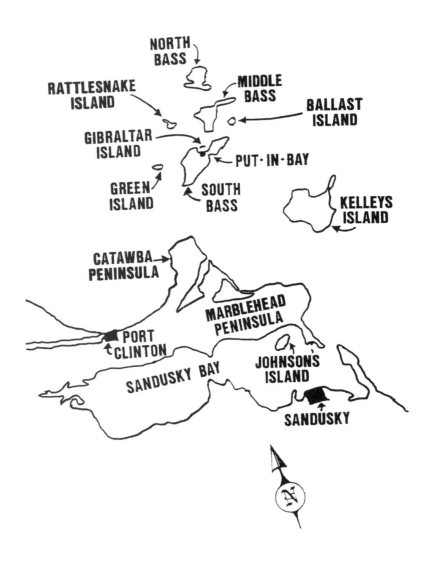

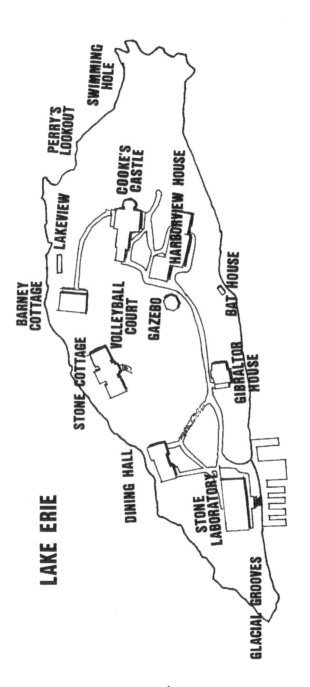

Gibraltar Island

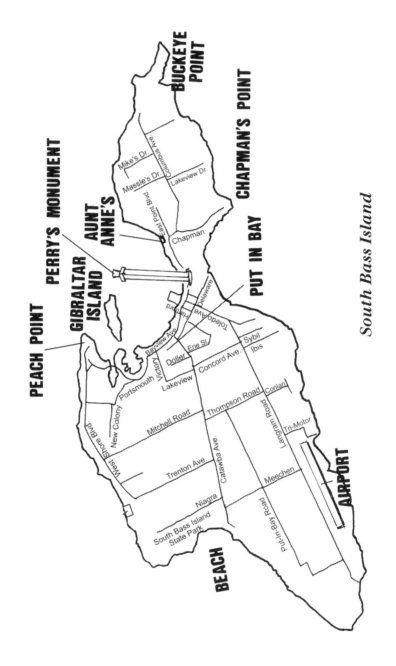

South Bass Island

Put-in-Bay
South Bass Island, Lake Erie

"I'm scared! You have to come home. Come home now," she pleaded. She moved to the window and nervously pulled the curtain aside so that she could peer out. "He's here again!" she screamed.

"You're sure it's him?" her husband asked as his blood pressure began to skyrocket.

"I'm positive. Who else would follow me like that? I tell you he's stalking me!" Stepping away from the window, she wiped away the tears streaming down her face. She began to shake. "I need you to come home now!"

"Where is he? I'll run him down with the truck!" her husband replied as he stood from his desk. He reached to his chest and ripped off his badge, throwing it onto the wooden desk. It bounced twice on the desk and then onto the floor where it spun into a corner. He decided that he wouldn't need his badge for what he was about to do.

"Across the street. He's leaning against the light pole," she sobbed.

"When I'm done with him, he'll be part of the light pole!" He paused for a second, then added, "Permanently! Stay put! I'll be there in two minutes." He threw the phone onto its cradle and began to race through the station.

Seeing the strained look on the officer's face, Put-in-Bay Chief of Police Chet Wilkens asked, "Larry, what's wrong?"

"It's that kid again! He's stalking Cindy!"

Wilkens raced across the room and grabbed one of Larry Straylor's arms to restrain him. "You're not running out of here like that! Especially when I see that your badge is missing." Looking more closely, he offered, "Probably ripped it out by the looks of it." Turning he yelled to two nearby officers, "Come on boys. Larry needs back up."

The four police officers raced up the steps from the basement station and to the Chevy Suburban parked in the alley. They quickly pulled onto Catawba Avenue and drove the four blocks to the Straylor house.

As they approached the house they saw the lanky, seventeen-year-old youth. He had a sarcastic grin on his face as the Suburban screeched to a halt in front of him. He barely flinched.

The officers poured out of the vehicle and surrounded the youth.

Before anyone could speak, the youth asked, "Isn't this a bit of an overkill? Four policeman to take down one kid?"

Straylor stepped forward. His face was beet red with anger. "I don't need any help on this one, guys."

"You need more than you think," Wilkens said as he clamped a firm grip on Straylor's shoulder and restrained him.

Straylor twisted to the right and freed himself. He started for the kid. "You stay away from my wife, Eastwood."

"I can't. She's my teacher," Eastwood smirked.

"Don't get smart with me. You've been stalking her. Wherever she goes, she sees you watching her."

Straylor was stretching the truth.

Eastwood pushed the envelope. "But she's such a pretty lady."

The comment pushed Straylor over the edge. He attacked Eastwood. His hands went to Eastwood's throat and began choking him. The two fell to the ground. Eastwood was twisting to escape. As they grappled, the other officers moved to separate them. Within a minute, the two were pulled apart. Eastwood had blood dripping from a blow to his nose.

"Put him in the Suburban," Wilkens ordered and the two officers lead the subdued teenager to the vehicle. Eastwood willingly sat in the back seat and watched as Wilkens and Straylor walked across the street to the Straylor home. Wilkens was lecturing Straylor as they walked.

"You need to restrain yourself. You can't let that kid push your buttons."

"But look at what he's been doing to Cindy."

"And what is that?"

"The stalking. He's everywhere she goes. Mind me, it's only a matter of time before he does something physical to her."

"Why do you say that?"

"He's always leering at her in class. He flirts with her. He's seeing how far he can push this and then, he'll take the next step. But, I'm not going to let that happen."

Wilkens looked at his hotheaded friend. He tried to go the extra mile whenever he could, but attacking a kid the way Straylor had was not acceptable behavior for a police officer. Wilkens sighed as they climbed the steps to the house. He knew that he'd have to take disciplinary action against Straylor. Straylor had crossed the line in attacking the youth.

"Hello, Cindy," Wilkens said as the woman stepped out of the house. She was sobbing as she threw her arms around her husband. Her husband responded by hugging her as he tried to comfort her.

"Honey, everything's going to work out," Straylor said as his lips brushed his wife's left ear, which was partially hidden by her thick, blonde hair. "I kicked his ass. He'll leave you alone now."

"I'd suggest dropping that talk, Larry," Wilkens said sternly. Wilkens looked at Straylor's wife. "Did Eastwood come on your property?"

"No," she said as she wiped the tears from her eyes and turned to face Wilkens.

Wilkens couldn't help but notice how attractive she was. Her long hair framed a porcelain-like face with pouty lips. Although she was slender, her frame carried her large bust well and the tight tee shirt seemed to draw attention to it. Her blue eyes were red from crying.

"Has he made any threatening remarks to you?" Wilkens asked as he began to take notes on the notepad, which he had extracted from his pocket.

"Not threatening, but it seems like he is always looking for an opportunity to flirt with me."

"Is he saying anything inappropriate?"

"He doesn't have to. The kid's creepy," Straylor interrupted.

Wilkens threw him a look. It told Straylor to shut up. Straylor wanted to hear the questions and answers, so he held his tongue.

"Once again, has Eastwood said anything inappropriate?"

"Yes."

"Like what?"

"I like your outfit today. You hair looks nice. I love your blue eyes. Stuff like that."

Writing quickly in his notebook, Wilkens continued. "Has he touched you?"

Straylor's eyes were riveted on his wife. His face began to redden again as he anticipated the response.

"He's brushed up against me a couple of times, but that's it."

Straylor couldn't contain himself and he burst out, "I'll kill that little piece of…"

Wilkens interrupted him. "Larry, that's quite enough out of you. I've respected our relationship and allowed you to remain here as we go through the questioning. I can't have you making threats, especially as a police officer." Wilkens turned his head and called to one of the two policemen standing next to the Suburban. "Don, can you come over and walk Larry back to the station?"

"Sure can," the officer said as he walked over to the porch.

"Larry, I want you to go with Don. You're too much of a distraction here. We need to focus on the facts of the case."

"I don't think so. I'm staying with my wife," Straylor retorted angrily as he pulled his wife's body against him. "She needs my support."

Wilkens stepped over to the couple and gently began to separate them. "Come on Larry. Work with me on this."

Straylor allowed them to be pulled apart and walked down the steps. "Chet, I expect this to be resolved. If you can't do it, I will."

Wilkens nodded to the other officer, who guided Straylor to the sidewalk and began walking him to the police station. Wilkens turned back to Cindy, who was now sitting on the porch railing.

"So, he brushed against you? Has this happened often?"

"Just a couple of times."

"And did he say anything to you after he brushed against you?"

"No, he just leered at me for a moment and then turned away."

"Were there any witnesses to the times he brushed against you?"

Cindy thought for a moment. "No, there weren't. The kid's pretty smart about that."

Wilkens closed his notepad. "It's going to be difficult to do anything about it at this point. I'm sure that's not what you and Larry want to hear."

"It isn't," she replied with a look of concern on her face.

"The only thing I can counsel you to do, as best you can, is to make sure that you're not alone with him. If he's stalking you, make a note about it and call us. We'll see what we can do."

"Thanks, Chet," she said as Wilkens began to walk down the steps.

"Wish we could do more at this point, but I'm afraid that we can't. Maybe we could do something about him loitering in front of your house."

"Anything would be appreciated."

Wilkens walked over to the Suburban and opened the rear door. He stared at the occupant in the back seat. "Think you're pretty smart, don't you?"

Eastwood didn't reply. Instead he threw a sarcastic look at Wilkens.

"Let me give it to you straight, son. We've got a couple of things going here. First, we're going to build a case against you. Larry and his wife are good people on this island. I'm going to make sure that nothing interferes with their quality of life. So, you better watch what you do. Understand me?"

Eastwood remained silent.

"Second, you've got a very angry and armed husband, who would like nothing better to do than kill you. So, if I was Mr. Cody Eastwood, I'd be real careful about what I did on this island. I might also think that it'd be a damn good idea to move to a healthy climate. You catch my drift?"

Eastwood nodded his head affirmatively.

"Now, get out of my vehicle. I'm probably going to need it disinfected after having vermin like you sit in it."

Wilkens was very pointed in his comments as he strived to underscore the seriousness of the situation to Eastwood. Eastwood slid across the seat and stepped out of the vehicle. Without saying anything, he began walking home.

Wilkens didn't need any stalkers on his little island paradise, especially one who'd stalk a police officer's wife.

The popular island resort village of Put-in-Bay is located on South Bass Island, about three miles off the Catawba Peninsula in the western basin of Lake Erie. South Bass and its neighboring islands are about an hour west of Cleveland and forty minutes east of Toledo. Visitors, fishermen and boaters from throughout the Midwest are attracted to the islands for numerous recreational activities and sometimes a wild nightlife with partying in the bars and on the docks and the boats in the harbor. Put-in-Bay is known as the "Key West of the Midwest." Like its namesake, it has its share of island characters.

Somewhere in the Mideast
Eight Years Later

The large air-conditioned room offered a respite from the rising heat outside the low narrow building. From the outside, it looked nondescript, fitting in well with the area buildings. Standing in front of the doors, lounged a uniformed guard. His AK-47 was leaning casually against the doorframe, as he took a deep draw on his cigarette.

Across the street was another plainclothes guard. His AK-47 was stashed within arm's reach in a tall box. He didn't want to draw any attention to himself. If the first guard incurred any trouble, he would provide back up support.

Inside the building were a number of small offices and a state of the art data center. The data center provided the support for the largest room in the building. In that room worked thirty teenage girls. Each sat at a desktop computer.

Sixteen-year-old Aisha adjusted her headscarf as she sat back for a moment. She was proud of her work. The government had been teaching her English since she was twelve and it had been twelve months since she had been recruited for her new job.

She was taught computer skills and trained in the art of internet searching using Google. She had been provided with a list of key words and phrases to search. Using specially designed hacking software, she was adept in mining information from blogs, Facebook, My Space and Linked In on targeted subjects.

Even if the targeted subject didn't have an account or page with blog, Facebook, My Space and Linked In, she could search for data, which was innocently posted by family members, friends or business acquaintances. She could create accurate profiles of targets by pulling together the data and photos. The profiles would be augmented with information gleaned from newspaper stories and photos or public records. Aisha was constantly amazed by the details naïve Americans posted to public websites.

Working diligently, Aisha had quickly become one of the top researchers in her unit. She and her family had received several financial awards, but she was focused on being rewarded with a nicer apartment for her family and more state-paid education.

For the last two months she had been given instruction to focus on Detroit, a city in the United States. The city name was familiar to her as she remembered the terrorist attempt to blow up a landing jetliner on Christmas Day, in 2009.

Her fingers flew across the keyboard as she searched the key words: military, defense, financial difficulty and boat. Her efforts had rewarded her with two potential targets and she had been building a profile on them. They were Dan Delton and Bruce Carlyle. Both men worked for defense contractors and were bloggers.

From their careless posts to blogs, she was able to pull blog comments like: "I can't say how I know," "big military projects," and "security clearance." One day, she had a hit on the same thread with Carlyle. It read "financial difficulty."

As she read the blog closely, she was startled to hear her supervisors voice over her shoulder. "Aisha?"

"Yes," she responded as she jerked back from her computer screen.

"Don't waste any more time on this Delton file."

Aisha nodded her head. Her place was not to ask questions. Her supervisor was aware that Delton had died unexpectedly, but he saw no need to tell the sixteen-year-old.

"I just found new information on Carlyle," she said as she pointed to the blog where Carlyle had made a passing comment about personal financial difficulty.

"Good." A smile crossed the supervisor's face. "Stay with it," he encouraged her as he turned and walked back to his office.

Once he was in his office, the supervisor accessed Carlyle's on-line profile and began to read the intelligence, which had been captured by Aisha's internet research. Carlyle was in senior management at a defense contractor in Detroit. He resided on a small island south of Detroit. It was called Grosse Ile. He was married to Donna and had two children. Jimmy was ten and played in a baseball league on the island. Michelle was eight and took dance lessons. There were photos and clippings from internet stories and the local newspaper, The Ile Camera.

Carlyle lived in a large waterfront home on the east side of the island on East Shore Road and belonged to the Grosse Ile Yacht Club. He owned a large boat which he kept docked at the club or, sometimes, at the dock in front of his home.

Personal financial difficulty, the supervisor smiled sinisterly as he typed an e-mail and forwarded the file to his boss. This is exactly what they were looking for.

The Restaurant
Alexandria, Virginia

For the tenth time in the last five minutes, the white-haired man in the rumpled blue suit checked his watch. Where could he be? he wondered to himself.

"More coffee?" the waitress asked as she appeared magically at the tableside.

"No," Jim Benko growled impatiently as he rubbed his unshaven face. He had taken a cab directly from Dulles Airport to the restaurant after he had arrived from his red eye flight from the west coast. He didn't like to be up and about looking unkempt. It ran contrary to how he had been trained.

With a scowl, he glanced toward the entranceway and saw a tall, distinguished figure in a gray pin stripe suit talking to the hostess. She pointed to Benko's table. The new arrivee thanked her and walked confidently through the crowded restaurant.

Benko watched the tall praying mantis approach his table. His hair was getting thinner and the ashen face had a few more wrinkles on it since the last time the two of them had seen each other. It had been five years ago. They had been roommates together during their college days. And though they had taken different paths, they still managed to get together every once in a while to catch up, or at least to talk about matters which they could without breaking any confidentiality or security clearance restrictions.

"You're looking scruffy," he said, thrusting his hand out.

Standing, Benko grasped his old friend's hand. "It was the flight. Everything okay?"

"For the most part," the visitor said as he quickly scanned the restaurant to see if he knew anyone or whether anyone was taking undue interest in them.

"Why are we meeting here and not your favorite place for breakfast?" Benko asked.

"Too many folks in the business there. The odds were higher that we'd bump into someone I know."

Benko wrinkled his brow. "Must be something important that you want to discuss."

"To an extent, yes." Before he could continue, the waitress re-appeared and took their order. The visitor moved his chair closer to Benko and leaned toward him. "I'm sorry you didn't get the promotion."

A scowl crossed Benko's face. "Politics. That's all it was. You know, sometimes I hate my job."

"I understand."

"You of all people would certainly understand. I do my best. I keep a low profile."

"As you must."

"And they promote Arness. Mr. Kiss Up!"

The two of them watched as a man in a wheelchair navigated his way through the restaurant to the table next to them.

"You know, Jim, I've always wanted the best for you. I've been a friend and supporter of yours over the years."

Benko nodded his head.

"Jim, if there was anything I could do to take your pain, I'd do it."

"I know."

The man in the wheelchair had placed his order and pulled out his iPod, inserting the ear buds into his ears. His head began to move to the beat of the music as he listened.

Ignoring the man at the next table, the conversation continued. "Jim, I may need your help with something."

"Yes?"

"This is big." He looked directly into Benko's soul. "This is very big and, once I tell you, there's no turning back."

Benko lowered his eyes and stared at the white tablecloth as he thought. He knew that they could trust each other and he also new how lethal his friend could be. He looked at his friend. "If you didn't think I'd be interested, you'd never have contacted me. So, it must be good. What is it?"

He leaned closer and began to outline the plan. As he listened, Benko's eyes widened in disbelief at what he was hearing.

"Are you sure?"

"Yes. He's a traitor and there's a small group of us who mean to address it." The visitor leaned closer and gave him more details.

"But certainly Congress will want to be involved. They'll want to take action!"

"It would be a long drawn out affair and hurt the strength of the county. Our plan provides for a quiet alternative. No fuss. No messy situations to clean up."

Benko sat back. He was stunned at the audacity of the plan. "How do you know that you can trust me with this information? This is much more serious than I guessed."

"Come on, Jim. How many years have I known you?"

Benko smiled weakly.

"I'm not worried that you'd do something stupid with this information."

The waitress, who had reappeared with their meals, interrupted them as she set the order on the table.

"I lost my appetite," Benko said as he pushed the plate of ham and eggs away from him. He picked up the white porcelain cup and sipped the black coffee.

"To continue what I was going to say, I'm not worried about you, Jim. Besides, I know where your mother is living now. It's at Shady Lawn Assisted Living, isn't it?"

Benko's head snapped around as he stared directly into the visitor's eyes. "You leave my mother out of this. And don't you think for one second that I'd tolerate you harming her."

"I didn't mean for you to feel that I was threatening her," the visitor lied as he smiled at Benko's reaction. He had scored a direct hit.

"You stayed at my house one summer. She cooked your meals. She did your laundry. And now, you're threatening to harm her?"

"I didn't say that."

"Cut the crap! You and I both know what you're doing. We've been in the business too long to play games with each other," Benko stormed. He took another drink of his coffee as his eyes glared over the cup's rim at the visitor. "Cut to the chase. What do you want from me?"

"Help. I'll be in touch when I need it. Can I count on it?"

"I'll think about it."

"Just be sure you do your thinking quietly," the visitor warned as he stood and threw cash on the table to pay for the uneaten breakfast. He hadn't touched his food either.

Benko jumped up from his chair as he faced the master of deceit in front of him. He jabbed his finger into the other man's chest. "Don't threaten me." He turned and walked briskly out of the restaurant.

The visitor watched Benko walk out. He knew that their conversation would remain confidential. A smile crossed his face as he smiled at the progress he had made in their first meeting. It had progressed as he had expected. Benko could be emotional and hotheaded at times. He had been like that since they had first known each other.

"You didn't like the breakfast?" the waitress asked as she began to clear the table.

"We both had some bad news and lost our appetites."

"I'm sorry," she said as she continued to clean the table. The visitor turned and walked out of the restaurant area.

A few minutes later, the man in the wheelchair pulled his ear buds out of his ears and switched off the iPod. He paid his bill and wheeled himself out of the restaurant. As he passed through the lobby area, he exited the door into the parking lot. It was a beautiful spring morning. The cherry blossoms were budding throughout the city. He wheeled himself behind the building to where his car was parked, partially hidden.

As he approached the car, he pulled the key fob from his pocket and popped open the trunk. He stood from the chair and collapsed it. Next, he threw the wheelchair into the trunk and closed it. He casually walked to the driver's door and pulled it open, smiling to himself as he did. He was anxious to return to the office and reveal what he had discovered. This was huge.

He was so caught up in his thoughts, that he lost touch with his surroundings. He didn't hear the approaching footsteps. Before he could enter the car, the barrel of a pistol with a silencer affixed was pressed against the back of his head. Before he could react, the trigger was pulled and the gun fired, ending the agent's life. The agent's body dropped to the ground.

With an evil smile, the gunman quickly searched through the pockets of the man's jacket and found the iPod. He quickly examined it and smiled. "Just as I thought. A listening device."

He pocketed the iPod and walked to his Mercedes. His hunch had proven itself. But then again, he was a survivor. He had spent his life using his specially honed skills. He started the car's engine and drove away as a pool of blood seeped from the dead agent's head and flowed like a small red stream into the parking lot.

William Harrison Taggart turned left as he exited the parking lot and pointed his car toward Washington and his final destination, the White House.

Grosse Ile, Michigan
A Few Weeks Later

Grosse Ile is the largest of several islands in the Detroit River. They are south of Detroit and north of the mouth of the river where it flows into Lake Erie. They are much more heavily populated than the Lake Erie islands. Grosse Ile is filled with large homes owned by executives in a variety of industries who worked in nearby Detroit.

At the rear of a large home fronting the Detroit River, the garage door shut on its well-oiled hinges. A late model white Cadillac eased down the driveway and paused at the end. Its driver gazed at the main channel of the Detroit River for a moment and then drove south along East Shore Road.

Bruce Carlyle was deep in thought as he drove. His mind was disturbed with issues regarding an upcoming renewal of his company's defense department contract. If it wasn't renewed, it'd create additional financial stress for Carlyle. So engrossed in thought was he that he didn't notice a white Nissan Altima, which had been parked along the river's edge, pull in behind him and begin to follow him at a discreet distance.

Carlyle's Cadillac traveled across the island on the Grosse Ile Parkway and the Free Bridge, also known as the lower bridge. He sped toward his office in Flint. Thirty minutes later, he pulled into a parking garage. The white Nissan parked in a space outside of the garage and its occupant waited.

Following his daily routine, Carlyle emerged from the parking garage and walked directly across the street to the Das Koffee House to grab a cup of Columbia brew and a Danish roll to take back to his office. A few moments later, he paid for his purchase and turned abruptly, knocking into a nicely dressed gentleman. His coffee swished over the edge and onto the man's tie and shirt.

"Oh, I am so sorry," Carlyle apologized as he reached for a napkin to wipe the stain from the gentleman's tie and shirt.

"Not to worry," the man responded. "It's an old shirt and I never did like the tie. My mother-in-law bought it for me for Christmas," he smiled at Carlyle.

Smiling weakly, Carlyle responded, "Yeah, I know how it is with those mother-in-law gifts." He looked at the coffee stain on the shirt and tie and reached into his pocket to extract a few bills. "Let me at least make a donation toward your next purchase."

"I wouldn't hear of it," the gentleman said. "The next time I see you in here, you can buy my coffee."

Glancing at his watch and seeing that he was running late, Carlyle readily agreed. "Fine, then. Next time. The coffee is on me."

The gentleman smiled, "As long as it's not on me again."

Carlyle shook his head. He raced for the door and headed toward his office.

Two days later, Carlyle walked through the door of the coffee shop and saw the victim of the spilled coffee. The man was standing two ahead of him in line. Carlyle excused himself as he brushed by the people and made his way to the gentleman.

"My turn to buy," he said as he eased up next to the man.

"What? Oh, it's you," the man said with feigned recognition. Little did Carlyle know that the man had been watching for Carlyle to cross the street from the parking garage and then had taken his place in line to purchase coffee. "Spill any more coffee on people?" he joked.

"Nope. Been very careful." Carlyle saw that they were approaching the counter and asked, "What will you have?"

"Columbian."

"Make mine a morning blend," Carlyle said as he placed his order.

While they waited, the gentleman introduced himself. "By the way, my name is Al Hanna."

"Glad to meet you, Al. I'm Bruce Carlyle." Carlyle paused and then continued, "Were you able to get the stain out of your shirt and tie?"

"I didn't even try. Just tossed them in the trash." Hanna looked around the room and then lowered his voice as he pitched his bait. "My company is having a very good year. The defense industry has been very good to us."

Carlyle's eyes widened. "You're in the defense industry? So am I!"

The server interrupted them as she set the order on the counter. "Keep the change," Carlyle said. Turning to Hanna, he asked, "Do you have a few minutes to talk?"

Hanna looked at his watch and responded. "Certainly."

"Good." Carlyle spotted a couple getting up from a table near the front window. "Let's grab that table."

The two men moved quickly to the table and sat.

"What type of contracts are you working on?" Carlyle asked.

Before responding, Hanna scanned the room. "I'm not in a position to discuss it, if you know what I mean," he said in a hushed tone.

Nodding his head, Carlyle said, "I get it. Intel, huh?"

Hanna would only raise his eyebrows in response.

His mind raced about the possibility of building a relationship with Hanna in case he lost his job. Who knows, he thought, maybe Hanna could help him find a job with his company. Hanna could be his safety net.

"Business is doing very well?" Carlyle asked.

"Very well, as I mentioned earlier."

"Wish I could say the same, Al."

"Tough year?"

"You know competition."

"Do you work near here, Bruce?"

"Across the street." Carlyle pointed at the office complex.

Hanna looked toward the building and back at Carlyle. "What type of work do you do? Are you in finance, purchasing...?"

Carlyle interrupted him. "My degree is in aerospace engineering."

"What a coincidence! So am I." Hanna's intelligence on Carlyle had already provided him with the information, but he had to act surprised. It was all part of the plan to reel him in. "I'm a Virginia Tech grad."

Beaming at the disclosure of the information, Carlyle responded, "University of Michigan grad. I stayed local."

With the bond growing between the two men, Hanna needed to advance to the next step in his plan. Hanna gazed across the street at the large building for a moment before speaking again. "With your business being down, it must hit you hard in your wallet."

Nodding his head slowly, Carlyle commented, "That's an understatement. I'm not sure that I'm getting a bonus this year. That's going to kill me." Carlyle was surprised at himself. He did not normally share information about his finances with anyone, but for some reason, he felt comfortable with the affable Hanna.

"That's tough." Hanna sipped his coffee. Placing the cup back on the table, he looked at Carlyle and lowered his voice as he spoke. "From time to time we have projects that we need help on. I could pay you for your help. I could do it under the table so that you wouldn't have to claim it on your income tax return." Hanna lifted his cup to drink again; his eyes looking over the rim of the cup at Carlyle to see if he'd take the bait.

Carlyle stared at his coffee for a moment as he gathered his thoughts. He knew that he needed the money to maintain his lifestyle on Grosse Ile. His wife had been pushing to have their daughter take expensive ballet lessons from an instructor up-river. He was also more worried about his other financial obligations, including the cost of running his boat.

He raised his eyes and looked around the room before asking his next question. "What kind of projects are they, Al? You know, I couldn't do anything which would violate the covenants I've signed with my employer or the Department of Defense."

"Bruce, we wouldn't want you to do anything that would compromise any covenants or what you work on currently. I could call you and explain what the project is and how many hours we'd need your help. You could then decide if there are any conflicts and whether you'd like to work on the project."

"Sounds fair." Carlyle took another sip of coffee. "Have you given any thought as to the pay for these projects?"

"If we could outsource them to you and you could have them done in a week or so, the pay could range from a couple of thousand to ten thousand. It just depends on the project."

Dollar signs flashed across Carlyle's mind. He sighed at the thought of having additional cash flow coming in to meet their obligations. "Count me in."

"Good," Hanna said as a smile filled his face. "We have a project now which we need help on. Could I bring it to your house tonight to discuss?"

Thinking quickly, Carlyle remembered that his wife and children would be at a ballet event that evening. "That would be fine." Carlyle produced a business card and wrote his home address and cell phone number on the back of the card. He then handed the card to Hanna.

Looking at the back of the card, Hanna feigned surprise as he exclaimed, "You live on Grosse Ile?"

"Yes, I do."

"I'm envious. My family and I plan to purchase a home there. It's been a dream of mine to take a boat ride around the island and down river to Lake Erie."

Carlyle had no idea how well he was being played. He responded to the bait. "I can help make that boat ride dream come true!"

"No way!"

"Yes. I have 62-foot Azimut, which I keep at the Grosse Ile Yacht Club. It's at the south end across from Sugar Island. I'd be happy to take you for a cruise. After we review the project parameters tonight, I'll take you out."

"This is absolutely unbelievable. I am so happy to have met you." Raising his cup, he toasted Carlyle. "To Bruce, may we have a long and mutually rewarding friendship."

Carlyle raised his cup and responded, "Here. Here. Next time, though, we need something stronger in our cups."

"I'll bring along wine tonight." Hanna reached into his pocket and extracted a business card for the dummy corporation they had set up. He handed the card to Carlyle. "Here's my contact info in case you need to get in touch with me."

Carlyle looked at the card and was curious when he didn't see a street address. The card showed a post office box. "No street address?"

"No, we don't provide one because of the nature of our business. You know, the Black Ops stuff."

"Oh, yeah."

The two closed their meeting and Carlyle walked across the street to his office. The missing street address on the business card nagged at him. He sat down at his desk and Googled the company. He saw that there were numerous references to the organization and hit on a few to see what he could learn. Although the information was limited, Carlyle told himself that it was due to the secrecy of the projects, which Hanna's company worked on. Little did he know that Hanna and his co-conspirators had been very thorough in setting up the dummy corporation and web site information. It was all a part of the plan.

Over the next few weeks, Hanna and Carlyle spent a significant time together evenings and weekends. They worked on projects and took numerous boat rides. Hanna made sure the projects paid handsomely. Carlyle didn't have a clue how he was being pulled into a spider web filled with intrigue and backstabbing.

Hanna didn't reveal that his real name was Eliazor Rahim. Benjamin Hanna was his deep cover alias. He had been in a Dearborn sleeper cell for years. Covertly he made several trips back for additional training. He had been comfortable with his ability to hide his identity and to blend into the community while waiting to be activated.

That day came sooner than expected when his cover was blown. He hadn't realized how effective the U.S. intelligence team was. Now, he had been turned and he was working for a special U.S. unit on a dangerous assignment. It was that or having false information fed back to the Taliban so that they could take repercussions on his mother and three sisters. Besides, the special unit had promised to extricate his mother and sisters from their perilous situation and bring them to the United States if he was successful with his mission. And he had every intention of being successful.

Put-in-Bay
South Bass Island
A Few Weeks Later

The rays from the early morning sun cast a warm glow on the mixture of watercraft bobbing gently at their moorings in the harbor. There was a hint of a westerly breeze.

On board one large boat, a small dog, wearing a red scarf, bounded onto the deck. Its ears perked up and it sniffed the air warily. A slight growl emerged from the terrier's throat as it stepped onto the swim platform and stared into the water. It paced back and forth on the swim platform as it growled. Seeing a ripple in the water, it paused and stared at the water. That was the terrier's mistake. With an anguishing bark, the small dog disappeared from the swim platform.

"Booty? What's wrong, girl?" the dog's owner called as he emerged from below deck onto the craft's main deck. He quickly scanned around for his little pet, but couldn't spot it.

As he moved toward the stern, he did spot something. Tears welled up in his eyes. Floating in the water, near the swim platform was a red scarf. It was Booty's scarf. He knelt down on the swim platform and bent over to retrieve the floating scarf, calling for his dog as he did.

"Booty. Booty. Where's my Booty?"

Just then the water at the stern of the boat swirled and churned. Out of the water surged a 40-foot tall, dark green sea monster. Its jaws were open, displaying two rows of sharp, pointed teeth. From its mouth a large roar erupted as one of its claws swept through the air. The lethal claw captured the stunned boater in its grip. It pulled the struggling and screaming boater to its mouth where it consumed its second meal of the day. The dog had been nothing more than an appetizer.

The sea monster's roar combined with the screams of the boater caused other boaters to race to their decks to see what was amiss. They stood in shock at the sight before them. Seeing more food to sample, the sea monster began making its way from boat to boat, smashing its claws through boats, grabbing their screaming occupants and sinking the boats as it gorged itself on the tasty morsels.

"Emerson, how can you sit there and watch something like that?"

Emerson Moore hit the off button on the remote and sat back in his chair. "I was just enjoying the special effects from this old movie. It's fun to watch how out of sync the movement of the Japanese actors' mouths is to the English voiceovers. It just cracks me up, Aunt Anne."

Emerson glanced at his Aunt Anne who was dusting her knick-knacks. "Maybe we've got a sea monster killing the fish here," he teased. "Maybe it's the Erie Dearie."

Moore was a *Washington Post* investigative reporter, who resided with his aunt on South Bass Island's East Point, which overlooked the resort town of Put-in-Bay and its inviting harbor. Moore had been filing stories on the massive fish kill on Lake Erie and had been working with The Ohio State University's Stone Lab on Gibraltar Island to determine the cause.

Aunt Anne paused and looked fondly at her tanned, 6-foot-2 nephew with glossy black hair and dark brown eyes. "Did you see the Cleveland Plain Dealer this morning?"

"Not yet."

"You might want to take a look at it. We've got fish kill here and they've got doctor kill in France," she responded.

"Another one?"

"Yes. That makes six of them. Why would anyone kill a doctor?"

"Over charged the patient?" Moore asked weakly.

"Emerson, that's not nice! They've got someone killing doctors in France and you joke about it!" She stormed out of the room in mild indignation.

Moore stood up and walked into the warmly decorated kitchen. He saw the newspaper on the table and picked it up. "I'll read it now," he said as he walked through the front room and onto the screened porch.

Sitting down, he allowed his eyes to gaze across the alluring harbor of Put-in-Bay. The Jet Express was rounding Gibraltar Island and approaching the harbor with a boatload of tourists. The docks at Axel and Harry's were filling with boats. He could see other craft at the city docks and at the mooring buoys.

Across the harbor on Gibraltar Island, he saw several people scurrying from the water taxi across the dock and up to Stone

Lab. Probably more technical people trying to determine the source of the fish kill.

The phone in the borrowed office began to ring and Moore set his coffee cup on the desk in front of him. Reaching for the phone, he answered it on the third ring.

"What took you so long, Moore? We don't run this operation on island time, you know!" the voice bellowed through the phone.

"Jamaica me happy, boss," Moore responded in the rhythmic style of a Caribbean islander.

"Cut the crap and come down to my office," John Sedler, Moore's editor, seethed as he slammed the phone on his desk and faced the doorway, waiting for Moore's arrival.

Moore replaced the phone in its cradle and looked at the clock on the wall as he stood. It read 9:00 a.m. Moore stretched and thought about his flight the previous afternoon and dinner last night with fellow reporter, Carrie Cupples. She had caught him up on the latest office gossip and a number of stories, which were in the works. He had known the dark-haired Cupples for ten years and they were good friends.

Moore walked to the end of the hallway and into Sedler's office.

"Close the door behind you," Sedler barked at his top investigative reporter.

Moore did as he was instructed and then sank his lanky frame into a chair in front of Sedler. He slowly raised one of his legs and placed his shoe on the top corner of Sedler's desk. It was something he did every time he spent time in Sedler's office because it always solicited a reaction from Sedler.

"How many times do I have to tell you? Don't put your smelly feet on my desk!"

"Oh, sorry, John. I always forget. I just forget where I am. At home on the islands, I don't wear shoes so you can be glad that I have them on today," Moore teased as he removed his shoe from Sedler's desk.

"I don't want to hear it!" Sedler said as he leaned forward in his chair and looked at Moore. "What I do want to hear is what's going on with that fish kill?"

"Don't know. I've been interviewing the fishing boat captains and what I'm hearing is that it's just affecting the perch. They're pulling in dead perch every day."

"And no one has any idea what's causing it?"

"Not really. I've got a follow up meeting with Jeff Reutter. He runs Ohio State's Stone Lab. It's on Gibraltar Island and across Put-in-Bay's harbor. They're heading up the analytics on this and coordinating all agency activities."

"I understand that it hasn't spread to all of Lake Erie or to any of the other Great Lakes."

"That's correet, John. It appears to be isolated in the western basin of Lake Erie, at least that's what I'm told by the fisherman."

"Think it's a virus?"

"Not sure what to think?"

"Terrorism?"

"No evidence of it yet."

"I want you to stay on top of this. For once, it looks like you're at the right place at the right time," the editor groused as his blue eyes peered from under thick eyebrows at Moore.

"You still want me at the convention?" Moore had been scheduled to cover President Benson's renomination to a second term at the national convention. It was being held an hour east of the islands in Cleveland's downtown convention center.

"You and everyone who's available. If Benson keeps Moran as his running mate, he'll lose for sure in November. He'll be a one term President just as his predecessor was with his national healthcare mess, high unemployment, the war overseas and his stimulus act."

"Do you use stimulants?" Moore teased.

Sedler glared at Moore. "Okay, that's enough out of you. Time to return to your island paradise, isn't it?" the crusty editor asked. "Finish your work here and get me that story on the fish kill!"

"I'm on it." Moore stood and walked over to the door where he paused as he looked back at Sedler. "You'll get your story." He smiled and walked out of Sedler's office to the office, which he had borrowed for the morning.

Sedler watched him walk away. He liked Moore. Moore reminded him of himself twenty years ago and he envisioned Moore replacing him at some point, if he'd be willing to leave his islands and return to Washington. But, Washington may be too much for Moore with the memories of his dead wife and son.

An hour later, Moore stepped out of the elevator and into the main lobby on the first floor. He walked past the security booth, which guarded the entrance to the elevators. He turned to his right and walked down four steps, where he paused to survey his surroundings.

He looked over his head at the newspaper's name, lettered in black. It stood out prominently against the building's tan bricks. The building on 15th Street stood upon the site of the original Saint Augustine Catholic Church, the oldest black Catholic Church in the nation's capital. It had been relocated to a new building in 1947 at 15th & U Street NW.

Moore's eyes took in Lee's Tailoring across the street, which reminded him that his slacks were fitting him a bit snuggly. He better watch what he was eating more closely, he thought to himself. He decided against going to Jack's Famous Deli, which he could also see across the street.

To the right, he could see Starbucks at the intersection with K Street; he knew that Caribou Coffee was located at the corner of 15th and M Street. Today, he opted for Caribou.

He glanced at his watch as he walked and planned the rest of his day. Once he had his coffee, he planned on driving over to the cemetery to visit the gravesites of his wife and son. They had been killed in a tragic auto accident years earlier. Their unexpected deaths had torn out Moore's heart and led him through several months of alcoholic despair.

Maple Hill Cemetery
Alexandria, VA

The rental car moved slowly through the tree-shaded winding lane of Alexandria's Maple Hill cemetery. The driver was struggling with his emotions as he neared the graves of his wife and son.

Mentally beating himself up, he felt that he had sacrificed time with his loved ones to cover stories and focus on his career. After their burial, Moore drowned himself in a sea of alcohol and self-pity. He would have lost his job had it not been for a very understanding Sedler cutting him some slack. Sedler had helped him qualify for FMLA and drove him to the alcohol abuse counseling center as well as to the psychologist, who had helped him with the emotional loss. It had been a long haul for Moore, but he had put it behind him.

The car slowed and pulled to the side of the lane where it parked. Its engine quieted as the driver turned the key to off. Behind the wheel, Moore wrestled with demons as his hands gripped the steering wheel. Long forgotten emotions rose to the top. This was the first time that he had visited the cemetery since their burial.

He sat quietly in the car, unable to move. He felt like a huge weight was on his shoulders and he couldn't exit the vehicle. He decided that he couldn't do it. He reached for the ignition key and started the car. His hand reached for the gearshift to put the car in drive. Then he stopped. He turned off the ignition and looked toward the verdant green knoll where his loved ones were.

He unhurriedly opened the door and began to plod toward the burial site. Reaching it, he looked down at the two grave markers and the names inscribed there, Julie Moore and Matthew Moore. Dropping to his knees, he ran his hands across each marker as if he could send positive touches to their bodies. They had been married for twelve years and Matthew was four-years-old at the time their lives had been snuffed out.

"I miss you both so much, " Moore murmured as he sat between the two graves. A sense of sadness began to overwhelm him as the emptiness he felt took control. His mind twisted like the center of a tornado as emotions began to overcome him. His head dropped and he sobbed.

Thirty minutes later, a voice called from behind Moore. "Tough, isn't it?"

Moore recognized the voice. Without turning around, Moore asked, "How did you know I would stop here today?"

"I didn't know for sure. Just had a feeling that you might this time. You've been dancing with the demons for too long. You need to release them." Sedler looked around the serene cemetery. "This is the first time you've been here since the funeral, right?"

There was a pause before Moore replied. "Yes."

Moore felt a hand grip his shoulder in a comforting way. "It's one day at a time, Emerson. I didn't lose my wife in an accident, but it's still tough."

"I remember. It was cancer."

The man next to Moore sighed. "Yes. And I'm still dealing with the loss every day. Boy, did I love that woman! Oh, the good times we had!" Sedler allowed a small smile to cross his usually stern face as he fondly recalled the special moments the two had enjoyed together as husband and wife.

Moore looked sideways at the black man, who was now standing next to him. "How did you know that I'd be here today?" he asked again, forgetting that he had asked previously.

"I just had a feeling when you left the office that you might head over here. I thought you could use a little encouragement so I left for the day," Sedler answered solemnly. "It sure took you awhile to get here. I thought I misread you."

"I stopped for coffee first. Then, I took my time driving over here. It wasn't easy. I started to turn back several times."

"I watched you pull up and gave you some private time before I walked over. Today was an important first step. I'm proud of you." Sedler patted Moore's shoulder. "I'm going to leave you now."

"I think I'll go too. I don't want to overdo it," Moore said.

Sedler faced Moore. "Stop running, Emerson."
Nodding his head twice, Moore responded, "I'm trying. Next time I'm in town, I'll come back here."

Sedler began to walk to the top of the hill to retrieve his car, which was parked on the other side. As he walked away, Sedler said, "That would be a good thing."

"John?"

Sedler paused at the top of the hill and turned. "What?"

"Thanks. I beat a few devils today."

"I'm glad I was here for you." Sedler turned and continued walking to his car. Moore headed to his car and then to the airport.

As he drove, he felt he was progressing. But it was a long road. He deeply missed his wife and son.

Cleveland Hopkins Airport
Cleveland, Ohio

After finishing his business in Washington, Moore caught a return flight to Cleveland where he retrieved his dark green Mustang convertible with its tan top. It was a warm and sunny afternoon so Moore decided to put the top down for the hour ride west to catch the ferry to South Bass Island.

He drove to the end of the Catawba Peninsula and pulled up to the Miller Ferry ticket booth where he produced his season pass. He was directed to lane #1 on the steel reinforced and concrete dock. There were two cars in front of him and within minutes ten cars had pulled in line behind him.

The loud blast from the ferry's horn announced the arrival of the *Wm Market*. Moore never tired of watching the ferries dock nor the rides back and forth between the mainland and South Bass Island. He found every ride to be idyllic and peaceful although a ride from the island to the mainland on a Saturday evening could be interesting. Then the ferry's main deck was filled with rowdy passengers, who had spent a significant part of the day at the island wineries and bars.

Like the three other ferries in the fleet, the *Wm Market* was painted in white and trimmed in bright blue. She was 96-feet long, had a beam of 38-feet and drew eight feet. She could carry 18 cars on her main deck and 280 passengers. The passenger deck was the deck raised over the rear third of the main deck. Perched above the passenger deck was the pilothouse.

The *Wm Market* had been built in 1993 in Sturgeon Bay, Wisconsin. Twin 3412 DITA Caterpillar diesel engines provided 1,300 horsepower of thrust to the two 42-inch props, pushing the craft through the strong current in the South Passage which runs between Catawba Peninsula and the Lime Kiln Dock on the south side of South Bass Island.

During the winter of 2009/10, her sister ferry, *Put-in-Bay*, underwent a mid-body extension to increase its length to 136-feet overall. Now it was able to carry up to eight additional full size automobiles and an additional 100 passengers.

The Miller Ferry business began in 1905 when two men, William M. Miller and Harry Jones, began harvesting ice in the bay and selling it to fishermen in the summer. They expanded their business to six charter boats for fisherman and provided water taxi service. When they realized there was an additional business opportunity, they attached a scow to one of the boats and began to ferry up to eight cars at a time to the island.

In 1978 Bill Market and his wife purchased the ferry boat company. Bill had been the manager of the business and a captain. When Bill Market passed away in November 2006, his three children, Bill, Scott and Julene, began to run the ferry business.

Of the three children, it was powerfully-built Bill Market with whom Moore had developed a strong friendship. It wasn't unusual to see Moore camped out in Market's Lime Kiln dock freight office talking up a storm. Market was well-read and enjoyed brainstorming story ideas with Moore when he worked on stories for the newspaper. Market also regaled Moore with lake stories and his personal adventures on the lake and the island. And Market had quite a few personal adventures to share!

It wasn't unusual to see the two of them in deep discussion at the end of the day while seated at The Goat Soup and Whiskey Restaurant on Catawba Avenue in Put-in-Bay between Heineman's Winery and Mother of Sorrows Catholic Church. In the winter, the two played highly competitive raquetball in the racquetball court behind Put-in-Bay's Crew's Nest.

Moore watched as the steel ramp was lowered from the arriving ferry's bow and the deckhands scurried to guide the vehicles onto the dock. Once the vehicles had driven by, there was a mass exodus of tourists from the upper and main decks. They walked across the ramp, past the line of waiting vehicles and up the hill to the parking lots where they had left their vehicles.

After a short wait, a Miller Ferry worker motioned to the first car in line to move forward and the vehicle boarding process commenced. Moore wheeled his convertible on deck and was directed to a space at the very stern of the ferry which suited him well. Cars parked near the bow had a tendency to get drenched when waves broke over the bow. By being in the stern, he didn't have to put the convertible top up.

Moore stepped from his car and took a position on the starboard side where he could enjoy the fresh lake breeze. As he leaned against the boat's frame, he watched as the passengers boarded and took the stairs to the passenger deck's seating area.

When the last of the passengers had boarded, the deckhands raised the ramp at the bow. The captain sounded three short blasts on the horn to signal that the ferry would be reversing its engines. The ferry began backing away from the Catawba Dock. Once they cleared the dock, the captain pushed the twin engines forward and the ferry headed due north at 10 miles per hour past Mouse Island for the 18-minute run to Lime Kiln Dock, which was at the southern point of South Bass Island.

From his vantage point in the stern, Moore looked toward a group of passengers, who had eagerly staked out positions at the bow of the boat. Moore smiled to himself as he waited for the ferry to hit the waves in the South Passage. He didn't have to wait long before the bow dropped suddenly. A massive amount of water sprayed over the bow, wetting the now shrieking passengers, who were hurriedly making their way aft to a dryer vantage point.

Moore chuckled. He could always spot the first-time ferry boat riders. They almost always received a water spray as part of their initiation to the islands. He turned back to watching the sea gulls. Their cries filled the air as they followed the ferry in hopes of enticing passengers to throw snacks at them. Moore always enjoyed the relaxing ferry boat rides.

The Park Hotel
Put-in-Bay

The golden rays from the early morning sun cast a warm sheen on her nude body as she stood at the bathroom window overlooking DeRivera Park and the harbor beyond. As she nervously talked in a hushed tone, she gazed at Gibraltar Island across the harbor.

She heard a noise behind her and spun around. Standing in the doorway, she saw her disheveled lover. He was only wearing his white dress shirt. Looking past him, she could see that the covers from the hotel room bed were strewn about the floor.

"What are you doing?" he asked.

"Nothing," she responded awkwardly as she snapped shut the cell phone and cast a quick glance to the park where she saw her caller standing next to an oak tree.

"I wouldn't say that talking on your cell phone is nothing," he said with a raised eyebrow as he approached her.

"I was just checking my messages."

He carefully grasped her arms and pulled them behind her back as he looked into her eyes before kissing her. "Are you sure you were just checking your messages?"

As their lips met and parted, she allowed a low moan to escape.

Smiling, he pulled back and looked into her eyes. "So, does that moan mean that there's nothing for me to worry about?"

"What do you think?" she asked and she pulled his taut body against hers and opened her mouth to kiss him deeply.

It was now his turn to moan. "Ready for round four?" he murmured.

Playfully breaking off the kiss and pushing him away, she asked, "Don't you ever get tired?"

"Not with you!"

When he tried to embrace her again, she squirmed out of his grasp. "You're going to make me miss my ferry ride. I've got to take my shower."

"Take the next ferry," he suggested as he began to close the space between them.

"I'll be late for work. No can do," she said firmly as she stepped into the shower and pulled the brightly colored curtain closed.

In seconds, the small bathroom was filled with the noise from the shower and her singing as she washed.

Seeing the cell phone on the window ledge, he walked over to it and picked it up. With the skill of someone trained to handle investigations, he quickly accessed her cell phone history. There he spied the call, which she had just ended. Both eyebrows rose when he saw the number. It was a number with a Washington area code.

He walked out of the bathroom and to the nightstand next to the bed. Picking up a pen, he jotted down the phone number and slipped it into his shirt pocket. Returning to the bathroom, he placed the cell phone on the window ledge and looked from the second floor room into the park below.

Because of the noise from the running water in the shower and her singing, he didn't hear the hotel room door open. He also didn't hear the intruder quietly stride across the room to the bathroom doorway. He did hear two soft coughs as the silenced gun was fired, but couldn't react as the two bullets entered the back of his head, killing him instantly. His body crumbled to the floor.

The intruder casually leaned against the white sink and waited for her to finish her shower. He didn't have to wait long as he heard the water turn off and the singing cease.

The curtain pulled back and she saw the body on the floor. Blood was coagulating on the white tile. Turning her head, she smiled at the intruder. "Good shooting!"

"It was a clean kill," he smiled.

"Too bad. He seemed like a nice guy, too."

"Yeah, they all do, don't they?"

"But this one was different."

"He had to be. Look at what his job was."

"True." She looked into the room and asked, "Did you bring my final payment?"

"Yes, I did," the intruder said coldly as he quickly raised the gun with its silencer. It coughed once, sending a bullet with deadly accuracy into her left eye.

Her body fell to the floor where it partially sprawled across the dead man's body. The intruder watched as her blood mixed with the first victim's and discolored the white tile floor.

The intruder carefully stepped around the two bodies and grabbed the cell phone from the ledge. He stuffed it into his pocket and walked into the room where he rifled through her purse and extracted her wallet. He saw a large bag of clothes, which the woman had purchased from Tamar and Danny at Lovella, the fashion apparel store a few doors away from the hotel. He searched through the bag in the event anything had been hidden there.

He went through the dead man's belongings and took his wallet and cell phone. Better to make this look like a robbery, he thought to himself as he stuffed the items and his weapon into a small backpack, which he had been wearing. He opened the room door and hung a Do Not Disturb sign on the outside door-knob.

Housekeeping is going to have their work cut out for them when they do finally decide to check the room, he mused to himself as he walked down the back stairway. He took off his gloves as he descended and stuffed them in the backpack.

Emerging at the rear of the building, he glanced around to make sure that there was no one around. He then began to whistle as he walked down the side alley and turned right onto Delaware Avenue. He stopped at the Village Bakery and pur-chased a cup of black coffee and one of Pauline's tasty baked goods.

Police Station
Put-in-Bay

"Chet?"

"Yes," Wilkens responded.

"Guess who's back on the island?" Donna Goodwill, the pretty green-eyed, red-haired dispatcher, teased.

"The mayor? Gee, I don't know."

"Cody Eastwood," she responded triumphantly.

"What?" Wilkens stood up from his chair and walked out of his office to the dispatcher.

"Yeah, that's right. I just got a call from one of my lady friends. She rode over with him on the Miller Ferry last night."

"Is she sure?"

"Oh, yeah. That's why she called me. She wanted to alert us to any potential trouble."

"Oh, boy," Wilkens said as he walked back to his office. "I better let Larry know."

Before he could call Larry to his office, his phone buzzed. It was Goodwill calling him. "Chet, it's Deb at the Park Hotel. They found two people murdered in a hotel room."

"What?"

"That's right. They've got two down. She said that one's a Secret Service agent. He'd been on the island for two days."

"Tell her not to let anyone go into the room. We'll be right there."

Wilkens stood from behind his desk and strode out of his office. "Larry, I need you to come with me. We've got two down at the Park Hotel."

Wilkens quickly explained what little he knew as they went up the steps and to the police vehicle.

"What's a Secret Service agent doing on the island?" Straylor asked.

"Don't know. He didn't check in with me, but Deb knew he was one." Wilkens turned left onto Catawba Avenue and drove quickly to the Park Hotel on Delaware. "Larry, there's something else I've got to tell you."

"Yes?"

"Cody Eastwood is back on the island."

Straylor's entire countenance changed. "What's that little S.O.B. doing back here?"

"It's probably just something to do with his parents' estate," Wilkens said as he parked the vehicle and the two men stepped from it.

"He had better stay away from my Cindy," Straylor fumed as they walked into the hotel lobby. "I bet the kid's gone postal and that's why we have two murders here."

"You're jumping to conclusions." Wilkens turned to hotel manager Deb Cook, who was consoling a crying housekeeper. The housekeeper had found the bodies. "Deb, can you give me the names of the two?"

"For one I can. His name is Steve Sorenson. The other was a visitor and she wasn't registered. Must have spent the night with him."

"Which room, Deb?"

Cook provided the room number. "Second floor, overlooking the park," she added.

Wilkens and Straylor started up the steps.

"Deb?" Wilkens asked as he paused.

Cook looked up at Wilkens. "Yes?"

"How did you know he was Secret Service?"

"When he was checking in, I saw his gun when his jacket opened. I confronted him about our hotel weapons policy and he produced his identification. He swore me to secrecy. I didn't even tell my husband, Bob."

"Thanks, Deb."

Wilkens and Straylor resumed climbing the stairs to the second floor and walked down the hall to the room. The room's door was left ajar by the shocked housekeeper. They carefully entered the room and made their way to the open bathroom door.

"Messy," Straylor said as they looked at the two bodies on the floor.

"Very," Wilkens agreed.

"I wonder who the female was," Straylor said as he looked at her naked body.

"Might have been an unlucky tourist he met last night," Wilkens surmised. "Let's get busy."

The two officers began to investigate the scene to determine what evidence was available. Wilkens placed a call to the police station and requested that the county coroner fly over from Port Clinton to assist.

As he examined the man's shirt pocket, he extracted a slip of paper with a phone number on it. He slipped the paper in a plastic bag and labeled it.

"Looks like a robbery gone bad," Straylor said from the hotel room.

"Why do you say that?"

"No wallets. No identifications."

Wilkens just nodded his head in acknowledgement. He looked again at the plastic bag in his hand and the handwritten phone number.

Hours later, Wilkens settled in his chair in his office. All he had were a lot of unanswered questions in front of him. It was highly unusual for the resort village of Put-in-Bay to experience a double homicide. Wilkens toyed with the plastic bag as he thought. He'd already completed a reverse phone number search. He found the caller's ID blocked. Wilkens reached for his phone and dialed the phone number. The phone was answered on the second ring.

"Yes?" a deep voice answered.

"This is Chief Wilkens with the Put-in-Bay Police Department."

"Yes?"

"To whom am I speaking?"

"Why do you need to know that, Chief?"

"We're investigating a crime on South Bass Island and found your number at the crime scene."

The man swore and then asked, "And what do you need from me?"

"First of all, I'd like to know who you are."

"No one you should mess with. Next question."

Surprised by the response, Wilkens sat up in his chair and probed. "Why shouldn't I mess with you?"

"It's classified. Drop it or you'll get in over your head. Goodbye." The phone went dead.

Now Wilkens' suspicions ran rampant as he began to assess what he heard during the conversation. His thoughts were interrupted when his phone rang.

"Yes?"

"Chet, you've got a call holding on line one. It's the White House!" the dispatcher said excitedly.

"Now what?" he said aloud into the phone. "Put them through." There was a click on the line and the line went live. "This is Chief Wilkens."

"Wilkens, this is Bill Taggart. I head the Secret Service's Presidential Protection Detail."

"Yes, Bill. I presume you're calling about your agent's murder."

"Yes, I'm aware that Agent Sorenson was murdered. We called his hotel when he didn't check in today and heard about it. I've got a team of our investigators in the air now. They'll be arriving at your airport shortly. And Chief, you should have notified us as soon as you became aware of the murder of one of our agents," Taggart fumed.

"I was about to call you," Wilkens replied. He wasn't lying. It had been on his list.

"We're taking over the investigation."

"No offense, Bill, but that's a jurisdictional matter."

There was a pause on the other end of the line.

"I said that we are taking over the investigation. This may tie in with an assassination plot during his visit to your island."

Stunned, Wilkens shot forward in his chair. "What visit?"

"That's the second reason I'm calling you. President Benson and Canadian Prime Minister Hargraves are having a bi-lateral conference on the fish kill matter. They're planning on being there in three days. So, we have a lot of work to do. And I'll need your cooperation to make sure that the island is secure for the President's visit."

"Sure. Sure. Whatever we can do. My men and I are at your disposal. And we can help with the murder investigation, too. Not sure who the female victim is yet."

"Don't worry about any of that. We'll get a debriefing from you when my team arrives. Agent Sorenson was one of our top agents. He was particularly adept at assessing potentially dangerous situations for us. That's why he was there. He and his partner, who didn't make the trip because of the flu, go in first. They evaluate any place, which we are thinking about taking the President, and provide an analysis of potential threats. They are backed up by teams here who run background checks of folks whom the President may be exposed to in one way or another."

"I see," Wilkens said. "Bill, could you help me out with something?"

"Sure. What is it?"

"We found a phone number in Sorenson's pocket. I know you folks have access to data we don't have. Could you have someone run it down for us?"

"I can do it. I'm at my desk. Give me the number."

Wilkens provided the number and he listened as Taggart's fingers tapped his keyboard.

Taggart swore. "It's classified, but let me see what we can do to track it down. Nice job in coming up with this."

"Like I said, we can work together on this."

"Good, we'll need each other's cooperation. Over the next 24 hours, you will see massive activity as we set up mobile command posts and bring equipment onto the island. We're planning to set up our media center and forward command post at Peach Point on Ohio State's premises. We're also using the Ohio Department of Natural Resources building there." Taggart quickly rambled off the first steps in setting up protection for the President.

Continuing, Taggart said, "We'll make arrangements with Miller Ferry to ferry equipment to their downtown docks so that it will be closer to Peach Point for us." Taggart paused for a second. "Chief Wilkens?"

"Yes?"

"Prepare to be invaded!" Chuckling, Taggart hung up. Then, swearing under his breath, Taggart ran the paper with the number jotted on it through his shredder. He had recognized the number.

Stone Lab
Put-in-Bay

Of all the Great Lakes, Lake Erie is the southernmost, warmest and the shallowest and contains the most nutrients. While the other lakes are more than 750 feet deep, Lake Erie's deepest point is in the Eastern Basin where it is 210 feet deep. The Western Basin, where the islands are located, has an average depth of 24 feet.

This shallowness can be troublesome for boaters and fisherman when sudden storms quickly create large waves of eight feet or more. Because the lake is shallow, the waves are poorly formed so the boater never knows whether his bow is going to go up or down.

Lake Erie's watershed is dominated by agricultural and urban land unlike the forest ecosystem watersheds surrounding the other Great Lakes. This results in more sediment draining into Lake Erie. Toledo's Maumee River alone deposits more sediment in Lake Erie than all of Lake Superior's tributaries combined.

Lake Erie is a strategic asset supplying drinking water to 11 million people. It also produces more fish for human consumption than all of the other Great Lakes combined. It's a fisherman's haven. At least it was until this summer.

It started slowly a few weeks ago when fishermen noticed small amounts of dead perch floating on the Lake's surface. As time passed, more and more of the perch were dying. They were washing onto the beaches, floating in the harbors and filling the air with a deadly stench.

When the first dead perch began to appear, the staff from The Ohio State University's Stone Lab began to scoop them up and take them back to Gibraltar Island for analysis.

Stone Lab is a part of the Ohio Sea Grant College program at The Ohio State University. It supports one of the country's premier research, education and outreach programs focused on the environment, the economy, and education in partnership with governmental and the private sectors. Each year it offers workshops, field trips and conferences for children in grades four and up as well as adult programs and summer college courses.

Their research projects have included elimination of the "Dead Zone" in Lake Erie's Central Basin, developing new vaccines for fish diseases, developing new sensors to detect toxins, eliminating harmful algae blooms in the Western Basin, investigating the viral hemorrhagic septicemia fish disease, understanding ecosystem changes due to the effects of the zebra mussel infiltration, and developing new techniques to remove Microcystin – a toxin produced by harmful algae.

Stone Lab is located on 6.5-acre Gibraltar Island in the mouth of Put-in-Bay's harbor. In 1925, the island was sold to Julius Stone by the Cooke-Barney family, daughter and son-in-law to Jay Cooke, the island's previous owner.

Julius Stone, an Ohio State University trustee at the time, donated the island to The Ohio State University to be used as a Lake Laboratory for the purpose of teaching, learning, and research. The Franz Theodore Stone Laboratory was built on the island in 1929, and was named in honor of Julius Stone's father. Gibraltar Island is the highest land elevation in the Put-In-Bay area and became a lookout point for Commodore Oliver Hazard Perry in the fight against the British during the War of 1812.

Perry and his men defeated a fleet of British sailing vessels during the famous Battle of Lake Erie on September 10, 1813. Gibraltar Island received its name because the eastern edge of the island rises out of the water in a similar manner to the more famous rock of the Mediterranean.

The island's facilities included a stone 21-room research laboratory and classroom building, a library, a dining hall, five dormitory units, and historic "Cooke's Castle." Sandusky-born Jay Cooke, who helped finance the Civil War during his banking career in Philadelphia, built the Castle as his summer residence.

The island's facilities were augmented by additional offices and research facilities across the channel on South Bass Island's Peach Point. The facilities were easy to spot. They were painted in Ohio State's scarlet and gray colors.

Lake Erie and all the Great Lakes are vulnerable to invasive species that hitch rides in the ballast water, which oceangoing vessels discharge into the Great Lakes. The EPA's National Center for Environmental Assessment has identified 30 species, which had a likelihood of reaching the Great Lakes.

The economic impact of the species that are now in the lakes is estimated at $5.7 billion per year. The costs include covering water intake pipes due to the tendency of the zebra mussels to clog the pipes; the killing of sport and commercial fish by sea lampreys; and zebra mussels, quagga mussels and round gobies outcompeting sport fish for food.

Recent regulations require oceangoing ships to flush their ballast tanks while still at sea. Ballast water exchange at sea should eliminate 99 percent of invasive organisms.

The door to Stone Lab's first floor lab opened and Moore entered the room. "I thought I might find you here."

An athletically built, gray-haired-man with an equally close-cropped gray beard stepped back from the lab table where he had been looking at a report with three co-workers. It was Jeff Reutter, Director of Ohio Sea Grant College Program and Stone Laboratory for The Ohio State University, and a long time friend of Emerson Moore.

He smiled. "I expected that you'd be showing up for an update."

"Anything new?"

"Not yet. We know that it's not the viral hemorrhagic septicemia virus. You may recall that VHS was responsible for killing perch a few years ago. We examined perch from different areas of the lake. There's been no evidence of bleeding in the eyes, skin, gills or at the base of the fins. So, we're pretty comfortable with our diagnosis at this point."

Reutter was referring to the virus, which was deadly to fish, but didn't affect people. The virus eventually disappeared after a few seasons of large die-offs as the fish population gradually built up immunity to the virus. They were continuing to test fish to make sure that the virus did not return.

"But this fish kill is much more massive than the VHS was," Reutter added.

"Think it's another virus?"

"Not sure. We've got the boats out collecting and tagging dead fish." Reutter was referring to the three workboats used in their operations. The *BIOLab* was a 37-foot commercial trap net boat. They also had the 42-foot *Gibraltar* and 27-foot *Erie Monitor*.

"Step over here, Emerson." Reutter said as he walked to a monitor.

Moore joined Reutter and looked at the image on the monitor.

"These are satellite images of Lake Erie." He tapped on one of the keys and zoomed in. "We get these from the National Oceanic and Atmospheric Administration's satellite. See these images in black?"

Moore bent over and squinted. I've got to get those reading glasses, he thought to himself. "Yes."

"Those are dead fish floating on the surface. If you notice, there's a pattern. It's starting close to the mouth of the Detroit River, just below Grosse Ile."

Moore nodded his head.

"It then fans out and continues with the current toward the eastern end of the lake, but it's concentrated here at the western end."

"You think it's bioterrorism or is someone dumping chemical waste?"

"Not sure. We are still trying to determine if it's a virus although we are exploring every possibility."

"There's no fish kill in the Detroit River or in any of the other lakes?" Emerson probed.

"None whatsoever. The *BIOLab* is collecting data near the Detroit River. We are dropping floating sensors to transmit data to us for evaluation." Reutter depressed three keys and a new image appeared. "Take a look at this. The other image was from three days ago. This is from this morning. See any difference?"

Moore studied the display in front of him. "Yes. Looks like you have a swath of death emerging from the Maumee River in Toledo."

"Exactly."

"Mutant gene?"

"Good guess. But I don't think we would see the massive fish kill the way we do. You'd expect to see that develop slowly and the fish kill to build. If it was a mutant gene, you'd see cells dividing and replicating the problem. None of the specimens we've examined showed any evidence of mutant genes. Neither did we see any evidence yet of a mutant strain of the VHS." He paused as he stared at the monitor. "This perch kill happened almost overnight and seems to be growing."

"So, that should bring you back to bioterrorism, right?"

Reutter looked Moore squarely in the eyes. "We don't know and we don't need to create panic based on false assumptions."

An approaching student interrupted them. "Dr. Reutter?"

"Yes?"

"Governor Coughlin is on the phone for you."

"I'll be right there. Emerson, I've got to run."

"Sure, I understand," Emerson smiled as his friend ran off to take the call. The two had become friends when Moore was researching a story on Lake Erie algae bloom. It had shown up as a green blob extending from Toledo's Maumee River to the Lake Erie islands and east toward Cleveland.

Normally the algae were non-toxic. But sometimes, it changed and became toxic. It didn't kill people, but it did cause rashes and made people sick if they swam in the water, immersed their head, or ingested the water.

The algae eventually died and decomposed. That was an oxygen consuming process as it drifted toward the lake's central basin. It contributed to the oxygen-depleted dead zone in Lake Erie's central basin. Scientists and researchers were still trying to identify what was triggering the algae to become toxic.

Moore returned to the dock where he surveyed Put-in-Bay's harbor and the boats at their moorings and at the waterfront docks. He thought to himself how fortunate he was to have been able to move to this touch of paradise. He untied the line to his Zodiac and sat on the stern's seat where he engaged the dinghy's Mercury outboard and eased away from the dock. He pointed the little craft toward East Point and his aunt's house.

Reutter was on the phone with the governor. "They want to come here for a briefing and a press conference?"

Coughlin responded, "Yes, and he wants to spend a few days fishing for walleye and working on his renomination acceptance speech. Think you could put him up at Cooke's Castle?"

"Sure can," Reutter agreed eagerly.

"You heard the rumors that he might dump Moran?"

"Yes, I have. I also heard a rumor that you may be replacing him on the ticket."

"That would be my dream."

"Let's see what we can do to encourage that," Reutter said.

"Much appreciated. By the way, I've already called over to Gee's office and cleared this with him. I asked him if I could call you direct as I wanted to let you know what was transpiring and he agreed." Coughlin was referring to Gordon Gee, President of The Ohio State University.

"Okay. We'll make sure the place is shipshape. I'm sure the Secret Service advance teams will be here doing their preliminary checks."

"Wouldn't surprise me if they already have a few folks there incognito," Coughlin chuckled. "Good luck and get to the bottom of that fish kill, would you?"

"We're working on it. I'm optimistic that we'll identify the source."

The White House
Washington, D.C.

"There are three things I want to accomplish on this trip to Gibraltar Island, gentlemen." The President paused as he surveyed his advance planning team for his meeting with Canadian Prime Minister Peter Hargraves. "First, I want the prime minister and I to hear the progress being made by Ohio State's

Stone Lab and the EPA in identifying the source of this fish kill mess and what we need to do to resolve it."

"Got it, Mr. President," his clean cut Assistant Deputy Press Secretary Jon Hertrack nodded. Hertrack was covering for Press Secretary Wilson Gauche. Gauche was at Bethesda Naval Hospital, recovering from a near fatal heart attack a week earlier.

"Second, I want to issue a joint statement with the prime minister following the briefing. I want the public to know what we know and what we are doing about it."

Hertrack nodded his head. As the President began to walk out of the room, Hertrack called, "And the third item, Mr. President?"

A smile filled the President's face. "Besides working on my acceptance speech for the convention, Hargraves and I are going to get in some walleye fishing with my old friend, Emerson Moore." The President left the meeting room. "I need to show the public that fishing is safe and I want them to see me eating the fish I pull out of the lake."

Hertrack's eyes scanned the room's occupants. There were representatives from the National Security Council, Department of Defense, Homeland Security, Coast Guard, Secret Service, EPA and the Intergovernmental Affairs Office. Because of the international involvement with Canada, representatives were also in attendance from the State Department, including the Chief of Protocol's Office. There would be additional coordination requirements with the Canadian governmental agencies, Canadian Coast Guard and the Royal Mounted Police.

Planning presidential trips required many long hours and attention to detail. First an advance team comprised of military members and secret service agents would set up camp on Gibraltar Island and Put-in-Bay. They'd land on a C-141 in Port Clinton and motorcade equipment to Put-in-Bay via the Miller Ferry. Rather than unloading the equipment and motorcade at the southeast side of South Bass Island, the Miller Ferry would deliver its passengers to its downtown Put-in-Bay docks for the short drive to Ohio State University's buildings just alongside the water's edge on Peach Point.

The advance team would be comprised of a dozen Secret Service agents, six members of the White House staff, four members of the State Department and two dozen military members from the White House Communications Agency. They'd be responsible for establishing the communications links and setting up appropriate radio towers on Gibraltar Island and at the OSU complex on Put-in-Bay. The press would be provided with a story-filing center at the OSU complex.

Gibraltar Island would be subject to close inspection by the Secret Service. They would scour the island for potential threats and secure it for the President's safety. Bomb sniffing dogs would scour the island to make sure that there were no threats. Buildings would be inspected. Background checks would be run on people who worked on the island. Badges would be prepared for anyone expected to be on the island while the President was there.

A series of perimeters would surround the island. Close in would be the Secret Service with their powerful chase boats. Then, there would be the ring of Coast Guard assets such as cutters and helicopters. The next ring would be local law enforcement officials and the Ohio Division of Watercraft officials in their watercraft, all combining to make a series of impenetrable rings to stop any potential intruders.

Divers would submerge and check under the docks in front of Stone Lab as well as the hulls of nearby boats. Sailboats, which usually were tied to the mooring buoys near Stone Lab, would not be permitted to tie up there while the President was in residence.

Secret Service agents with binoculars would be stationed throughout the island to keep an eye out for potential intruders.

Counter sniper teams of a spotter and shooter would be stationed strategically around the island and Put-in-Bay.

Every precaution would be taken to protect Walleye, the code name given to Benson by the Secret Service Presidential Protection Detail. Presidential code names had been used for years by the Secret Service as a quick way to identify the President and other key government officials. A few of the names used in the past were Renegade for Obama, Tumbler for George W. Bush, Elvis for Clinton, Timberwolf for George H.W. Bush, Rawhide for Reagan and Deacon for Carter.

Aunt Anne's House
Put-in-Bay

"I'm coming. I'm coming," the elderly aunt said as she moved at a pace, which would surprise people if they knew her age. She picked up the ringing phone. "Hello. Yes, he's here. And who should I say is calling?" She caught herself as she was shocked by the caller's identification. "Could you repeat that?" She listened very closely and then asked, "Is this a joke?"

"No, this is not a joke. This is Jon Hertrack calling from the White House on behalf of President Benson. I'd like to talk to Emerson."

"Sure. Sure," she mumbled. "Hold on a second and I'll get him." She took the portable phone with her as she walked out to the detached garage. "Emerson?"

"Yes?" He answered as he stopped waxing his deceased uncle's 1929 Ford Model A truck. The classic cream vehicle had a tan top and green fenders. His uncle had replaced its original 40 horsepower 4-cylinder engine with a 289 cubic inch V8 engine. He had also replaced the standard three-speed transmission with an automatic and a floor shifter. The truck was tricked out with lots of chrome and a spotless rich brown leather bench seat.

"It's for you. I think it's a prank. Guy says he's calling from the White House."

"Is it the President?"

Moore wouldn't have been surprised to receive a call from President Richard Benson. The two had met years earlier when then-Senator Benson was head of the Senate Homeland Security and Government Affairs Committee. Moore conducted a number of interviews with Benson resulting in a series of articles, supporting Benson's position on increasing Homeland Security spending.

During the time they spent together, the two had become fast friends. They both had something in common. Both had lost wives and children in an auto accident.

"Mercy no, I'd know his voice. I've been hearing it on the TV for four years now."

Moore took the phone from her and answered it. "This is Emerson Moore. Can I help you?"

"Hi, Emerson. It's Jon Hertrack."

A smile crossed Moore's face. "Hi Jon. Long time since we talked. How's Wilson doing?"

"They think he's going to make it. Man, did that ever catch us by surprise."

"I bet. How are you holding up with your additional duties?"

"Good, actually. A bit hectic with that fish kill mess you guys have out there and trying to get ready for the President's re-nomination."

"The folks at Stone Lab seem to be right on top of this. I'm sure that they're on the verge of a breakthrough."

"That's what we're counting on and that's part of the reason I'm calling."

"Oh?"

"It hasn't been officially announced yet, but the President and the Canadian Prime Minister are having a bilateral conference on Gibraltar Island in a week on the fish kill issue."

"Just before the convention in Cleveland?"

"Yep. The President wants to show everyone that we are fo-cused on resolving this issue and he wants to prepare his re-nomination acceptance speech on the island."

Moore interrupted. "And I hope he plans to announce that he's dumping Vice President Moran from the ticket." Moore pushed. "Anything developing in that area?"

"Easy does it. You know I can't comment on what he will do in that regard."

"If he's smart and he listens to the polls, he'd dump him. He needs to put in someone like Coughlin. Coughlin could replace him in four years. The party needs someone with some smarts and integrity."

"My call isn't to discuss his running mate. I called to extend an invitation to you."

"For another fundraising dinner at $500 a plate, which is not in my budget?" Moore teased.

"No, actually the President wants you to join him and the Canadian Prime Minister for some walleye fishing while he's there. You up to it?"

"With Dick, anytime. Then I can get some one-on-one time with him to tell him to drop Moran."

"Don't you ever let go?"

"Nah. That would be too easy." Moore was grinning to himself. "Give me the dates and I'll block out my calendar."

When Hertrack provided the dates, Moore groaned.

"What's wrong?" Hertrack asked.

"That's the wrap up of Pirates' Week."

"What's that?"

"It's a week long celebration of being a pirate. We've been doing it on the island for the last several years. They'll be firing cannons from ships in the harbor."

"I'll mention it to the President and Secret Service. That should make the agents real jumpy if you're firing cannons."

"Keep them on their toes," Moore grinned.

They chatted for a few more minutes before ending the call.

Moore set the phone on the workbench and picked up his polishing rag. He bent over the truck to finish his waxing. Moore looked forward to seeing the President. He planned to do his best to persuade Benson to drop Moran from the ticket. Moore's mind began to race with ways to convince Benson to make the change to the ticket.

Mouth of the Portage River
Port Clinton, Ohio

A brisk breeze was blowing from the west. The waves disturbed tranquil Lake Erie. The waves shimmered in the moonlit night as fishermen sat patiently in their boats off the mouth of Port Clinton's Portage River. The fishermen were hoping for a big catch despite the massive fish kill, which had been tormenting this Lake Erie fishing wonderland for several weeks.

They weren't the only ones planning on a big catch. A large Tiara had slowed its engines as it entered the fishing area from the west. Four scuba divers edged off the craft's swim platform and dropped silently into the warm water. Adjusting their masks, the divers submerged and began their surreptitious swim toward the mouth of the Portage River. The Tiara's engines roared as the boat virtually leaped out of the water and headed westward.

Carefully following each other, the divers swam into the river and against the current. They went past the dock where the Jet Express would be returning within a half hour with partyers from an evening of carousing at Put-in-Bay's bars. The four swam underneath the drawbridge where they surfaced momentarily in its darkened shadows to take a visual read on their target, the President's yacht. It was a 42-foot Grand Banks Classic Trawler, which had been loaned for the President's use by two wealthy Grosse Ile islanders, Kevin and Tawnya Kissell. They were big contributors to his last campaign. The boat was named *Estorel*, Calusa Indian for where the river meets the sea.

It was a hundred yards up river and tied to the dock. The infiltrators saw two armed guards patrolling the dock and two more walking the yacht's main deck. Another guard leaned against the entryway to the yacht's radio room.

The divers submerged and continued their journey. In a few minutes, they found themselves at their dispersion point. It was under the ship's bow. With a nod from their leader, they split up and moved to complete their deadly assignments.

Two divers positioned themselves below the dock's edge where the two guards were talking as they smoked. The other two made their way to the yacht's stern and were about to ascend to its swim platform when the lead diver suddenly grasped the arm of his partner. He pointed downward and up river.

The two moved away from the stern and swam up river. Within 50 feet they swam under a dock and surfaced.

"What's up?" the partner asked.

"They had a little surprise waiting for us," the leader grunted as he lifted his mask and peered out of the river's surface.

"What do you mean?"

The leader pointed. "There. In the sailboat's shadow."

His partner followed to where he was pointing. He then saw the Zodiac. The inflatable boat with a Mercury outboard had two more guards. Both were wearing night vision goggles and were scanning the water's surface for intruders.

"How did you know?"

"Just had a funny feeling," the leader replied.

"Amazing."

The leader smiled as he began to replace his mask on his face. "Can't go after the President until we take them out. Let's do it."

The two submerged and swam quickly across the river's current and to the rear of the Zodiac. Before ascending, the two divers released their HK MP5N submachine guns and set them to fire three-round bursts.

On board the Zodiac, the two guards were talking in hushed tones. "See anything yet?"

"Nope."

"Me neither." A thumping sound from the stern caught one guard's attention and he began to turn in its direction. "What in the hell?"

That's as far as he got as he found himself staring into the deadly end of a submachine gun. He raised his hands quickly to avoid giving the gunman a reason to unleash its lethal 9mm parabellum rounds. The other guard followed suit and raised his hands.

Within a few minutes, the two divers had boarded the craft and secured the guards with plastic ties and gags. Seeing that all was in order, the two divers reentered the river. They allowed its current to carry them to the yacht's stern where the two divers slipped off their masks, fins and BC's, buoyancy compensators. The BC's had small dive tanks affixed to them. They secured their equipment to the swim platform and eased onto the platform.

The leader cautiously peered over the edge of the stern and ducked down. "Clear," he mumbled softly.

The two divers quickly swung over the stern. Holding their submachine guns at waist level, the leader quietly padded to the port side while his partner hurried to the starboard side. Seeing an open doorway, the partner dodged inside where he waited.

He didn't have to wait long before the starboard guard began his return walk to the stern. His attention was focused on the surface of the river and he was shocked when he felt the cold, wet gun barrel press against the back of his neck.

"I'll take your weapon," the diver ordered.

The guard's head began to turn as his mouth gaped open in amazement. "But, how...?"

"Quiet! Just hand me your weapon."

Reluctantly, the guard handed over his rifle. Taking the rifle and placing it inside the doorway, the diver produced another plastic tie with which he secured the arms of the guard. He slipped a piece of tape across his mouth as a gag. He then prodded him with his gun barrel towards the stern as he walked to catch up with his leader.

The leader had a more difficult task in front of him. As he peered onto the dock, he saw that one guard's attention was focused outward while the other guard was watching the port side of the yacht. The leader would be unable to walk along the yacht's port side, so he hid and waited for the shipboard guard to make his walk to the yacht's stern. In a matter of minutes, the guard obliged him and he repeated the actions of the first diver in securing the guard.

The leader then made his way along the starboard side to the other entrance to the radio room. Quietly, he padded across the deck and stuck his gun barrel into the back of the guard's neck. Meekly, the guard surrendered and walked to the stern area of the craft where he was also bound.

With all three guards in front of them and gun barrels pointed at their backs, the two divers stepped portside and called to the two guards on the dock. "Time to throw them down, boys, or we'll take out your friends," the leader yelled.

At the same time, the two divers who had been patiently waiting underneath the dock appeared over the dock's edge. In their hands, they also held HK MP5N submachine guns. They were pointed at the two dockside guards.

At that moment, the entire scene was lit up by large floodlights and the divers and guards were greeted by the sound of several pairs of hands clapping.

"Very well done," Presidential Protection Detail Special Agent Patrix Heschel called out. "I don't think your boys were ready for them, what do you think, Sheriff?"

Ottawa County Sheriff Tom Tschudy wasn't clapping. Neither was he smiling. A large scowl was displayed on his face. Before the practice attack on the Presidential yacht, he had been boasting about the prowess of his officers over that of the Presidential Protection Details agents. Now, he was eating crow. "No comment," he responded gruffly as he eased his large frame out of the chair where he had been sitting for the last four hours.

Heschel called to the divers on the yacht. "Hope this helps with your story, Emerson!"

"Oh, it will. It will indeed." Moore replied. "Readers find Presidential security issues very interesting. Especially since we had two crash the Obama state dinner a few years ago."

Moore was pleased that he had been invited to participate in the evening's mock attack on the Presidential yacht.

"E, did you have fun with this?"

Moore chuckled to himself as he turned to look at the dive leader and ex-Navy SEAL, Sam Duncan. The powerfully built, blonde-haired 39-year-old Duncan had been a close friend of Moore's for years. He lived most of the time in a mobile home on United Street in Key West, but seemed to spend a lot of time working on special, confidential projects. Moore assumed that he worked in Black Ops and for DEA on a contract basis since he'd clam up when Moore pushed for information.

"Yes, I did. Thanks for inviting me along, Sam."

Duncan was on special assignment to assist in protecting the President while he visited Gibraltar Island and during his time at the convention.

"Like I could invite anyone else? You'd have killed me if I came all the way up here and didn't get you involved in something."

Moore smiled. He knew that his irascible buddy looked for any excuse to visit Put-in-Bay. Put-in-Bay had its wild side and its mild side, which seemed to help with its magical allure. And Duncan liked its wild side from the bars to the dancing to the stage acts to partying on the boats rafted six deep in the bay.

"Like you had to work hard for an excuse to visit here!" Moore teased.

Duncan smiled and shrugged his shoulders.

Seeing the Sheriff moving toward his car, Moore called over, "Sheriff, don't forget you've got two men in the Zodiac!"

The sheriff glanced toward the river as he opened the cruiser's door and sat inside. "We'll get them." As he started the engine, he continued, "In the morning." He was laughing to himself as he squealed his tires and pulled abruptly out of the parking lot.

"Where are you going?" Duncan asked as he saw Moore walk to the stern.

"Be right back. I'll free those two deputies."

Before Moore could dive into the river, the two were distracted by a red Mustang convertible, which pulled into the parking lot.

A tall blonde stepped out of the car and waved at the two men, who returned the wave.

Moore was the first to comment. "I don't know her. Do you?"

"Yes. They're both mine," Duncan grinned.

"She's a nice hood ornament," Moore teased. "Where did you find her? E-Harmony?"

"Nope. Got her on E-Bay. Both of them," he joked back. "Want to join us over at Bootleggers? I asked Johnny to hang around tonight."

Moore looked at his watch. "You sure that he's still there? It's late, or I should say almost dawn."

"Well, if he's not, I'm sure I can find something to do," Duncan said as he eyed the blonde. "She makes my heart beat as fast as a hummingbird's wings!" Duncan sighed.

Moore groaned at the last comment. "You say that about every woman you meet! I'll pass on Bootleggers this time. Go have your fun."

"Oh, I intend to, E," Duncan said as he licked his lips.

"Will you have time to come out to Put-in-Bay this week? It's Pirates' Week. There will be all kinds of goings on. Pirate costumes, parades, contests, sword fighting. The guy who provided the cannons for the film *Master and Commander* will be there with his cannons."

"Oh, man, I hate to miss that. I'll be at the convention, working at setting up security."

"You sure get some exciting assignments," Moore said as he looked at his friend.

"What can I say? When you're good, you're good," Duncan said as the blonde began to help him slip out of his wetsuit.

"Have fun at the convention." Moore eyed the blonde. "And tonight."

Moore turned around and executed a clean dive into the river. Surfacing, his powerful arms catapulted him toward the anchored Zodiac and the officers waiting to be freed.

Police Station
Put-in-Bay

"Larry!" Chief Wilkens called with an urgent tone in his voice.

"Yeah?" Straylor replied.

"Better come with me. Your house is on fire!" Wilkens said as he rushed by Straylor and charged up the steps. He threw a quick glance at his dispatcher. "You heard?"

Goodwill nodded her head as Straylor raced around the corner to catch up with the chief.

"What? My house? But everything was okay an hour ago when I met Cindy for lunch."

Reaching the top of the stairs, Wilkens added, "It's not only your house. It's also Cheri's house next door."

A cold chill ran up Straylor's spine. "Is Cheri home?"

"Don't know?" Strange, Wilkens thought to himself as he sat behind the wheel of the Suburban, Straylor didn't ask about his wife's whereabouts.

"I bet that Cody Eastwood has something to do with it. This is revenge for what we did to him. I'm positive. First the Secret Service agent and that woman, now this. I'll kill that little S.O.B.!" Straylor said as he sat next to the chief and the vehicle pulled out of the parking lot for the short trip down Catawba Avenue to the burning homes.

Wilkens remembered the case from several years earlier. Eastwood was a high school student who stalked Straylor's wife, a teacher at the Put-in-Bay high school. Eastwood's parents, who were now deceased, had sent him away to live with relatives in southern Ohio. The last anyone had heard was that Eastwood had joined the service and was overseas when both of his parents died a year ago. The Eastwood's home on Mitchell Road had been closed up since then.

"I wouldn't be jumping to any conclusions, Larry," the chief said as he took a quick glance at Straylor whose face was a brilliant red. It was a sign that everyone on the island knew. It meant that Straylor's legendary anger was about to erupt.

"Easy does it, Larry. Calm yourself down."

"I tell you it's that kid. I'm taking him out," Straylor boiled.

They could see black smoke billowing skyward as they neared the blazing houses. The two houses sat on well-manicured lots, which were shaded by large oak trees. Where beautiful flowers had grown in front of the houses, there were now remnants of brown, burnt flowers.

Parking the vehicle along the street, they walked briskly to Fire Chief Folger.

"Are the ladies safe?" Wilkens asked. He realized that he didn't need to ask. The look on Folger's face told the story. Straylor saw it too.

"Which one didn't make it?" Straylor asked anguishly.

"Neither. I'm so sorry, Larry," Folger said as he went to put his hand on Straylor's shoulder.

Straylor pulled away. "I'll be back!" he stormed.

"No, you're not going anywhere." He motioned to one of the approaching police officers and quickly told him what had happened. "Stay with Straylor and make sure that he doesn't go anywhere or do anything stupid."

The officer nodded his head and stood next to Straylor.

"Now is not the time to do anything stupid, Larry. Stay put," Wilkens ordered as he turned back to Folger.

"One more thing," Folger said quietly so that Saylor wouldn't overhear.

"Yes?"

"You've got a homicide here?"

"What?" Wilkens asked, stunned.

"Yeah. One in each house."

"Both Cindy and Cheri?"

"Yeah. They found Cindy on the floor in the kitchen."

"What about Cheri?"

"They found her on the floor in her bedroom."

"Crap."

"Apparently, someone set the fires, hoping that their bodies would be burned and that no one would know that they had been murdered."

Wilkens thought to himself, if it was Eastwood, why would he also murder Cheri? The common theme between the two women was that they were both attractive blondes.

"I already called for the coroner," Folger added.

"Thanks." Wilkens turned to look at Straylor, who was now seated on the ground. He was sobbing.

With the fires being doused, the crowd began to dissipate. A lone figure, which had been leaning against a lamp pole a hundred feet up the street, stepped away from the lamp pole and sat on his bicycle.

Straylor saw the figure. He began to run towards it, pulling his handgun as he did. "Eastwood, you're dead meat!" he yelled as he approached Eastwood. Eastwood stood frozen in his tracks as he watched Straylor stop and take aim at him.

As Straylor's finger began to squeeze the trigger, Straylor found himself tackled from the side. His gun fired, but the bullet missed its target and buried itself in the trunk of a nearby maple tree. Straylor found himself in a battle for control of his weapon.

"You need to think before you act," Moore said as he wrestled the gun away from Straylor's grip. Two passersby had now joined Moore and helped restrain Straylor until Wilkens and another officer appeared to help.

"That was a stupid thing to do," Wilkens admonished Straylor as he cuffed him. "I'm doing this for your own good." Turning to the other officer after they helped Straylor to his feet, Wilkens said, "Take him to the Suburban and drive him back to the station. I want him in my office, waiting for me."

The officer nodded and walked away with Straylor.

"Thanks, Emerson," Wilkens said as he took possession of Straylor's gun which Moore had just handed to him.

"It looked like Larry's emotions whacked him out! I did it for his own good," Moore said.

"It's that temper of his," Wilkens explained.

"What's the deal here? Is that the kid who was banished from the island?" Moore asked as he pointed at Eastwood.

"Not sure that I'd say he was banished, but that's him. And I need to talk with him." He waved Eastwood to join them.

Eastwood rode his bike to where they were standing and before Wilkens could say anything, Eastwood looked at Moore. "Thank you for taking him out. I owe you one. I'm Cody Eastwood."

"Emerson Moore," Moore responded as they shook hands.

"Yeah, I've heard about you."

"Oh?"

"I've stayed somewhat in touch with the island over the years. I used the internet and my folks used to send me copies of *The Put-in-Bay Gazette* until they passed away."

Wilkens interrupted. "So, what brings you back here?" Wilkens had noticed a change from the smart-mouthed teenager to a more mature, self-confident young man.

"Got a few things to do to close up my folks' estate. I'll be putting the house up for sale."

"You're not planning on staying?"

"No longer than I have to. I have other interests now, but I'll miss the island," Eastwood replied.

Wilkens looked at the firemen who were finishing extinguishing what little remained of the fire. "You have anything to do with that fire?"

"I was wondering how long it would take before you'd ask me. Mr. Wilkens, my answer is no, I didn't have a thing to do with either fire. In fact, I've been catching up with Maggie at the Chamber of Commerce and Pauline at the Bakery. They were friends with my folks. You can check with them."

"I'll do just that," Wilkens said. "How long were you with them?"

"I'd say about two hours."

"Did you have any contact with Cindy Straylor since you returned?"

"No, but I had planned on it."

Both Moore and Wilkens had surprised looks on their faces.

"You were?" Wilkens asked incredulously.

"Yes, sir. I was going to apologize to her. I was so disrespectful and inappropriate to her when I went to school here. She was too kind of a lady to have to put up with someone like me. What I did was wrong and I wanted to apologize. Is she okay? I didn't see her." Eastwood was peering around Wilkens and toward the Straylor house.

Two firemen appeared in the doorway of the house. They were carrying a stretcher. On the stretcher was a closed body bag.

"That's her," Wilkens said as he turned and pointed at the body on the stretcher. "She didn't make it."

"I'm truly sorry to hear that. Under the circumstances, I'd appreciate it if you could pass along my apology to her husband. I better not talk to him."

"Good idea," Wilkens said. "You staying at the house?"

"Yes, sir. I hope to be off the island in the next two or three days."

"Check in with me before you leave in case I have any more questions for you."

"I'll do that." Turning to Moore, Eastwood said, "Pleasure meeting you, Mr. Moore. And thank you again for disrupting his aim."

"You're quite welcome and good luck."

Moore and Wilkens watched as Eastwood pedaled away on his bike.

"I am going to follow up on his alibi."

"I never doubted for a moment that you would, Chet."

Cooke's Castle
Gibraltar Island

The Cooke Mansion, more commonly known as Cooke's Castle, was built in 1865 as a summer vacation home on Gibraltar Island by Philadelphia banker and Civil War financier Jay Cooke. Cooke was born in nearby Sandusky on the mainland and enjoyed returning to the area and the recreation it offered. Many of his influential friends including William Tecumseh Sherman, Salmon P. Chase and U.S. Presidents Rutherford B. Hayes, Grover Cleveland and Benjamin Harrison, would visit Cooke's island haven. After many years, the island was again the site of another presidential visit.

The 15-room, three-story limestone castle was built on a ridge near Perry's Lookout. Its landmark feature was the octagonal tower that stands high above the island. Its rooftop deck provided magnificent views of the lake, Put-in-Bay and the surrounding islands. It would provide a lofty perch for one of the presidential counter sniper teams.

Inside the tower and on the first floor was the tower library, which was surrounded on three sides by tall narrow windows. It had bookcases made of pine wood and a desk where Benson would work on drafts of his renomination acceptance speech. The advance team had set up computers and communications for the President's use.

Across the hall from the library was a parlor with a dining room next to it. Servants' stairs were at the rear of each floor as were servants' quarters. Another set of stairs led to the five bedrooms on the second floor. The President would be occupying Jay Cooke's bedroom and the Canadian Prime Minister would be staying in the turret bedroom.

The balance of the rooms on the second floor and the additional bedrooms on the third floor would be used by staff members. The third floor reading room in the turret had been turned into an office for the staff members to use. It was also filled with computers and other electronics.

The kitchen area was located on ground level with stairs leading to the dining room. Below ground level and with a door facing the north side was the wine cellar, which had been stocked with a variety of Lake Erie island wines for the Presidential visit.

The day was a busy one at Carl R. Keller Field Airport in Port Clinton whose runway had been recently lengthened. First, the plane carrying the press corps landed. It taxied to an area where five Marine helicopters waited. The doors opened and the plane emptied out as 100 members from the media walked by the first helicopter, which was Marine One for the President. They transported their gear to the other four helicopters and boarded them.

Next, Air Force One landed at the airport and taxied over to where the press corps plane had parked. The portable stairs were rolled over to the plane and staff members descended. They carried gear as they headed to Marine One. They were quickly followed by 15 members of the media, who had ridden on Air Force One with the President. They walked over to the other helicopters and boarded.

After Benson's staff members and advisors deplaned, Benson appeared in the doorway. He gave a brief wave to airport personnel who had gathered to watch the operations and then descended the stairs. He walked confidently across the tarmac to Marine One and boarded it for the ride to the islands.

In a matter of minutes, the helicopters were airborne and heading for the Miller Ferry's downtown dock on Bay View in Put-in-Bay. Marine One's pilot flew the President around the Lake Erie Islands for a quick aerial tour while the other copters landed and disembarked their occupants and gear.

Waiting vehicles took the first arrivees to their hotel rooms and then to the press headquarters, which had been set up on Peach Point. Several of the camera crews and TV/cable news reporters remained on the dock to film Marine One's landing for news footage.

Marine One appeared on the horizon as it approached Gibraltar Island and flew low around the island. It then flew close to Perry's Monument and over downtown Put-in-Bay before it landed on the Miller Ferry downtown dock. When the President and his immediate staff emerged, they were escorted to waiting water taxis, which took them on the short ride across the harbor to the Gibraltar Island dock in front of Stone Lab. Standing on the dock to welcome Benson to the island was Jeff Reutter.

"Mr. President," Reutter started. "Welcome to The Ohio State University's Gibraltar Island and Stone Lab."

Taking the outstretched hand, Benson beamed, "It's good to be here. I'm anxious to hear firsthand what you've discovered about this fish kill matter."

Seeing Hertrack nod his head, Reutter said, "Let's walk over to the lab and we'll give you an update."

"Splendid."

Benson and Hertrack accompanied Reutter to the lab for their initial update. Hertrack looked at his watch to make sure that everything was running on time. The Canadian Prime Minister was due to arrive within the hour.

Walking through the ground entranceway, Reutter led Benson into the first floor lab. "This is the lab we've used for our testing," Reutter said as they stood inside the doorway.

"Impressive," Benson said as he surveyed the room full of testing gear, fish tanks with live perch and large containers holding dead perch. "And what have you determined is the source of this fish kill?"

"Not sure yet. It has some tendencies of the VHS which killed a number of fish a few years ago, but this is different."

"How's that?" Benson asked.

"The VHS virus wasn't selective. It killed all species of fish. Whatever this is, it's only affecting the perch. There is a slight possibility that it could be a derivative of VHS, which is now just targeting perch. We're still evaluating all possibilities."

With a nod to Hertrack who had provided him fish kill briefing material, Benson asked, "And am I to understand that this problem is primarily limited to the western basin of Lake Erie?"

"Yes, so far."

"Hargraves is here." Hertrack called from the doorway. "He's early."

Within minutes, the portly Canadian Prime Minister walked through the doorway and joined them. "Gentlemen, got it solved yet?"

"Welcome to our islands," Benson greeted Hargraves. "We were just getting an update from Jeff about possible sources of the fish kill."

After brief introductions were made, Reutter continued with his explanations about the various tests and analysis, which had been conducted. "We're still working our way through this."

Nodding his head, Benson said, "We appreciate everything you and your staff are doing here. How about taking a break from your work and giving the Prime Minister and I a brief tour of the island before we head to the Castle for our meetings."

"Be glad to," Reutter responded and he began to escort the men out of the Stone Lab building.

Later that evening, Hertrack placed a call from his third floor bedroom in the Castle. He was calling the Death Watch team at the media center on Peach Point. The team was put in place after the Kennedy assassination due to an agreement between the Secret Service, the media and the White House.

It was comprised of a small media pool of rotating members. It had representatives from one newspaper, radio, network and wire service. They were created in part to avoid the Hollywood paparazzi approach to news coverage. The team was stationed in the third car, the camera car, of presidential motorcades and also covered the President during golf outings or meetings. After the events, they'd prepare a pool report for release to the other members of the media.

The phone at the media center was answered on the first ring. "Yes?"

"It's Hertrack. You can put a lid on it for the day. The President's in for the day and we don't expect any more news this evening."

"Thanks," the reporter responded. "We'll try to grab some sleep on these old Army cots you guys provided us."

"I'll see if I can get them replaced. Let me see what I can do in the morning," Hertrack responded.

Mitchell Road
Later That Night

Gunning the police car, Straylor shifted the car into neutral and turned off the ignition. He did the same with the vehicle's lights. The police car coasted quietly down Mitchell Road until Straylor brought it to a stop across from the Eastwood home. Straylor settled back in his seat as he looked through his open window. With his right hand, he took the cigarette from his tightly drawn lips and exhaled, watching the smoke dissipate in the warm evening air.

Most homes on the dark street had their lights off. It was after one in the morning. But the lights were on in the Eastwood house. Straylor's eye narrowed as he tried to see Eastwood through the curtainless and open windows. A TV was on in the front room and its sound carried over to the police car and through the open window on the driver's side.

A storm had been brewing in Straylor since the death of his wife and the neighbor lady. For some reason, its intensity seemed to overwhelm Straylor that evening as he cruised the island, watching the late night antics of party goers as they stumbled from the bars and along the sidewalks.

Straylor had decided to park in front of Eastwood's house so that he could plot his retaliatory action against Eastwood. It had to be something safe, something that wouldn't cause a direct link back to him. Everyone would suspect him, of course. That's why he had to be clever in designing Eastwood's death.

Straylor's eyes darted between the house and his rearview mirror. If a vehicle pulled onto Mitchell Road, Straylor planned to start his car and move along. He took another long drag on his cigarette as he fought to overcome his animalistic desire to storm onto Eastwood's porch. He imagined himself withdrawing his service revolver and placing the barrel tightly under Eastwood's chin, then pulling the trigger. It's what he would have preferred to do.

Two taps against the police car's roof caused Straylor to snap back to reality. He had been mindlessly dreaming as he looked down the road in front of him. When he turned his head to identify the source of the tapping, he found himself confronted with the open end of a deadly weapon. Caught off guard, Straylor thought about going for his own weapon, but he wouldn't have had a chance.

"What's this all about?" Straylor queried the shadowy figure as he noticed that the weapon was equipped with a silencer.

The figure didn't respond.

"Who are you?" Straylor asked nervously as fear edged into his voice.

This time, the figure answered. "Too bad that I saw you park here."

Straylor's eyes widened in terror. He was speechless.

"I know all about you."

Straylor was frozen in place as the gun's barrel dropped and aimed at his crotch. Straylor followed the barrel and then looked back at the figure. "Please," he pleaded, "I'll do anything you want."

The shadowy figure answered by pulling the weapon's trigger. A bright flash momentarily filled the interior of the police car. Filled with pain, Straylor twisted in the car seat as he grabbed his crotch and opened his mouth to scream in agony. As his mouth opened, a soiled rag was shoved in to silence him.

Writhing in pain, Straylor looked at his assailant and saw that the weapon was now pointed at his face. Straylor shook his head from side to side as he silently pleaded for his life.

"Nothing like payback," the assailant grinned as the trigger was pulled one final time. The body slumped against the driver's door and slid down. The assailant reached in and retrieved the rag from Straylor's mouth. "Serves you right for all the grief you've caused me."

Looking up and down the road to make sure that there were no approaching cars, the assailant walked to the rear quarter panel of the vehicle. Opening the gas filler panel, the assailant twisted off the gas cap and stuffed the rag down the filler pipe. The assailant struck a match and ignited it. Taking a final look around, the assailant turned and disappeared into the night.

A few minutes later, the police car exploded as the gasoline ignited. The noise from the explosion could be heard for several hundred feet and awoke the residents in several of the nearby homes. When they saw the flames, they called the fire and police departments and rushed from their homes to see if they could provide assistance.

Hearing the explosion and seeing the fire, Eastwood walked onto his front porch. The shadows from the flames did a macabre dance on the front of his house. Eastwood began walking to the fire to join his neighbors. As he did, he called the Put-in-Bay fire department on his cell phone to make a report.

"Yes," the dispatcher answered. "We've had a couple of reports. The trucks are on their way."

One of the neighbors yelled and looked at Eastwood, "There's someone in the car."

Knowing that he needed to react, especially in front of his neighbors, Eastwood ran up to the car. The back seat was ablaze and flames were advancing on the front seat. Eastwood wrenched open the door. As he did, Straylor's upper body fell out. Ignoring the blood from the head shot, Eastwood grabbed Straylor's arms and pulled him out of the car and dragged him to a spot, which was twenty feet away.

Speaking to no one in particular, Eastwood said, "It's Straylor. He's dead."

"Son, you have some explaining to do."

Eastwood looked up as he stood and saw two EMT's rush by him to examine Straylor. Standing in front of Eastwood was Chief Wilkens.

"Straylor's dead," one EMT confirmed. "Looks like he took a bullet to the face and one to the crotch."

Wilkens nodded his head. From a psychological standpoint, it sounded like someone with a deep emotional link to Straylor had killed him. The shot to the crotch was the critical clue. Wilkens eyed Eastwood. "Did you have anything to do with this?"

"Now, wait a minute! I was in the house. I didn't even know that he was here."

One of the neighbors overheard the confrontation and added, "I saw Cody run out of the house to help."

Wilkens nodded his head and looked back at Eastwood. "You're sure that you didn't know he was here?"

"I'm not that stupid, Chief. If I was going to go after Straylor, I certainly wouldn't do it in front of my house."

"Unless you're using the obvious to throw us," Wilkens mused.

"I'm not," Eastwood responded firmly.

"Just the same, I don't want you leaving the island unless you clear it with me."

"I was planning to leave in a couple of days. I've just about got everything cleaned up regarding my parents' estate."

"Like I said, clear it with me." Wilkens looked toward the now smoldering police car as the firemen finished dousing the flames. He saw that two of his officers were taking statements from the neighbors and smiled at their efficiency. When he looked back at Eastwood, he saw that Eastwood had begun walking back to the house.

"Eastwood!" he yelled.

"Yeah?" Eastwood paused and looked back at Wilkens.

"Would you mind if I searched your house?"

"You'd need a warrant to do something like that," Eastwood replied.

"Yes, I would."

Eastwood smiled. "Come on over. I don't have anything to hide."

"Thanks, I appreciate it," Wilkens said. He called to two officers to accompany him. The three followed Eastwood to the house to begin their search.

The Next Morning
Put-in-Bay Police Department

Parking the old pick up truck behind the police station, Moore walked through the warm morning sun to the stairs, which led down to the police department. Moore stopped at the top of the stairs as a young man was climbing them.

The man looked up and greeted Moore. "Emerson, what a surprise to see you here."

"Good morning, Cody," Moore said as he greeted Eastwood.

"You here to do a story on Straylor's murder last night?"

"What?" Moore asked with a stunned look on his face.

"You didn't know?"

"No," Moore responded.

"Yeah, it happened in front of my house. Wilkens thinks I did it. Like I'd be stupid enough to kill him in front of my house, if I was going to do something like that." Eastwood shook his head from side to side. "I can't catch a break on this island. Next thing you know, I'll be blamed for this fish kill stuff."

"So you didn't kill him?" Moore pushed and watched Eastwood closely to see if he could pick up any unconscious signals from Eastwood that he was lying.

"No!" Eastwood replied emphatically. "I didn't like the guy, but I wasn't out to kill him."

Glancing at the stairway and back to Eastwood, Moore asked, "Were you in for questioning?"

"Yeah."

"How did it go?"

"Okay as far as I could tell. I'm trying to cooperate with them. Last night, Wilkens asked if he could search my place and I let them. I guess they were looking for the murder weapon."

"Without a search warrant?"

"Yeah. I don't have anything to hide. I didn't do it."

Placing his hand on Eastwood's shoulder, Moore tried to calm the frustrated young man. "Sounds to me like you're doing all the right things to help them."

Eastwood grimaced and again shook his head from side to side.

Moore decided to make a bold statement. "For what it's worth, Cody, I believe you."

"Thank you, Emerson. My parents told me about you and your reputation on the island as a straight shooter. That means a lot to have someone like you believe me."

"The best piece of advice I can give you is to continue to cooperate with Wilkens and stay out of trouble," Moore cautioned.

"You can count on that," Eastwood said as he walked toward the bicycle rack. He retrieved his bike and mounted it. "I've just about finalized my parents' estate. Thanks again, Emerson," he said as he began to pedal his bike onto Catawba Avenue.

"Good luck," Moore called as he turned and descended the stairs to the police department. He entered the department lobby and was greeted by the dispatcher.

"Hello, Emerson. What brings you here so early in the morning?" Goodwill asked as she batted her green eyes at Moore and looked him up and down.

"Good morning, Donna. Is Chet in?" Moore said as he ignored her flirtatious look.

"Yes, he is," she responded as she winked at Moore. "Let me see if he can visit with you. Give me a second." She called Wilkens' office as Moore took a seat in the spacious lobby.

In a moment, Goodwill was calling Moore. "He can see you. I'll buzz you in."

"Thanks," Moore replied as he walked over to the door and opened it when he heard the buzz, signaling that the door had unlocked. He made his way down the narrow hall to Wilkens' office. "Morning," he said as he walked in and sat in a chair.

"What brings you to my office so early in the morning?" Wilkens asked his friend.

"I'm heading over to the press conference and thought I'd check in with you to see if there were any new developments with the fish kill that you could discuss with me. But it sounds like you have a different type of kill on your hands."

"You heard about Straylor, then?"

"A few minutes ago when I bumped into Eastwood on the stairs. You think it was him?"

Wilkens' eyes looked directly at Moore and a smile crossed Wilkens' face. "You know better than that. I can't discuss details while we're in the middle of an active investigation, no matter how good of a friend you've become."

Moore smiled back. "But you can discuss what's in the public domain. What's the Reader's Digest as to what happened?"

Briefly, Wilkens gave Moore an overview of what happened.

"Heard you conducted a search of his house. Find anything?"

"Emerson, you know I can't answer that question." Wilkens smiled at the probing reporter.

"So, he's your number one suspect?"

"Let's just say that he's a person of interest," Wilkens responded.

"What you're actually telling me is that you don't have enough evidence to book him, otherwise he wouldn't be walking around. You have a motive in that he's had a history of run-ins with Straylor, but you don't have evidence," Moore hypothesized.

"Not yet. We're still investigating."

"Busy week. Pirates, Presidents, fish kill and murder."

"You could say that," Wilkens sighed.

"For what it's worth, I don't think that young man killed Stray-lor," Moore offered.

"Everyone's entitled to their opinion," Wilkens said.

Changing the topic, Moore asked, "How's the week going with the rowdy pirates on the island?"

"We've got a few more locked up in the drunk tank than we usually do. But other than that, it's been typical. The pirates on the island are making the Secret Service antsy, though," he observed.

"I saw a few pirate wenches walking on Delaware that would make any guy antsy," Moore smiled.

"As long as we keep all of these pirates away from Gibraltar Island and the President, we should do okay."

"Any news on the fish kill? I'm going to check with Reutter at the Stone Lab, too."

"Nothing yet. I hear that they're still investigating it."

Moore looked at his watch and stood from his chair. "You coming to the press conference?"

"Nope. Better stay here."

"Good luck with the Straylor murder investigation. But like I told you, I don't think it was Eastwood."

"We'll see," Wilkens said as he began to go through his notes on his desk.

Moore walked down the hall and left the police department.

The Gazebo
DeRivera Park

Cutting through DeRivera Park and carrying a fresh pizza from Frosty's, Moore stepped into the large white gazebo and leaned against the rail. Eating a slice of pizza, he stared toward Gibraltar Island, which was bustling with activity as workers and security personnel prepared for the President's press conference. To his right, Moore could see the tall masted *Niagara* at its berth. Later that day, she would be sailing back into the harbor with her cannons firing as part of the Pirates' Week festivities.

The screams of several female tourists behind him caused Moore to whirl around. Riding his bike at breakneck speed through the park and scattering tourists was Mike "Mad Dog" Adams, the legendary island entertainer at the Round House bar and good friend of Moore's.

Easily, Adams jumped his bike up the two steps to the gazebo and slid to a stop about six inches from Moore.

"Nothing like a little morning bike ride to put hair on your chest," Adams growled as he took a slice of pizza from the open box extended by Moore.

"You had those women scattering like pins taking a direct strike at the bowling alley," Moore grinned at his rowdy friend.

"You going to the press conference with El Presidente?"

"I'll be there. It's later this afternoon."

"Listen, Emerson. You need to come with us at one o'clock for the pirate attack on the Bay. Most of the island entertainers are going to be on board the *Niagara*."

"Sounds like fun, but I don't have any pirate gear."

"You come over to the Round House with me. I've got some extra stuff in the truck and I bet that Teri Remington has some stuff she can loan you. Wait until you see Maggie Beckford from the Chamber. She's got the real deal going with her costume." Adams paused and looked closely at his friend. "You up to a little pirating?"

Before he could reply, an Island Cab honked its horn at the two men in the gazebo. They both waved and Adams yelled, "Coconut Pomps, you come back when you have a load of women with just enough room for me to squeeze in and I'll ride with you!"

Adams turned to Moore and explained. "You ever ride in Coconut Pomps' cab?"

Watching the shuttle type vehicle drive by, Moore responded. "No, why?"

"Oh, I'm telling you man, you are missing it. You need to ride with him after the bars close and he fills it up with a bunch of drunken women. He's got the only cab on the island with a stripper pole. In fact, he has two in the cab. It gets very interesting in that cab late at night as he drives them back to their lodgings." Adams allowed a deep laugh to emit from his mouth as he reached for another slice of pizza.

"You've ridden with him?"

"Oh, yeah. Several times. My man, Tim, calls me on his cell when it gets real interesting and I'm at the curb, waiting to ride with him." Adams leaned toward Moore. "It's a wild time," he said as he winked slyly.

"It's funny that this is the first time I've heard about that. Sounds like I need to do some field research," Moore teased. "You never know what to expect here!"

"That's what I like about Put-in-Bay. It's like Key West on steroids or Disneyland for drunks! And the women who live here are just screaming beautiful. I think they should change the name of South Bass Island to Cougar Island!" he grinned slyly.

They watched as two boat babes walked up from the docks.

"And the island visitors aren't that bad looking either," Moore observed as he finished the last piece of pizza.

"There you go! Now, let's go get a pirate outfit for you." He looked at his watch. "Time is running out."

The two headed toward the Round House Bar.

Aboard the Niagara
Off Gibraltar Island

"Bring her about and fill her sails," the pirate captain shouted to the helmsman.

Adeptly shoving over her rudder, the helmsman brought the *Niagara* about. Crewmembers in the topsails set their lines and the breeze filled the sails of the square-rigged brig. The double-masted vessel was 198 feet long with a 30-foot beam and carried four 32-pound carronades for armament.

The original *Niagara* had played a pivotal role in the Battle of Lake Erie during the War of 1812 when Commodore Oliver Hazard Perry defeated the British near the Lake Erie islands.

Standing next to the helmsman was the ship's pirate captain, Mad Dog Adams, with a gold earring in his ear. A gold coin was hanging from a chain around his neck. He wore a black bandanna on his head and a sleeveless black waistcoat aflame with red embroidery; beneath it was a worn white shirt with sleeves ending at the elbow. He wore dirty white trousers, which ended below the knees, and black, cuffed boots. In the red sash around his waist, he carried two pistols and a short sword.

Standing next to Adams was his friend Emerson Moore. Moore was wearing a dark blue woolen captain's coat with gold buttons. On his head he had a black tricorn pirate's hat, trimmed in white. Around his neck hung colorful beads and a pirate's skull and crossbones. He wore a blue-striped shirt, black pants to the shins and black, cuffed pirate's boots. His cutlass hung from a tan baldric and a pistol protruded from the bright blue sash around his waist.

"I meant to ask you, Emerson. Where did you get the spiffy attire?" Adams inquired as he eyed Emerson's gear. "You didn't like what Teri had for you?"

"I borrowed it from that best selling island author," Moore grinned.

"Hey, where is he? I thought Bob and his wife, Cathy, were going to join us today," Adams wondered. "That Cathy is hot!" he added.

"That she is," Moore agreed. "Bob is lucky to have landed that catch! They're over at Splash. She's keeping an eye on him because he's judging another bikini contest there."

"That Bob's got it tough! Today's pirate parade is going to end up at Splash's pirate ship, so we can catch up with them." Adams turned his attention to the crew scattered about the main deck. "Maybe we can kidnap a couple of bikinied wenches," he said with a mischievous glint in his eyes.

The ship was filled with regular crewmembers in their period uniforms as well as a number of islanders and island entertainers. Decked out in pirate gear were entertainers Pat Dailey from the Boat House, Ray Fogg from the Put-in-Bay Brewery, Westside Steve from the Crescent Tavern, Bob Gatewood from the Round House, Scott Allen the Island Doctor from the Crew's Nest, Alex Bevan from the Boat House and the Menus Band from the Beer Barrel.

Above the crew, Tim Goldrainer from the Menus was swinging and cavorting from a hastily rigged trapeze, just like he would do during his shows. In a small lifeboat, being towed astern was the Island Doctor, Scott Allen, from the Crew's Nest. The Doc was sandwiched between two pretty wenches, who were vying for his attention.

Adams raised his telescope to his eye.

"Mad Dog, what does ye glass tell ye?" Dailey called.

Adams lowered the glass for a moment and looked at his motley crew. "Half full," he said. "Are ye thirsty for a little blood today?"

"Blood? Hell no. We're thirsty for a little Grog. Grog for all, I'm buying," Westside Steve yelled as his long red hair streamed in the breeze. Rum magically appeared and was served to the rowdy pirate crew.

"Want a swig, Emerson?" Adams asked as he finished a pull on the flask, which had been hidden in his waistcoat.

"Aye. Don't mind if I do," Moore responded as he took a small sip from the offered flask and returned it to Adams, who took another long pull.

"Time to run up our colors!" Adams said as the vessel moved into the bay. Adams pulled out a folded flag and attached it to the lines. He then ran it up the line and the Jolly Roger unfurled in the breeze.

A bespectacled member of the ship's regular crew approached Adams. "Excuse me, but you're going to have to lower your colors."

"What do you mean lower our colors?" Adams asked with an intimidating look.

"Sir, the ship's name is misspelled."

With a feigned look of concern, Adams looked at the flag. Below the skull and crossbones was the ship's name. It read *U.S. Viagara*. "I don't know about that. It looks correct to me." Adams looked at the crewmember and without hesitation; he snatched the glasses off his face. "Take another look. Does it look better?" he growled as he began to toss the man's glasses overboard.

As the glasses sailed through the air, Moore leaped high and caught them. Handing them back to the man, he spoke to Adams, "You can't fly that. It'd make this the last year we use the *Niagara* for attacking the bay."

"Geesh, Emerson. You're ruining all of our fun," Adams said as Moore lowered the flag to the deck.

"Not quite. We're just making an adjustment here." Moore laid the flag on the deck and withdrew his cutlass. Quickly he cut off the bottom of the flag with the offending name and ran it back up the line. "There we go. Everybody's happy."

"Be careful how you use the word everybody, Emerson."

Moore turned and saw that Adams had drawn both pistols from his sash. They were aimed at Moore. Before Moore could respond, they were interrupted by a shout from Fogg.

"Land ho," Fogg yelled from the crow's nest.

"What kind of ho was that?" Adams asked with a wicked grin.

"It's a land ho!" Fogg called back from the crow's nest located on the 118-foot tall main mast.

"I think I met her," Pat Dailey yelled.

"It was Adams' sister," Bevan added.

"Store that chatter or I'll have ye all keelhauled and make ye into shark bait!" Adams snarled.

Seeing the ship sailing past Gibraltar Island, the temporary residence of President Benson, Adams ordered, "Okay men, it's time to salute the President." In unison, the pirates wheeled and faced away from Gibraltar Island. Then, they dropped their trousers and mooned Gibraltar Island.

"No, no, not that kind of salute. With the cannon, you dumb asses," Adams snapped. "Beat to quarters! Clear the decks for action and run out the guns!"

Under the supervision of the regular crew, the island entertainers prepared the cannon, Old Betsy, for firing.

Dailey rammed a powder charge deep in the cannon's barrel. "I rammed her," Dailey said to his gun crewmates.

Through the vent in the top of the cannon, Bevan pricked the powder cartridge and primed the cannon with gunpowder from his powder horn.

Gatewood and Bevan used handspikes to maneuver the gun in place and ran her out for firing. Acting as the gun captain was Alex Ford, who was attired in his Captain Jack Sparrow gear. His wife, Lisa, and the rest of the Pirates of the Caribbean look-a-like crew were also on board. Ford barked an order as he waved his cutlass, "Stand clear there, my mates!" He sounded like Captain Jack.

He pulled the lanyard and stepped back. The hammer with flint struck the primer pan, creating a spark, which ignited the primer in the pan. The flash flew through the flash hole and ignited the fuse, which, in turn, caused the cartridge's gunpowder to explode with a thunderous roar.

From the stern, Adams remarked with a grin to Moore, "I'd just love to see the faces of all those Secret Service guys right now. This cannon fire has got to make their blood pressure soar!"

Moore nodded his head in agreement.

"Reload," Ford commanded as Gatewood and Bevan began to maneuver the cannon for the reloading process.

"Let's put a live round in this time," Gatewood teased as the crew moved quickly to ram a damp sponge down the gun barrel to extinguish any burning debris before ramming another powder charge. The crew reloaded and fired three more times as the ship sailed toward Put-in-Bay's Boardwalk Restaurant and Bar.

With the breeze strengthening and the ship beginning to pick up speed, Mad Dog gave orders to the regular crew, "All hands, shorten sail!"

The regular crewmembers jumped to their assigned positions and began to lower the sails to slow the vessel.

Within a few minutes, Adams bellowed, "Drop sail."

The helmsman expertly maneuvered the ship alongside the Boardwalk's dock and dockhands secured the lines.

As the pirate crew prepared to disembark and join the tourist pirates to lead the parade, a blood-curdling scream rent the air. Everyone looked skyward toward the crow's nest. Their eyes were greeted by the sight of Fogg swinging on a line from the upper mast like swashbuckling Errol Flynn. Fogg's momentum carried him over the dock and over the Boardwalk's upper deck.

Fogg let go of the line and executed a midair somersault onto the upper deck. Bowing to the astonished faces and applause of the onlookers.

"Give him a perfect 10. Style was good. Landing was great. I rank him a 10," Adams teased from the ship's deck.

Fogg turned and was greeted by the Boardwalk's owner, Eric Booker. Booker shook his friend's hand and presented him with a glass of champagne. Fogg downed the champagne and raced to catch up with his crewmates to start the parade.

A large crowd had gathered underneath the Boardwalk arch at the end of Catawba. Some were in pirate attire while others were casually dressed. Both sides of Catawba Avenue were lined with people, ready to watch the pirate parade.

The pirate flag carried by Mad Dog Adams served as the rallying point and the island entertainers led the parade. As they walked, they threw candy and Mardi Gras beads into the crowd. They walked past the Beer Barrel, Tippers, the Put-in-Bay Brewery, Cellar Cache and Grand Islander Hotel.

Turning left on Erie Street they strode to the Islander Inn and walked through its parking lot to Splash's large pirate ship, the *Flaming Skull*, with masts 55 feet tall. The ship's 100-seat bar overlooked the pool and the large tiki hut perched over the world's longest swim up bar. Island entrepreneur Tim Niese had constructed this 97-stool, 62-foot long bar which was more lucrative than a Vegas slot machine.

Taking seats at the bar, the parade walkers quickly ordered rounds of grog and watched the antics in the 60,000-gallon pool below them. It was like MTV Spring Break as bodies in a variety of skimpy swim attire gyrated to music from popular island entertainer, JD Owen! JD was singing from a huge tiki hut, perched over the swim up bar.

Behind JD, a bevy of bikinied and tanned young women were lined up for a contest. The winner would take home $500 and appear on the cover of the Put-in-Bay author's next novel. The author's wife, Cathy, was paying close attention as the author sat in a chair so that he could be at hip level to more effectively judge the contestants' tan lines.

Standing behind the author was *Put-in-Bay Gazette* owner Barry Hayen. He was using a telephoto lens on his camera so that he could capture the contestants for the paper's next edition – that's what he told his wife.

Press Conference
Gibraltar Island

The white pavilion to the west of Cooke's Castle provided the perfect setting for the press conference. It was at one of the island's high points overlooking the lake and boaters on their way to or from Put-in-Bay. The sky was a brilliant blue and served as a perfect backdrop for the conference.

Red and gray colored chairs were arranged neatly for the media. A large white canopy offering refuge from the sun's strong rays also covered the media area. Security was tight as uniformed and plainclothes officers seemed to swarm the area.

Moore cleared security with the other reporters and accompanied them on one of Ohio State's workboats to the Gibraltar Island dock. They made their way up the hill to the gazebo where chilled, bottled water was available. Moore had taken one of the bottles and found a seat in the third row next to an old friend of his from the Associated Press, Dan Newsome.

"Think they've solved it?" Newsome asked.

"I hope, but I think it's still too early with all the analysis and testing yet to be done," Moore replied.

"Yeah, you're probably right. So, gimme the skinny. How are the locals holding up? And don't hold back," Newsome warned in a good-natured tone.

"Of course, they're upset as anyone would expect. The perch market is a big deal here. It's hurting the fishing industry badly."

"How about tourism?"

"I'd have to say it's up. Funny thing about bad news. A lot of people want to see for themselves. The hotels are booked full. The ferries to the island are full. People want to see what's going on. And they probably want to see Benson."

"Yeah, you're probably right about that."

"And the press are everywhere. You guys are like ants on a piece of discarded fruit. You're trying to find info from anyone."

"It's called research, Emerson. You know that."

Nodding, Moore continued, "I know. Some of the locals are getting their share of free drinks by spinning stories to you guys."

"Yeah, some of us are starting to catch on."

"I was talking to Denny Watson this morning. He's a local legend and the island genius, who runs Dairy Air out at the airport."

Newsome nodded his head as he listened.

"Watson is a great storyteller and one of my favorite people on the island. It seems that he had two reporters not only buying him drinks, but also a huge dinner over at Axel and Harry's waterfront restaurant last night. He spun a yarn about aliens being responsible for the fish kill. Funniest thing you ever heard. And he got free drinks and a meal out of it!"

A murmur arose from the seated media and Moore turned his head to the right. There, he saw the presidential entourage approaching. President Benson and Prime Minister Hargraves were chatting amicably as they walked. Following them were Jon Hertrack, the PM's press secretary, Taggart and several other U.S. and Canadian security personnel.

The President and Hargraves stepped inside the Lakeview Pavilion, which provided them relief from the warming sun. Before addressing the media, they paused to take in the view from the pavilion, which was perched on the cliff's edge.

"Beautiful, isn't it?" the President commented to Hargraves.

"Yes, it is," he agreed as he looked at the alluring lake.

Benson turned and looked at the group of media members and others with sufficient pull to get a seat.

"I thank all of you for coming here today so we can update you on the Herculean efforts we and our Canadian partners are making to identify what is killing the perch and our efforts to eradicate this scourge. We're also going to talk about the new measures we must take to preserve our clean water.

"We all understand the importance of clean water. It is about more than a precious natural resource. It is about more than our lakes and rivers and streams. It is important for our communities to have clean, safe water.

"And that goes beyond safe drinking water and water for recreational purposes such as boating and swimming. It's clean water from which we can harvest food for our tables. Today, we are faced with a crisis caused by this massive fish kill. While it only involves one species, perch, we need to resolve it. We need to find what is killing the perch, be it pollution or some virus. We are resolved to stopping it before it can spread to other species of fish or, worse yet, to compromise the safety of our drinking water.

"This morning, Mr. Hargraves and I met with Dr. Jeff Reutter." Benson paused for a moment and smiled at Reutter, who was standing near the gazebo with his staff and other agency representatives. "Dr. Reutter is the head of Ohio Sea Grant and Stone Laboratory for The Ohio State University.

"Stone Laboratory is The Ohio State University's Island Campus on Lake Erie and the research and education facility of the Ohio Sea Grant College Program. Sea Grant is the primary university-based program of the Department of Commerce's National Oceanographic and Atmospheric Administration.

"During our meeting this morning, Dr. Reutter and his team provided us with an update on the progress they've made toward solving this fish kill puzzle. And they have made progress. I wish I could tell you that we have solved the puzzle. But, we haven't. Dr. Reutter, his staff and a group of international agencies are focusing their efforts to resolve this. I have every confidence that they will solve it quickly. We are pleased to let you know that the fish kill has been isolated primarily to the Western Basin and has not spread up or down stream.

"This lake is bounded by four states and two countries. While it only contains 2% of the water in the Great Lakes system, it contains 50% of the fish in the Great Lakes. It's no wonder that fisherman descend in mass here. And I'm going to be one of those fishermen. I'm planning on catching walleye today in this lake, known as the Walleye Capital of the World.

"We remember a time when Lake Erie was dying. It had become the poster child for pollution problems. Too many communities didn't have clean, safe water they could depend on. That's all changed, thanks to regulatory actions on both sides of the border and investments from both the public and private sectors.

"First, we must protect the public health. People shouldn't have to worry about whether the water they drink is safe, or whether the fish from our waters can be served to our children. Over 11 million people count on their water supply from this lake. Twenty power plants, over 300 marinas and 40% of the charter fishing boats in the Great Lakes are on Lake Erie. Its $1 billion sports fishing industry makes Lake Erie one of the world's top ten fishing sites.

"Second, we must do more to prevent polluted run off from contaminating our waters. Of the Great Lakes, Lake Erie's tributaries carry more suspended sediments to it than any of the others. This is due to the agricultural areas near the lake. Those sediments carry nutrients, chemicals, pesticides and raw sewage into the lake. Despite that, the lake is still the most biologically productive of the lakes.

"Third, we need a comprehensive approach to water quality which brings together all levels of government, and all concerned members of our communities to share ideas and approaches, to pool resources, and to develop a truly comprehensive strategy to safeguard our water.

"Years ago, America had a change of heart -- and a change of course. Instead of polluting our waters, we decided to clean them. Since the passage of the Clean Water Act, we have stopped billions of pounds of pollution from flowing into our rivers, lakes, and streams; and doubled the number of waters safe for swimming and fishing.

"People, who grew up in the Cleveland area, remember the Cuyahoga River catching fire. Because of the Ohio Environmental Council, we have witnessed the restoration of the Cuyahoga

River and other rivers. The Cuyahoga has been revitalized and the harbor in Cleveland is alive with boaters and tourists.

"These case histories tell stories that will make us proud. But problems persist. For all our success, there are still dangerous run offs of toxins and pollutants into our streams; communities that don't have the knowledge or the resources to fully protect their water; regions where the wrong kind of development threatens our hard-won progress. We need to recommit ourselves to the vision of the Clean Water Act -- and we need new action to move it forward.

"Of course, a strong vision is not enough. We must act to make that vision a reality. That is why I am directing the relevant federal agencies to take a series of actions that will preserve and extend a quarter-century of success, to make our water even cleaner for the next 25 years.

"We know that the best ideas don't necessarily come from Washington, but from the communities that are confronting these challenges every day. So we will seek input and opinion from all of you. We specifically invite Congress to work with us in strengthening and codifying a new national commitment to clean water.

"Today, we are announcing a bilateral agreement with our Canadian neighbors. Prime Minister Hargraves and I have signed a joint agreement to create a $100 million fund to accelerate efforts to identify and resolve this fish kill problem and ensure safe water. This follows up on previous administrations' efforts with the enactment of the Safe Drinking Water Act and the Clean Water Act. We will be asking for emergency action by Congress to approve this funding.

"We will get to the bottom of this fish kill issue. Thank you for listening -- and to the various agencies working on this, I say, keep up the good work. I'll now turn the podium over to Prime Minister Hargraves."

Moore took a swig on his water bottle as Hargraves replaced Benson at the podium and began his speech, which echoed Benson's comments. Hertrack must have been busy last night and this morning coordinating the speech preparation and fine-tuning them for both officials, Moore thought to himself.

At the conclusion of Hargraves' speech, Benson joined him at the podium and stated, "We're open for questions."

A reporter from one of the cable news channels was the first to raise a question. "Mr. President, we haven't heard any comments from you or indications from Dr. Reutter's team that rule out bioterrorism. Can you rule it out?"

"To answer your question, we can't say that we can rule it out, but we don't suspect that it is the source. We are investigating every aspect and leaving no stones unturned."

"So, then one could say that bioterrorism is a possibility."

Benson stared at the questioner. "What I am saying is that we are considering and reviewing all possibilities. We feel stronger about some than others."

Another reporter stood. "Mr. President, could you explain why the FBI is involved? Is it because you do fear that it's bioterrorism?"

Although he was becoming exasperated, Benson responded calmly. "Gentlemen, we are pursuing all avenues in this investigation. I'm confident that we will have an answer shortly."

After a few more questions, the two men concluded their press conference.

As Moore stood, Newsome spoke to him. "You were quiet today, Emerson. No questions for Benson? Not like you," Newsome observed.

A smile crossed Moore's face. "I've got several tough ones to ask him, but I'm saving them for tomorrow."

"Tomorrow? Is there another press conference tomorrow?"

"I'm going fishing with Benson tomorrow. I hope to land a big one," Moore replied.

"Yeah, fishing for information like you always do, right Emerson? I forgot that you and Benson were buds. Nice to have a one-on-one with him," Newsome teased.

"I'll see what I can stir up."

"Let me know what you find out, would you?" Newsome asked as they walked down the slope to the dock where boats were waiting to transport the reporters back to Peach Point's media center.

"Sure. It'll be in the *Post* the next morning," Moore grinned.

The Presidential Fishing Boat
Off Put-in-Bay

The early morning sun cast a warm glow across Put-in-Bay as the boats rocked gently at their moorings. It would be a peaceful morning after a night filled with partying for many of the boaters.

The scene at Gibraltar Island's dock was quite different as Secret Service men peered diligently around the surroundings and the last of the snacks and beverages were stowed on board the *Estorel*, which had been designated as the presidential fishing boat. The 42-foot Grand Banks Classic Trawler with twin 425-horse diesel engines had been loaned to the President by Kevin and Tawnya Kissel from Grosse Ile.

Standing on the dock and awaiting the presidential fishing entourage was Emerson Moore. Moore had motored over in his Zodiac from his East Point residence. On the way he was stopped twice and asked to show identification to the Coast Guard and Secret Service agents on a patrol boat. Security was tight.

A burst of activity from Secret Service agents as their radios came alive and the movement of a group of walkers from Cooke's Castle signaled the pending arrival of the President.

Moore saw Benson talking animatedly with Canadian Prime Minister Peter Hargraves as they neared. Everyone was dressed Put-in-Bay style: tee shirts, and khaki shorts with either boat shoes or tennis shoes.

Seeing Moore, the President called out, "Emerson, it's good to see you." He walked over to Moore and tilted his dark sunglasses from his tanned face to his head full of curly black hair. Shaking Moore's hand, he asked, "Ready to land some big ones today?"

Grinning, Moore responded, "Anytime, Mr. President."

Benson shot Moore a quick glance. "Cut the Mr. President crap, Emerson. You've known me way too long."

"Just showing you a little love and respect, Dick," Emerson replied.

Benson shook his head and turned to Hargraves. "What do you do with guys like this?"

"Keep them around. They usually give it to you straight. No sugar coating!" Hargraves extended his hand to Moore. "Glad to meet you Emerson. Dick told me about you over breakfast this morning. But don't let it go to your head. We spent most of our time talking about walleye." Hargraves was an avid fisherman.

"Is there anything better to talk about when you're boarding a fishing boat?" Moore replied as he followed the two leaders on board. The Canadian Prime Minister was followed closely by one of his Royal Canadian Mounted Policeman, who made up his protective detail.

Standing in the stern as Secret Service agents untied the lines and another took the helm, Benson introduced Moore to two other agents. "Emerson, meet Bill Taggart. He's heading up my protection detail these days. It's a wonder that I'm allowed to stand at the urinal by myself," he said with mock indignation.

"Got to protect you, Sir," the steely-eyed Taggart replied. He had an abrasive edge to his voice. "We've met before, as you may recall."

"I do," Moore acknowledged.

He had encountered Taggart when Taggart had headed the vice-president's protective detail. During one confrontational interview two years ago, Moore had drilled in with a series of uncomfortable questions to the Vice President. Moore had been trying to demonstrate that the Vice President was involved in a cover up when he was governor of Nevada.

Taggart had abruptly ended the interview and sharply elbowed Moore in the ribs as he walked away. Moore had filed a protest with the Secret Service, which resulted in a less than heartfelt apology from Taggart. Taggart had steadfastly claimed it was unintentional, but Moore knew better.

The President continued. "I believe you've bumped into Kenfield Valero a few times when you and I have been together."

"Yes, we have," Moore smiled. "Good to see you, Kenfield."

"It's been a while, Emerson," Valero grinned confidently.

Valero was the direct opposite of Taggart in personality. Taggart was cold and seemed to be constantly looking over his shoulder and not just for potential threats to the President. It was known amongst Washington insiders that Taggart had desires to move up the ladder and run Homeland Security. The advancement from protecting the Vice President to heading the presidential protection detail was seen as a step in that direction.

Valero, on the other hand, had been a dedicated agent, who felt his life's calling was to serve The Office of the President. He enjoyed the travel and the challenge of staying abreast of technology advances, which could pose a threat to the President.

Moore had taken an instant liking to Valero when they first met ten years ago. The five-foot-seven-inch tall Valero had an amiable personality.

"Hey, anyone for coffee?" Benson asked as the craft picked up speed, rounding the eastern edge of Gibraltar Island.

Magically, one of the White House staff members appeared with coffee for everyone. Benson, Hargraves and Moore had settled into seats in the stern. Taggart had moved to the helm where he was communicating with a Coast Guard helicopter overhead. Valero had taken a position near the stern from where he cast a wary eye around their surroundings for potential threats.

There was an unlikelihood of anything happening as they were surrounded by a flotilla of watercraft. Leading the presidential fishing boat was the Put-in-Bay Police Boat. Two U.S. Coast Guard patrol boats flanked the presidential watercraft. Each of the boats was also staffed by one Secret Service agent as were two Canadian Coast Guard boats, which followed astern.

Following the fishing boat was another larger boat, which carried additional, heavily armed Secret Service agents, a doctor and nurse. Behind this boat was the press boat, jammed with photographers, awaiting permission to pull abreast of the presidential fishing boat to get a few pictures of Benson and

Hargraves pulling in fish. Once they got their obligatory shots, they would be ordered a safe distance away from the President so that the presidential party could fish in peace.

While Hargraves was talking on his cell phone, Benson leaned toward Moore. "So tell me, Emerson, how do you like island life?"

"It's just wonderful. We have fresh breezes from the west. I live over there." Moore pointed to his aunt's waterfront home on East Point.

"With a relative?"

"Good memory, Mr. President. Yes, it's my Aunt Anne. She's getting up there, but has enough energy to tire out both you and me."

"The view of the harbor must be fantastic from there."

"It is," Moore agreed. "From the front porch or the dock, you see the boats in the Bay. There's just something relaxing to me about watching the boats move around the harbor. And the sunsets are unbelievable!"

"Sounds relatively stress free," Benson sighed as he thought about the responsibilities he faced. "One thing about being President though."

"What's that?"

"Once you get sworn in, then all you get is sworn at!"

Nodding his head in understanding, Moore added, "It is relatively stress free here. I'm fortunate that the *Post* allows me to work from here. But then again with all of the technology, it doesn't matter where I'm domiciled. Besides, I'm on the road a lot too as I research stories."

"And this time, we bring the story to you," Benson grinned.

"Awfully nice of you," Moore grinned back. "And it allows us to catch up on some good fishing."

"So, tell me Emerson. How do the locals really feel about the efforts being made to resolve this perch kill?"

"Honestly, they wanted it resolved yesterday. They know that everyone is focused on identifying the source and finding a way to eradicate whatever it is, but they want it done faster. Anyone would."

Benson nodded his head in agreement as he continued to listen.

"The charter boat captains have switched to walleye fishing just like we are going to do. Tourism on the island is still strong. It helped a lot when the papers announced that whatever it was, was not harmful to humans. We've got a bunch of curiosity seekers on the islands, too."

"But we have got to get to the bottom of this!"

"I agree wholeheartedly. Jeff Reutter and his team at the Stone Lab are working long hours to resolve it." Changing topics, Moore asked, "How's the acceptance speech coming?"

"I haven't had a chance to focus on it. Hertrack gave me a rough draft to review, I'm going to start on it later today."

"Still keeping Moran as Vice President? You haven't announced anything yet."

Benson was quiet. Then, he turned and looked directly into Moore's eyes. "You know I can't divulge anything to you at this time. It'd be premature and inappropriate."

Moore began back peddling. "Sorry. I didn't mean for it to sound like I was trying to get a jump on the story."

Benson sat back in his deck chair. "You might say I'm a bit sensitive on that topic. There's been a lot of pressure from both sides."

"Well, not to add to the pressure, but I think Coughlin is your man. More importantly Moran should be dropped from the ticket. You just can't trust the guy. There was that Nevada scheme."

The President stopped Moore with an upraised hand. "Emerson, I'm aware of all that. Let's not beat a dead fish here," he said as he interjected his strange sense of humor into the conversation. "Let's just drop it and have a good time fishing."

Reading Benson's attitude and posture, Moore realized that it was indeed time to drop the topic. "Sounds like a great idea to me."

Seeing Hargraves end his cell phone call, Benson said, "I sure hope they're biting."
Hargraves nodded.

The Presidential fleet slowed as they reached their targeted fishing site. It was northwest of North Bass Island and where the "F" can buoy once marked the boundary between the United States and Canada. Their fishing guide, John Hageman, made his way back to the stern of the trawler.

"If you folks are ready, let's bait those hooks," he said. "We'll be drifting with the wind today."

"What are we using for bait, John?" Benson asked.

"A May fly rig. We'll flavor the hooks with a small piece of Canadian jumbo nightcrawlers provided by our friend from Canada." Hageman was looking at Hargraves.

"Nice fresh ones, too," Hargraves added. "And today, it doesn't matter which side of the border we fish on!"

"As long as we catch fish today," Benson grinned.

Each of the three fishermen grabbed their poles and prepared their rigs and hooks. They then cast astern and against the wind. Their hooks settled to the depth, which Hageman had suggested based on his fishfinder observations. They began a slow retrieval of their lines back to the boat.

Benson felt extra weight on his line, which indicated that a walleye was mouthing the bait. It felt like the line was being pulled through Jell-O. Benson pulled back on his rod, setting the hook. He began to reel in the line as the walleye began a minor run.

When the fish sighted the boat, it made a sharp dive to test the line strength, the reel's drag and the skill of the fisherman. This walleye was no match for Benson. Knowing that walleye are typically done after one good dive, Benson pulled in the walleye.

As he reeled it in, Hageman netted the fish and brought it on board. He removed the hook and handed the fish to Benson. "Nice one, Mr. President. It's a plump 20 incher over 2 pounds," Hageman said with a large smile.

Within minutes, Hargraves was holding the walleye he had hooked. His wasn't as big as Benson's.

"Taggart."

"Yes, Mr. President."

"Why don't you call in the press boat so they can take our picture?"

"Will do."

"And tell that Coast Guard cutter to drop back. Otherwise, they'll be in the background of the shot."

"Got it," Taggart responded as he talked into his radio, barking orders.

Valero leaned toward Moore. "Want to step up toward the bow with me so you won't be in the photo?"

"Great idea!" Moore replied. He didn't need to be in those photos. It was a photo opportunity for the President and the Prime Minister.

Moore followed Valero to the bow. "How's the President really doing, Kenfield?"

"Fine. He's doing just fine," Valero answered.

Moore bore in. "Oh, come on now. You can give me the straight scoop. I'm not going to print it. I'm asking as a friend of his."

Valero stared at Moore for a moment before replying. "You can see him anguishing over making the right decision about keeping or dropping Moran. Other than that, he seems good."

They both turned their heads and looked toward the stern where the two heads of state were posing with their first catches of the day.

"He's a good man," Valero said.

"I know. They don't come much better than him. The integrity. The smarts. He's got it all."

"Needs to be careful with his talent selection skills," Valero murmured quietly.

"I know. But who could have guessed that the Vice President would turn out the way he did?"

"That's not who I was talking about."

Moore looked at Valero who was staring at Taggart.

"Taggart?"

Valero seemed to snap out of a daze. "I've said too much." Seeing that the press boat was beginning to pull away, Valero said, "Looks like it's back to fishing time. Let's get you back to your fishing partners." Valero started toward the stern with Moore closely following.

As he entered the stern area, Benson was removing his shirt. "I guess it's okay that I get more comfortable since the press have moved away." Benson was in good shape for his 48 years. His muscular chest was tanned and toned. "Got to catch some more rays," he chuckled.

"Fine with me, but my shirt is staying on," Hargraves said. He wasn't about to reveal his chubby Canadian belly to any photojournalist with a telephoto lens.

Benson turned away from Moore and bent over to secure more bait. When he did, Moore chuckled to himself as the rear of Benson's shorts gapped open. There in front of him and below Benson's tan line at his waist was the Presidential plumber's crack. Moore sensed someone else staring and he looked to his side. There, he saw Valero. He grinned back at Moore, having also spotted the Presidential plumber's crack.

The men continued fishing for another hour and then the entire flotilla headed back to Gibraltar Island's dock.

As the *Estorel* was secured to the dock, Benson leaned toward Moore. "Emerson?"

"Yes?"

"Hargraves leaves this afternoon and I'm planning on going fishing again tomorrow morning. Care to join me?"

"Sure. Is there some other reason for me going with you?"

A smiled appeared on Benson's face. "You are so suspicious."

Nodding his head, Moore replied, "Have to be in my business." He grinned back at the President.

"All right then. I want to bounce a couple of thoughts off you regarding my acceptance speech."

"About dumping the Vice President?" Moore needled his friend as Taggart appeared at Benson's side.

Ignoring the comment, Benson said, "I just want to talk about a couple of things."

"Mr. President?" Taggart asked.

"Yes."

"We're set to disembark."

"Good." Turning to Moore, Benson said, "Meet us here at 8:00 a.m. We'll see what we catch then. Taggart, make sure he has clearance for tomorrow."

Taggart acknowledged by nodding his head.

"See you tomorrow," Valero said to Moore as he followed the departing group.

"Tomorrow."

The boat emptied with the exception of John Hageman and Moore. "Good guy," Moore observed as the group climbed the hill toward Cooke's Castle.

"Yeah. First time I've been up close to a president."

"One thing, though," Moore said as he stepped off the boat.

"What's that?" Hageman asked.

"I don't like that Taggart."

"Me neither. I'd rather fall through the ice than have to spend time with him. There's something about him."

"Yes, there is, John." Moore approached his Zodiac under the watchful eyes of Secret Service agents on the dock. "See you tomorrow, John."

"Right."

Moore started the Zodiac and guided the craft toward East Point.

Early That Evening
Put-in-Bay Airport

The small plane circled the Put-in-Bay Airport one time before lining up for its approach from the lake on the south side of the island. As the plane descended on its final approach, the pilot lowered his landing gear. It touched down easily and taxied up to the Dairy Air hangar. With its twin engines still running, two passengers disembarked from the craft and hurried into the open hangar.

The plane turned and taxied to the southern end of the runway. It quickly lined up and took off. The plane's ground time was barely six minutes.

"Can I help you, boys?"

The two visitors spun around in surprise and faced the direction from which the voice had boomed.

The wily owner of Dairy Air, the only airline based on South Bass Island, was standing next to the fuselage of one of his planes. He was holding a wrench in one hand. With the other hand, he was pushing back the brim of his *Rainbow's End* cap.

"I said, can I help you boys?" Denny Watson asked again as he peered at the two men; one was clean-shaven and the other was bearded. They were both wearing dark sunglasses despite the approaching darkness. The bearded man, who was also wearing a hat, tightly gripped a briefcase.

The clean-shaven one spoke first. "We're waiting for our ride."

Watson stepped away from the plane and walked toward the hangar entrance. "The last time I checked with the FAA, they weren't allowing any taxis, buses or private vehicles to drive on the tarmac. There's a sign over there on that fence which states no vehicles beyond this point. If you're waiting for a ride, I'd suggest that you mosey over there beyond the fence to wait."

The clean-shaven one had removed his glasses. He gave Watson a cold stare. "We'll just wait right here until they pull up."

Watson rubbed his beard. "Well, I guess you could do that, but then again, I'd have to charge you a hangar waiting fee."

"This is government business."

"Oh, I know what you mean. I do government business, too. I work for the government in delivering mail to this island. The waiting fee is fifty bucks." Watson was grinning at his two unwanted visitors.

Suddenly, the clean-shaven one raised his arm and spoke into his wrist. "Hurry it up!"

"Secret Service, huh? You know, I thought I recognized you. I saw you in town before President Benson arrived. You were scouting us out." Watson was beaming at recognizing the agent. He had a good memory for people's faces. "Since you're Secret Service, the waiting fee is doubled," Watson chortled.

The sound of screeching tires as a car wheeled quickly into the airport parking lot interrupted Watson's banter.

"There's our ride," the clean-shaven one said as the two started toward the dark colored vehicle. "Bill me," he called over his shoulder to Watson.

Watson thought to himself, your day is coming.

"What took you so long?" the clean-shaven agent asked as the two men deposited themselves in the vehicle's back seat.

"Give it a rest, Benko," the driver said as he heard them shut the vehicle's doors. He knew Benko's reputation for being negative.

Agent Jim Benko looked out the window as the car sped toward town. He was agitated that the car had been delayed. He didn't want to increase the odds of exposing his quiet guest anymore than need be. His mission was to quietly escort this surprise visitor to Gibraltar Island to meet with the President. No one was to know about this visit.

Benko stole a glance at his visitor, who turned to look out of the vehicle's window. He was still wearing his dark sunglasses to help obscure his identity.

The vehicle continued along Langram Road and turned left onto Toledo Avenue. When Toledo dead-ended into Bay View, the vehicle turned left on Bay View and drove along the waterfront past Axel and Harry's Restaurant, the Jet Express dock and the village docks. The village docks were filled with boats and boaters in swim attire gyrating to the loud music blaring from the expensive sound systems on several boats.

The visitor muttered under his breath. "Beautiful."

Benko nodded and pointed to the other side of the bay. "That's Gibraltar Island."

The vehicle pulled to a stop in front of the Boardwalk and its two passengers stepped out of the vehicle and walked past Sonny's Ferry, which took passengers to Middle Bass Island. On the other side of it was one of the water taxis, which transported boaters between the island and their boats tied to the mooring buoys.

"Can you run us to Gibraltar?" Benko asked the helmsman.

"It's restricted. The President is staying there," the helmsman replied from the taxi.

Pulling his badge from his pocket, Benko flashed it at the helmsman. "I know. I'm Secret Service. So is he. Now, will you take us out there, pisshead?"

The helmsman winced, but recovered quickly. "Let me see his identification then."

The bearded visitor produced his Secret Service identification and displayed it to the helmsman, who quickly looked at it and returned it.

"Come aboard."

The helmsman would never know that the identification was counterfeit. It looked very much like the authentic identification.

As soon as the visitors boarded, the helmsman released the lines and put the water taxi in motion by nudging the throttle forward and adroitly spinning the wheel to take the craft away from the dock.

As he rounded the mooring buoys and pointed the taxi in the direction of Gibraltar Island, a police boat appeared almost magically. From its speaker came a command. "You're entering restricted waters. Stop and turn about."

The helmsman picked up his radio's mike and spoke into it. "I've got two Secret Service agents aboard. They're going to Gibraltar."

Interesting, the officer in charge thought to himself. None of the other agents were using the water taxi. They were being transported from the Ohio State docks on Peach Point. "We're going to board you. Idle your engine."

Benko had been closely observing the exchange. He didn't need this additional exposure for his visitor. He lifted his wrist to mouth and spoke into his radio. "Taggart."

"I'm here, Benko"

"Looks like we are going to be boarded."

"I see. I'm standing on the dock. I'll take care of it." Taggart gave orders to a nearby agent who rushed to the communications center to radio the police boat.

The officer in charge had stepped aboard the water taxi. When he did, Benko stepped up to him to buy time. "Here's my identification," he said as he thrust it into the man's chest so hard that he almost knocked the man back into the police boat.

Recovering his balance, the man stared hard at Benko. Two cold eyes returned the stare. Before a confrontation could develop further, a voice called over from the police boat. "They're cleared."

"But I haven't had a chance to..."

Benko interrupted him as he snatched his identification from the man's hand. "We're cleared. Now shove off, idiot."

The officer was fuming as he returned to the police boat which pulled away to allow the taxi to continue its short journey to the dock.

Benko allowed a grim smile to cross his face as he began to whistle and the water taxi resumed its journey to Gibraltar Island. In a matter of minutes, they arrived and were greeted by the waiting Taggart.

"Any problems, other than what just occurred?"

"None," Benko responded as he helped his passenger onto the dock.

"Good to see you again," Taggart said with a sly smile to the visitor.

"Likewise," the visitor mumbled as he looked around nervously.

Noticing the visitor's agitation, Taggart offered, "Nothing to worry about. I've given instructions, which will keep our security people away from us. We won't have any close encounters on the way."

"Good," the visitor commented. He was still nervous. He wanted to keep his identity concealed.

"Let's go then." Taggart turned and began walking the visitor up the sidewalk toward Cooke's Castle. They were closely followed by Benko.

As they walked past the gazebo and the entranceway to Harborview House, the Ohio State University dormitory, they didn't notice a figure standing inside the doorway. It was Kenfield Valero.

Valero looked at his watch and noted the time. He had seen the daily schedule when he had gone on his duty shift for the day. There were no notations of visitors scheduled for late in the day. He felt the hair on his neck stand. Not a good sign, he thought to himself. It was his sixth sense working again. And he usually listened to it. It had saved him before during his career in DEA and then the Secret Service.

It was the dark sunglasses the visitor was wearing which made Valero uneasy. He stepped out of the doorway and watched as the threesome approached and entered Cooke's Castle.

Five hours later, a knock on the President's bedroom door awakened him. "Yes? What is it?"

"Mr. President, it's Taggart."

"Yes. What do you need?"

"Sir, there's someone here to see you."

Benson glanced at the watch on his bed stand. "At this hour? Is there something wrong?" he asked as he shook his head to clear it from the deep sleep he had been enjoying.

"If you bear with me, I think you'll understand."

Benson ran a hand through his rumpled hair and then pulled on his slacks. He threw on a polo shirt and slipped on his boat shoes. "This had better be important."

"It is, sir."

Benson followed Taggart down the stairs to the first floor and then through the dining room and into the kitchen. Taggart opened the door to the wine cellar and descended with Benson.

At the bottom of the stairs, Taggart stood aside and allowed Benson to walk past him. He saw two people. "Good evening, Jim," Benson said to Benko.

"Mr. President," Benko nodded as he greeted Benson.

"And who do we have here that it was so urgent for me to be awakened from my sleep?" Benson asked as he looked at the back of the other person.

The second person slowly turned around to face Benson. When Benson saw who was standing in front of him, he stormed incredulously, "What is this all about?"

Wilkens' Office
Put-in-Bay Police Station

"This has been a week full of pirates and Presidents. And I'm not sure that there is any difference between any of them." Wilkens stormed quietly as he stood with his back to his desk, awaiting his visitor. "Add in a couple of murders, arson and fish kill and you'd think I work in Detroit rather than a quiet island paradise," he muttered to himself.

"Chief? You wanted to see me?"

Wilkens turned to face the doorway where he saw Donna Goodwill, his attractive dispatcher standing. "Yes, I do, Donna.

Come in and have a seat," he said as he pointed to a chair in front of his desk. Wilkens walked to the door, shut it and returned to his desk where he sat back in his massive leather chair.

"Is there something you need help with? We have more dignitaries coming?" she asked eagerly.

"No, it's nothing like that. I need to ask you a question."

"Oh? What's that?"

Wilkens picked up a letter from his desk. "I just received this confirmation e-mail from the FBI." He looked from the e-mail to Goodwill.

"Yes?"

"It appears that I authorized a down cell wiretap."

With proper authorization, the FBI can activate a person's cell phone without their knowledge and use it to listen in on the person's conversations. It was an effective tool for gathering evidence in terrorism, drug trafficking and other illegal activities.

"Yes?"

"I didn't authorize it." Wilkens peered closely at Goodwill. "It was on Straylor's cell phone and it was on the day before his wife and neighbor were killed and the two houses burned down."

Goodwill's face seemed worried. "What do you think that means? Was he drug trafficking here on the island?"

"I'm not sure. I'm also not sure who would have used my name to authorize the wiretap on his cell phone."

"Who do you think did it? One of those Secret Service guys? They certainly have enough law enforcement agencies on the island this week."

"I'm not sure. I might determine that once I figure out what the motive would be."

"That sure is strange," Goodwill said with a touch of nervousness. It wasn't lost on Wilkens.

"Are you done with me?" Goodwill asked as she stood and began to ease toward the closed door.

"Yes, Donna, I am."

Goodwill turned and placed her hand on the doorknob. As she began to turn the knob, Wilkens said, "Oh, Donna."

Goodwill grimaced before turning. When she faced Wilkens, the grimace had disappeared. "Yes?"

"One more thing."

"Yes?"

"Is there anything you need to make me aware of?"

Goodwill averted her eyes and looked at the carpeted floor. "Like what?"

"I'm not sure."

Thinking for a moment, Goodwill raised her head and looked directly into Wilkens' eyes. "You do know about Straylor's nickname on the island?"

Wilkens knew, but he wanted to hear her tell him. "What's that?"

"Straying Straylor."

There had been rumors for years about Straylor having multiple affairs, especially with the summer island visitors who were looking for an island fling. Straylor was cunning. No one had been able to catch him in the act.

"Yes, I do remember hearing that."

"I think just about everyone on the island knew about it. Can I go now?"

"Yes. Thanks for listening."

"Anytime, Chief. It's been a rough week," she said as she regained her composure and walked out of the office.

Wilkens spun his chair around and faced the cluttered credenza behind his desk. He was troubled by the cell phone wiretap. What was behind all of this, he wondered to himself? He reached for his phone and dialed his contact at the FBI to follow up on the authorization. In the last few days, he had three homicides on his hands and no answers. It was more like five homicides if he counted the murdered Secret Service agent and the woman at the Park Hotel. A voice answered the phone at the FBI.

Wilkens identified himself and explained why he was calling. His contact punched in several characters on the keyboard in front of him, and quickly identified the source of the authorization. Stunned, Wilkens thanked his contact and ended the call. He slumped in his chair and spun around to think as the reality struck home.

Ten minutes later, Wilkens made his decision. He spun around to face his desk and reached for his phone. He punched in two numbers.

"Yes, Chief?"

"Could you come to my office?"

"Be right there."

Less than a minute passed.

"You wanted to see me?"

Wilkens' face had a serious look. He was not relishing the confrontation, which was about to take place. "Yes, Donna. Please close the door and sit down."

Closing the door and approaching the chair, Goodwill asked nervously, "Is there something wrong? I can tell by your face." Goodwill sat in the chair across from the desk.

"Donna," Wilkens started, "you've been one of my most trusted employees."

"Yes. I've always thought we had a good relationship over the three years I've been here."

"You know, I would do anything I could to support you."

"Yes, and I'd do the same for you, Chief."

"I've always wanted you and the rest of the team to feel comfortable enough that they could come to me if there were any problems."

The anxiety level in Goodwill was building. "Okay Chief, what did I do wrong?"

"I just got off the phone with the FBI. I followed up on the authorization for the tap on Straylor's cell phone. They told me that you called it in and said that I authorized it. I never gave you those instructions."

Goodwill's eyes were now staring at the floor.

"Do you want to tell me why you would do something like that?"

The firm tone in Wilkens' voice reflected how serious the issue was. Goodwill looked up at Wilkens and swallowed. Before responding, she took a deep breath. "Sure Chief. My primary duty here has been at the front desk as a dispatcher. I wanted to show you that I was capable of doing more than that. I had growing suspicions that Straylor was involved with the murder of the Secret Service agent and the woman at the Park Hotel. So, I decided to prove to you that I could be a good investigator. I did take the liberty of calling the FBI and authorizing the tap, saying that you requested it."

Wilkens probed. "And what did you hear when you tapped in?"

"Nothing," she responded as her eyes returned to staring at the floor.

"What made you suspicious in the first place?"

"It was just woman's intuition. But, it turns out that I was wrong with my suspicions." Goodwill looked up at Wilkens. She flashed her pretty green eyes at him and said, "Chief, it won't happen again. I'm sorry that I broke your trust. It was stupid of me to do that."

Leaning back in his chair, Wilkens admonished her. "I can't have you or anyone else here authorizing actions under my name when I haven't given you permission." Wilkens leaned forward and picked up his pen and began to jot several notes on the pad on his desk. "I'm going to write you up for disciplinary action."

"I expected that would be necessary. It won't happen again," Goodwill said as a sigh slipped from her lips. She stood and walked to the door.

As her hand began to turn the doorknob, Wilkens surprised her with a question. "Donna, were you having an affair with Straylor?"

Goodwill froze. Slowly, she turned and faced Wilkens. "Why would you ask that?"

"Just a growing suspicion. Call it men's intuition or what my gut is telling me now," Wilkens replied firmly.

Goodwill was silent as she shifted from one foot to the other.

"Donna, I asked you if you were having an affair with Straylor. You haven't given me an answer." Wilkens' keen skill at observing people during interviews helped him in picking up subtle signals from her body language that she wasn't answering his questions truthfully. On several occasions, he noticed that her hands were shaking. She had appeared nervous to him. He also recalled an incident in the parking lot when he had observed Straylor and Goodwill in a heated conversation. There was something there. He was sure of it.

Goodwill's eyes were cast downward. Quietly, she answered the question. "Yes."

"Come back here and sit down."

Goodwill returned to the chair. Her body slumped as she sat.

"And what was the purpose of the tap?"

"I thought he was cheating on me."

"You knew that he was already cheating on his wife with you, so why would that come as a surprise?"

Goodwill didn't respond.

"Care to tell me what you heard on the tap?"

Goodwill was silent as a range of emotions swept through her.

"Donna, I need you to tell me what you heard."

Sensing that her world was beginning to crumble and Wilkens would find out anyway, Goodwill decided to be forthright. It would only be a matter of time before the Chief put together the entire puzzle. "I didn't hear anything during the day. I picked a day that his wife would be off island. But I did hear something that night."

"What did you hear?" Wilkens was now sitting straight up in his chair.

A look of fury burned in her eyes as she recalled the event. "I heard a woman. She was squealing like a pig in heat. I didn't know who she was until Straylor shouted her name."

A scowl filled her face and she virtually spat the name. "Cheri!"

"Straylor's neighbor?"

"Yes, the little slut," she replied with a distasteful tone.

Wilkens stood and walked around his desk. He stood next to Goodwill. "Donna, did you have anything to do with the fires and deaths of Straylor's wife and neighbor?"

Hesitating a moment before responding, she erupted angrily as her emotions overwhelmed her. "Yes, I did. He was going to divorce his wife. He promised me he would. He told me that he loved me. I was his soul mate. He was nothing more than a liar."

Grimly, Wilkens picked up his phone and punched in two numbers. When the phone was answered, Wilkens said, "Could you come to my office right away?" He replaced the handset in the cradle.

A few seconds elapsed before the door opened and officer Bob Cook walked in, closing the door behind him.

"Bob, I need you as a witness. Donna just confessed to killing Cindy and Cheri and I need to give her Miranda rights."

Shocked at the news about her, but understanding the procedure, Cook nodded his head.

"Chief, I waive my rights. It's all going to come out anyway. I'll cooperate and I hope you explain that to the judge and prosecutor," Goodwill said as her demeanor changed and she resigned herself to her fate.

"But, why did you kill Cindy and Cheri? Why didn't you walk away?"

"Come on Chief, I couldn't. I work with the guy virtually every day. If I couldn't have him to myself, I wasn't going to let them have him."

Deciding to probe further, Wilkens asked, "And so you killed Straylor and torched his car?"

"Yes, I did. I followed him that night and saw him pull up in front of Eastwood's house. I thought it'd point the blame at Eastwood."

"It didn't in my book."

"How's that, Chief" she asked confused.

"Crimes of passion leave telltale signs. It was the shot to the crotch that gave it away. Eastwood wouldn't have any reason to do that. It would have been from someone who was emotionally involved with Straylor."

Nodding her head, Goodwill allowed a wicked smile to cross her lips. "Yeah, I thought I'd teach the SOB a lesson for cheating on me. I put the first bullet there as retribution."

"Bob, I think we have enough for now. Would you relieve her of her weapon and lock her up?"

"Will do, Chief," Cook responded.

Walking with them to the office door, Wilkens said, "I'm going to Eastwood's house and let him know that he's off the hook."

Calling over her shoulder as they walked down the hall, Goodwill said, "You won't find him there. One of my girlfriends told me this morning that she saw him catching the Miller Ferry. He's off island."

"I told him he couldn't leave the island without clearing it with me," Wilkens fumed as he returned to his office.

The Presidential Fishing Boat
The Next Morning

"Morning, Emerson." The President said as he boarded the waiting fishing boat. "Looks like a grand day for walleye."

"I'm counting on it, sir." Moore replied from the stern where he was already sipping a cup of coffee. He had arrived early for the trip and John Hageman had provided him with fresh brew.

Taggart and another agent also boarded with the President.

"Good morning," Taggart said to Moore.

Moore nodded his head and asked as he saw the second agent, "Where's Valero?"

"He's on another assignment today. Meet Jim Benko."

Moore looked at the beady-eyed Benko and his first impression of the agent was less than desirable. Valero had seemed very positive about being on today's fishing adventure and his not being there was a surprise. Moore dismissed it and greeted Benko, "Good morning."

"Yeah, it is, isn't it?" Benko grunted as he walked past Moore and stood next to Hageman.

Serving the President a cup of coffee, Hageman asked, "Ready to push off, Mr. President?"

"Yes, let our fishing adventure begin," the President responded as Hageman returned to the helm. With lines tossed into the craft, Hageman pushed the throttle forward and the craft headed toward open water, followed by a small flotilla of security and the media boat.

In the stern, Moore turned to the President and asked, "Any more thoughts about our conversation yesterday?"

The President looked at Moore and responded by asking, "Which topic?"

"About tossing Moran from the ticket."

"None. I've decided to keep him," the President replied with a tone of strong conviction.

With a look of surprise, Emerson asked, "That's a dramatic turnaround from yesterday!"

The President looked at him with raised eyebrows. "Oh?"

"Yesterday, you seemed unsure as to what you were going to do."

"Emerson, you've got to understand. Sometimes I do my thinking out loud. That's what I was doing with you yesterday. I've thought more about it last night and reached my decision to keep him."

Moore was still struggling with the decision. "What sealed your decision in the last 24 hours?"

The President looked at Moore and smiled. "Keeping him on the ticket is paramount to us winning our reelection. I'm not changing horses in midstream."

"But the polls are showing that you'd be better off without him."

"If you believe the polls. Besides, that's what they say today. And don't forget the man is innocent until he is found otherwise."

"But, it will be a distraction to the campaign."

"That's why I'll be pushing for an immediate and full investigation of his alleged wrongdoings so that we can clear the slate. And clear it quickly, I might add."

"And if the results of the investigation warrant formal charges and a trial?" Moore pushed.

"Then so be it. But, I am confident that he will be exonerated of his allegations."

"And if he isn't, then you'll have to drop him during the campaign and replace him."

"That won't happen." The President sipped his coffee and then looked at Moore. "Emerson, don't you think that I've had the folks over in Justice take a close look at this? When Attorney General Deline is signaling me that she doesn't believe there is merit to the allegations, don't you think I'd get comfortable about keeping him on board?"

"But doesn't it make sense to eliminate the drama and replace him with a solid candidate? It will be nothing more than a distraction to the campaign. Your opponent will be all over this."

"Emerson, I appreciate your concern, but I'm not changing my mind. My decision is made and I will stand by it." The President took another sip from his coffee cup. "And I don't expect to see any parts of this conversation in the paper tomorrow." He looked straight into Moore's eyes, awaiting a response.

"You know me better than that. This is just a friendly jousting match between friends."

"Then, let's keep it that way."

"I'm not covering the election. I'm only doing the story on the fish kill."

"Did I hear someone say, it's time to fish?" Hageman called back to the stern.

"No, but is it?" the President asked. "Or, are we going to cruise all the way to Detroit before we drop a line?"

"No sir, we're there," Hageman offered as he brought the boat to a halt. "You can bait your lines though."

"Sounds like an excellent idea," the President said as he stood and approached the bait box with his rod in hand. He bent over the box. Moore chuckled as he did the previous day as the President's shirt rode up in back and his shorts gapped opened to reveal the Presidential plumber's crack again.

As the President straightened, Taggart approached him. "Excuse me, sir."

"Yes? What is it?"

"I just received a message from Jon Hertrack. He needs you to return to the Castle immediately. There's a small problem."

"And cancel our fishing time?" the President said as he turned to look at Emerson, who had now baited his hook.

"I understand. These things happen," Emerson said.

"I'm sure Jon wouldn't have interrupted if it wasn't urgent," Taggart continued.

"Okay then, let's turn this armada around and return to Gibraltar," the President said with a deep sigh. "We might as well sit back and enjoy the lake cruise, Emerson," the President said as he returned to his seat in the stern.

An Hour Earlier
Park Hotel

The golf cart parked in the small asphalt parking lot behind the Park Hotel. Its driver picked up the backpack on the seat next to him and slung it over one shoulder as he stepped from the cart. He looked up and saw the head of one of the counter sniper team members on top of the hotel's turret. From that position, the counter sniper team would be able to command a view of the park and the bay in front of Gibraltar Island. He expected that there were four men on the turret, which allowed them to keep the tops of the buildings along Delaware Avenue under surveillance.

From his earlier reconnaissance, he had confirmed the positions of the two remaining counter sniper teams. One had been obviously on top of Perry's Monument where a four-man team was located. He found the other team on top of the Fish Hatchery on Peach Point where the Secret Service had set up their mobile command post.

The man was wearing an Ohio State ball cap, white tee shirt and khaki shorts with brown sandals. He blended in with the summer crowd on the island, which had been his plan.

He entered the side door of the hotel, which was across the street from Pasquale's Restaurant. He had nourished a cup of coffee there earlier in the day. He had been studying DeRivera Park across the street from the restaurant and the bay on the other side of the park. It hadn't taken him long to spot the Secret Service agents in the park. He had casually walked from the restaurant and sat for ten minutes on the steps to The Country House Gift Shop so that he could confirm his sightings.

He waved to the desk clerk and climbed the stairs to the third floor where he walked over to the room located below the turret. He cautiously looked up and down the hall to make sure that no one was coming or observing what he was about to do. He pulled on a pair of plastic gloves and extracted a lock pick from his pocket. Before he inserted the device into the door's lock, he knocked on the door and listened.

There was no response to the knock as he expected. The Secret Service would have made sure that the third floor rooms overlooking the park, the bay and Gibraltar Island would be empty. He inserted his lock pick and expertly unlocked the door to the room.

Grasping the handle, he opened the door and stepped inside, quickly scanning the room to confirm that it was empty. He closed the white wooden door behind him and looked toward the window. It indeed did provide a view, the right view for him.

He glanced at his watch before slinging his backpack on the bed and opening it. Reaching inside, he withdrew the pieces to his RAP Model 300 sniper rifle. The Model 300 sniper was one of the first purposefully designed sniper weapons for the U.S. Army. All of the others had been a rework from an existing military, hunting or sporting rifle. The Model 300 also served as a test bed for development of the new long-range sniping ammunition.

The man began to assemble the rifle. It wouldn't take him more than three minutes to assemble. He had done it so many times that he could do it in his sleep.

His hands moved methodically as he assembled the deadly weapon. He screwed on the silencer and raised the rifle to his shoulder to test the adjustable stock. Lowering it, he made a couple of adjustments and raised the weapon again. Satisfied with the fit against his cheek, he set the rifle on the bed.

From inside his right front pocket, he withdrew two shells. They were .416 rounds which would provide improved accuracy to 1,500 yards, far better than the .308 Winchester round which was accurate to 1,100 yards. But today, his accuracy would be reduced to 1,200 yards because of the silencer. He slid open the bolt and inserted the first round.

The stock was fully adjustable and could be easily removed along with the pistol grip to make the rifle more compact for carry and storage. The trigger was also fully adjustable, and the rifle required no disassembly to adjust it. While the Model 300 featured no open sights, it had a quick-detachable scope mount, which required no re-zeroing after it was reinstalled. The scope base also featured a range-adjustable mechanism.

With the rifle fully assembled, he laid it on the bed and turned his attention to getting the room ready. He was careful to keep his distance from the window so that the agents in the park below would not see him in a room, which was supposed to be vacant. He carried an end table and positioned it three feet away from the front of the window. Next, he positioned a chair beside the table.

He glanced at his watch again and saw that the time was approaching. He grabbed the tool from his backpack and positioned himself next to the window as he waited for the next step in his plan to take place. He didn't have to wait long.

From the west end of DeRivera Park, came a series of loud pops. Immediately the Secret Service agents directed their attention to the west end and several in the park sprinted there.

As soon as he heard the first pop, the shooter cut a large hole in the lower right windowpane with his glasscutter. He extracted the cut glass into the room and quickly stepped away from the window. An open window would have attracted the attention of the agents in the park. But a hole in the pane would be difficult for them to detect.

He chuckled to himself as he imagined the interrogation the two teenagers were going through. He had given the boys twenty dollars a piece to set off the firecrackers at the precise time they did.

He picked up the RAP 300 from the bed and set it on the table after extending the folding bipod, which was attached to the forward receiver.

Standing next to the table, he lifted the scope to his eye and looked out of the window to check the environment as he prepared to set up for the shot. He confirmed the wind direction by surveying the movement of the trees in the park and the direction to which the flag on the Boardwalk was blowing. He confirmed it again by looking at the flags blowing from the masts of the sailboats on "B" dock.

He then focused the glass on Gibraltar Island's dock and began to calculate the distance for the shot. He was pleased that his estimates had been on target. His calculated distance was 1,200 yards. He then calculated the arc of the shot, working quickly through the math.

Placing the glass into the backpack, he sat down at the table and began setting his calculated adjustments to the weapon. As he adjusted them, he sighted through the Model 300's scope to make sure that his adjustments were aligning the weapon properly.

He saw a Secret Service agent walking on the dock, and zeroed in on him. He mentally pulled the trigger and imagined the bullet's trajectory as it sped to its target, impacting its target's head and causing an instant kill.

The shooter pulled back from his weapon and caressed its sleek lines as he would the body of a beautiful woman. He grinned to himself as he thought how deadly both were.

Sitting back in his chair, he watched Gibraltar's dock for the flurry of activity, which would signal the return of the President from his fishing trip. Within thirty minutes, he saw a number of Secret Service agents scurry onto the dock. Two minutes later, he saw the first of the protection craft cross his sight. Next, he saw the President's boat appear and begin to maneuver for docking.

The shooter leaned forward and slowly grasped the stock, pulling it close to his shoulder as he positioned his head so that he could look through the weapon's scope. He sighted on the docking craft and waited. It wasn't long before he saw the President. Through the crosshairs of his sight, he focused on the President's head. His trigger finger began to close on the trigger.

The Dock
Gibraltar Island

"We'll have to do this again sometime, Emerson," the President said as he stepped onto the dock and turned to face Moore, who had followed him.

"Yes, we will," Moore responded. There was a cautious tone in his voice. Moore's mind was racing to put the pieces of the puzzle together. Something was amiss – of that he was sure.

The President shook hands with Moore. "I need to get back to the Castle. Got to finish up my acceptance speech and work on my vice presidential selection announcement," he grinned.

"Good luck," Moore said as he watched a number of agents swarm around the President and escort him up the hill and back to the Castle. When Moore looked to his side, he saw Taggart. "There's something wrong with this picture."

Taggart ignored Moore as he looked across the bay.

"Fess up, Taggart. What's going on?" Moore asked.

"I don't understand what you're talking about."

Moore saw Benko move near them. "Let me whisper it to you." Moore leaned toward Taggart's ear and whispered his suspicion.

Taggart stepped back. "Why would you think that?"

Moore whispered his response.

"You've got a wild imagination, Mr. Moore," Taggart said sternly. "That imagination is going to get you in trouble."

"Lead me to trouble? You're right. But my gut is usually right and that carries over to some good stories for my paper to publish," Moore said firmly as he began to walk along toward the smaller dock where his Zodiac was tied up.

Taggart nodded to Benko, who caught up with Moore and spun him around to face Taggart.

"You're not going anywhere, but in protective custody!"

Moore was stunned by what he saw. Taggart had withdrawn his pistol and was now holding it in his right hand. It was pointed at Moore, but not for long.

The sniper's bullet grazed Taggart's shoulder, causing him to discharge the weapon as he dropped it. The weapon's bullet harmlessly embedded itself in the mass of undergrowth next to where Moore was standing.

Taggart swore and then yelled, "Assassin! He's trying to kill the President!"

Thinking quickly as Benko moved toward him, Moore reached into the undergrowth and his hand emerged with a mass of wiggling and angry Lake Erie water snakes. Moore threw them into Benko's face.

Benko stopped in his tracks and screamed as the angry reptiles snapped at his exposed skin before falling to the ground where they quickly slithered back into their safe refuge.

Moore took several steps and dove into the bay before Taggart had a chance to recover his weapon.

The Sniper's Nest
Park Hotel

"You owe me big time, Emerson," the sniper said quietly to himself as he began to break down the rifle. His plans had gone awry. All the sniper had wanted to do was to get the President of the United States in his crosshairs so that he had the personal satisfaction of knowing that he could have pulled it off had he wanted.

Through his scope, he had watched the scene unfold in front of him. He didn't know that Moore was on board the President's boat. After the President had left the dock, he had continued watching through the scope.

When he saw Taggart pull his weapon, he knew that he had to take action. He had smiled at himself for his accuracy. Trying to hit the pistol in Taggart's hand would have been a difficult shot. He had aimed for the shoulder. If Taggart had surprised him and moved to his right suddenly, he would have found that the sniper's bullet would have been embedded. Embedded in his brain. The grazing shot had worked.

The sniper worked quickly. He had limited time before the Secret Service agents would use lasers and trace the shot back to the Park Hotel. In less than three minutes, he had broken down the rifle, stowed it in his backpack and retrieved the shell casing. He slung the backpack over his head and onto his back. He placed his ball cap and sunglasses firmly on his head and face.

Slowly he unlocked the room's door and opened it. Peering into the hall, he saw that it was empty. He stepped into the hall and walked casually to the steps. He slipped off his gloves and stuck them in his pocket before descending the steps.

As he emerged in the lobby, he smiled when he saw that the front desk clerk was not in sight. He walked to his left and through the lobby filled with antique furniture and beautifully framed prints of Lake Erie scenes.

He pushed open the Victorian style white screen door and walked across the porch. He then stepped down to the street and walked behind the hotel to where he had parked the golf cart. He started its engine and drove off. To any passerby, he would have looked like a tourist on the island. But this tourist was a deadly tourist.

The Dock
Off Gibraltar Island

Two agents charged out of the Stone Lab building and raced to the dock.

"What happened?" one asked as he anxiously surveyed the scene in front of him.

Benko was standing to his feet as the last of the water snakes slithered quickly into the undergrowth. Bleeding snakebites covered his face. The snakes weren't venomous, but the bites from their tiny sharp teeth could break the skin and cause bleeding.

Taggart was tenderly rubbing his right shoulder where blood slowly seeped from the wound caused by the sniper's bullet as it grazed his shoulder. Taggart snarled in response. "Moore's involved in a plot to kill the President. He's got a sniper on his team and I took the bullet."

"Where's the sniper?"

"Don't know."

"I didn't hear a shot," the agent commented.

"Think silencer, stupid ass," Benko snapped as he wiped the blood from his face with the back of his hand.

Taggart pointed to the ground. "Find the bullet. It should be over there." He pointed to where he guessed the bullet would have hit the ground after grazing him. At the same time, he called into his radio. "I need the laser team on the Gibraltar dock now. We've got a sniper who missed his timing to take out the President, but got me instead. I need dive teams here now and boats in the harbor. Distribute photos of Emerson Moore from *The Washington Post*. He's involved in a plot to kill the President and he dove into the bay to escape. I want this bay shut down! Nothing creeps out of the water or sails out of the bay without us knowing. I want a cordon of security set up around the harbor. Get security established on Bay View Avenue now! I want Moore found and I want him found now!"

Finished with his tirade, Taggart strode angrily to the spot where he had been standing when the bullet struck him. He quickly scanned the bay as he searched for Moore's head to break the water's surface. Seeing nothing, he gazed across the bay and looked around the town for possible sniper nests. His eyes settled on the third floor of the Park Hotel. He picked up his radio and called to the counter sniper team on the hotel's roof and the agent in the DeRivera Park, who had been assigned to watch the front of the buildings in that sector.

"Did you see any open windows?"

"No," the agent in the park responded.

"Are you sure?"

The agent thought for a moment. "There was a commotion in the park when some kids set off firecrackers. It was called in according to protocol and I returned to my post. I did check the windows and confirmed that there were no windows open."

"Gorman?" Taggart called to the spotter on the roof of the hotel.

"Nothing. We didn't hear anything."

"Okay. Stay at your post."

Taggart ordered several agents to sweep the hotel rooms, which faced the bay. When finished he turned and saw that the laser team had arrived. They were going to use their lasers to pinpoint the source of the shot.

As the laser team began to set up, one of the agents shouted, "Here's the bullet."

"What do you have there?" Taggart demanded.

"It's a .416 round."

The laser team lined up with the round and Taggart's shoulder and they did a quick initial analysis. "It points to that tall, white building," the laser operator said.

When Taggart's head turned to look, he was pleased. The laser confirmed his original suspicions. It pointed to the Park Hotel.

Just as he raised his radio to bark additional orders, one of the agents sweeping the rooms called in. "We've got a room here with a circular hole cut out of the window pane. Other than that, the room looks like it's in order."

"The sniper's smart. He probably put everything back after he took the shot," Taggart growled. "I want a forensics team there to confirm what you've found and start interviewing any witnesses there about what they may have seen. See if the sniper's weapon is hidden in the building or if anyone saw somebody walk out, carrying something in which the weapon could have been concealed."

The Bay
Off Gibraltar Island

Moore surfaced on the far side of one of the sailboats, tied to one of the mooring buoys. He had deliberately changed direction while underwater and had begun swimming south. He guessed that any pursuers would expect him to swim east toward his residence on East Point.

He cautiously looked around to see if he had been spotted. He knew that he'd have limited surface time, as the counter sniper teams from their high vantage points would be searching for him to break the water's surface. He took several deep breaths and submerged, swimming underwater toward the docks next to the Boardwalk Restaurant and Bar which protruded into the harbor. To the side of the Boardwalk were docks owned by the Crew's Nest, the premier private club on the island. Those docks were Moore's targeted destination.

The Winter Bar
Park Hotel

Just behind the front desk in the lobby was the Winter Bar. Ordinarily it was not used much during the summer months since most folks frequented the Round House, which was connected to the front of the Winter Bar. When the Round House closed for the season, the Winter Bar became more heavily used. Today was an exception. Secret Service agents were interviewing a potential witness to the shooting. They had gathered everyone in the hotel and ushered them into the lobby area.

Other agents were doing a room-by-room search for the sniper's weapon. They had first searched the first floor and the kitchen behind the Winter Bar and were methodically working their way upward, floor-by-floor.

Agent Doug Plumly walked to the doorway, which separated the Winter Bar from the Park Hotel lobby. He looked at the list of names on the hotel's desk and called the next name.

"Teri Remington?"

"Yes?" the voice responded in a provocative tone.

Plumly's head swiveled to identify the source. Approaching him, he saw a svelte blonde with alluring smokey-blue eyes.

"Please follow me."

"Where to?" she purred as she followed him to one of the tables in the Winter Bar where a number of agents were conducting interviews. Before he could respond, she asked, "Could you have that handsome one over there frisk me?" She smiled as she continued tongue-in-cheek, "Or, maybe, he needs to strip search me."

The agent motioned to her to take a seat and looked her in the face. Her eyes were twinkling from teasing the agent. Plumly grinned back at her. "You going to make this difficult?"

"Not at all," she cooed good-naturedly. "You can interrogate me anytime you want. I bet you're a good interrogator," she smiled sensually.

"Okay then, what were you doing in the building?" Plumly ran his hand through his thick graying hair and then began to take notes on the pad of white paper.

"I manage the Round House Bar and the Winter Bar."

"And your name again is Teri Remington?"

"Yes, and be careful, I'm always loaded."

The agent shook his head from side to side as he noted her name at the top of the pad. He couldn't help liking the affable woman in front of him. Ignoring the quip, Plumly probed, "How long have you worked here?"

"A lifetime," she smiled. "I couldn't ask for a better job or place to work than here on Put-in-Bay."

"Okay, help me understand what you observed. Did you hear any gunshots?"

"No." When she had been herded into the lobby with the others, several rumors had buzzed around the group about someone trying to assassinate the President.

"Could you describe your actions over the last two hours?"

"Sure, I was going over the receipts from last night, checking our inventory and making sure that the food prep area and the kitchen help were ready to go for the day's crowd."

"Did you see anyone of a suspicious nature walk through this room?"

"Not this room."

Plumly raised his head when he heard the way she answered. He looked her directly in the eyes and asked, "How about any room?"

"There was one person, who was different."

"How's that?"

"I'm known for having an eye for detail, the little things rarely get by me. When I was standing near the door to the lobby, giving the hotel manager, Deb, a fresh cup of coffee, I noticed a young man walk down the stairs and out the door."

"And what was suspicious about him?"

"Most people, who stay at the hotel, will give you a glance. Sometimes you get a smile and sometimes, especially if they're nursing a hangover, they don't smile. But folks look around to see who's in the lobby. This young man kept his eyes averted. He actually lowered his eyes as he turned the corner and walked toward the side door."

Plumly waved for one of the agents at the back of the bar to join him. "You better listen to this." Plumly turned back to Remington. "Did you notice what he was carrying?"

"Just a back pack. Nothing unusual."

"Would you recognize him if you saw him again?"

"I think so. He looked vaguely familiar. He may have stayed at the hotel before."

"We'll want to check the guest register and run background checks on everyone in the hotel," Plumly said softly to the agent. "Could you describe what he was wearing?"

"Nothing special. He was dressed like most of the island's visitors. White tee shirt, khaki shorts and khaki ball cap."

"Anything else which might make him stand out?"

"No."

"Ms. Remington, I'd like you to take a seat in the lobby where you can see the side door and the steps to the second floor. I'm going to assign an agent to sit with you so that you can let him know if the man reenters the lobby. He'd be someone that we'd like to interview."

"I'd be happy to help in any way. But, if he is your sniper, I'd guess that he wouldn't be back."

"I agree," Plumly said as he stood. "But, we can't take any chances."

Remington stood and walked to the lobby to take up her position. As she did, Plumly heard the radio message that the sniper's lair had been located.

Stone Lab
Gibraltar Island

∽

"What do you mean you can't find Moore or the sniper?" Taggart snarled. "We have an attempt on the President's life and no one can find the trigger man?" Taggart's face had a deep scowl on it as he surveyed the men in front of him. "They found Oswald in a matter of hours after he killed Kennedy."

The ten men crowded into the small office represented five agencies.

"We know the sniper fired from a top floor window in the Park Hotel. Based on the trajectory of..."

"I don't care about the details!" Taggart growled, interrupting the head of the counter sniper team, which was assigned to protect the President. "I want results. Now, you guys go out there and find Moore and the sniper. Nothing moves off this island without being searched."

"The Coast Guard is pulling over every watercraft and searching them. We've got men at the Miller Ferry. They're searching all vehicles and passengers. The same goes with the Jet Express' passengers and the Sonny B. ferry," one of the agency representatives offered.

"What about the airport?" Taggart grumbled.

"We've got men there, too. Nothing flies out without being searched."

"Keep an eye on that guy, who runs Dairy Air. He gave Benko a hard time the other day. He might be linked to this somehow. He and Moore are buddies."

"You've got it!"

"Okay, everyone clear out. Go find them. Do house-to-house searches. I want every inch of this island searched. And don't forget to check the caves. They've got several here."

"We're on it." The ten men hurried from the office to carry out their assignments.

Taggart was still fuming when he walked into the building's first floor where the nerve center for the island's security was headquartered. For five minutes, he studied the monitors for the island's security cameras and there didn't appear to be any problems. He stormed out of the office and looked toward the dock where the green trash containers were being wheeled aboard a workboat for its run across the harbor.

Overhead, low flying helicopters were conducting air searches for Moore and anything suspicious. Coast Guard harbor patrol boats were boarding watercraft at the mooring buoys and searching them for Moore. Across the harbor, Taggart saw police and Secret Service agents conducting searches of all boats tied to the docks, which fronted Bay View Avenue.

Looking to the west, Taggart saw the men, who had just left his meeting, disembarking at the Ohio State University docks, where waiting members of the media were besieging them with questions. Brushing them aside, the men raced off to a series of trailers, which were cordoned off from the press and were serving as supplemental command posts.

Taggart looked at the Gibraltar Island dock, which was guarded by two Secret Service agents. He took in a deep breath and turned to begin the climb up the path to the Castle. A few minutes later, he walked past an agent guarding the entranceway and walked into the first floor. He walked down the short hallway and through the dining room. He passed through the kitchen and descended the stairs to the locked wine cellar door.

From his pocket, he withdrew a key and inserted it into the lock. Before turning the key, he said in a low voice, "Benko, it's me." He turned the key and pushed the door open, walking into the room.

As he did, he saw Benko lowering his weapon. "I wasn't sure who it was when I heard the key inserted."

"I know. I'd rather have you be cautious." Taggart looked around the dimly lit room filled with racks of Lake Erie wines. "Where is he?"

Nodding his head to a corner, Benko answered, "Back there."

"Any trouble?"

"None."

"Good."

"Any news on Moore or the sniper?" Benko asked.

"Not a thing! It's like they both disappeared into thin air."

"Both? Do we know that the sniper didn't have a spotter?"

"No, we don't know crap." Taggart then unleashed a torrent of expletives as he vented his frustrations and stormed around the room angrily. "We can't have anything go wrong. Moore may be sniffing out what's going on."

"How's that?"

Taggart shared what Moore had whispered to him.

"Oh, crap!"

"Yeah, that's what I thought. That's why we've got to get him."

"But he doesn't have any proof!"

"No, he doesn't. But you know about him as well as I do. Moore has a way of putting two and two together to get five. And the damn thing about it is that he is usually right on the money."

"We don't need that."

"No, we don't."

"We've come too far."

"Exactly. That's why we're going to nip this in the bud before tomorrow evening when the President appears at the convention to give his acceptance speech," Taggart said firmly. He cast a glance toward the corner and then said, "I'm going to head over to the Command Center on Peach Point. I'll be there if anything comes up on this end."

"Okay."

Taggart left the Castle's basement and headed down the hill to the docks to catch a ride to the Command Center.

Put-in-Bay Gazette Office
Overlooking the Harbor

The knife's blade easily sliced through the window's screen, allowing the intruder to climb into the combination office/home of the *Put-in-Bay Gazette* publishers, Barry and Sybil Hayen. The intruder quietly padded through the dining room and the front room.

He paused at the base of the steps and listened for any noises, which would have signaled that the home's occupants were awake. Glancing at his watch, he saw that it was two in the morning. He smiled to himself and walked through the kitchen to the bathroom where he discarded his wet clothes and toweled himself dry.

Stepping back into the kitchen, Moore carefully draped his wet clothes over the back of several kitchen chairs. By morning, they would be dry. Moore opened the refrigerator and helped himself to some cold cuts and a piece of pie, which Barry had been saving for the next day. Moore padded back into the front room and laid on the sofa, modestly pulling a blanket over himself in the event the Hayens discovered him in the morning. It was a matter of minutes and Moore fell into a deep sleep.

It was around six in the morning when a voice interrupted Moore's sleep.

"Who's been sleeping on my sofa? It certainly isn't Goldilocks!"

Moore sat straight up, almost knocking the blanket off of himself and exposing his naked body to the voice's owner.

"And it looks like he's naked! Not only do you try to assassinate the President, but now you break into people's houses and sleep naked. Man, you're turning into a real pervert."

Clutching his blanket, Moore looked at the lanky, graying owner of the *Put-in-Bay Gazette*. Barry, his wife and Moore had struck up a close relationship shortly after Moore had moved to the island and they often dined together. "Thought you'd be surprised to find me here," Moore grinned.

"You've got yourself into a fine mess on this one. What were you ever thinking? Trying to kill the President?"

"It's not like that."

"Yeah and now I'm involved. I'm allowing a would-be assassin to hide out here. The Secret Service and law enforcement officers have got this island covered like a blanket. You're in big trouble." Hayen paused for a moment and then continued, "No, that's an understatement. You're screwed!"

"It's really not that way. You know me better than that."

"I thought you and the President were friends! Again, what were you thinking?" Hayen had walked into the kitchen and returned with Moore's dry clothes, which he handed to Moore. "Here put your clothes on. You're making me feel inadequate." Hayen walked over to the large front window and peered out at the bay.

"Barry, you've got to trust me on this one," Moore said as he began to dress. "I can't get you any more involved than what you are. These guys play for keeps!"

"And that's another understatement!"

"Seriously, I can't let you know what's happening on this one. It would jeopardize your safety. If this heads the way I think it will, it will be a blockbuster story!"

"Yeah, you do have a knack for that," Hayen concurred. "And, who's your buddy?"

"My buddy?"

"Yeah, the sniper. What were you ever thinking?"

"I don't know anything about a sniper other than seeing Taggart's gun spin out of his hand. Things were happening so fast, I was just trying to get away from Taggart."

Moore explained how he had escaped and then played hide and seek under the docks with the dive teams, who had been searching for him. Hayen reciprocated by telling him about the search for the sniper and how the island had been shut down.

"Again, I don't know anything about a sniper."

"Oh, come on now. You don't expect me to believe that a sniper just happened to be there to protect you," Hayen groused.

"I don't know, but it does sound like I had a guardian angel watching over me. We'll try to figure out who that was when I get my issue with the President resolved." Moore glanced through the front window at Gibraltar Island. "I've got to get back on Gibraltar Island!"

"What? Are you crazy?" Hayen looked at Moore who had picked up a pair of binoculars and was raising them to his eyes. He was standing five feet away from the large picture window, which overlooked the harbor and Gibraltar Island.

Rolling his eyes, Hayen continued, "Why would you want to go back into that lion's den? This is a time to retreat, my friend."

"I'm not retreating. I'm just pausing to reload and go back to get the truth. There's something fishy going on."

Hayen groaned.

"Sorry, no pun intended," Moore interjected as he thought about the fish kill. "Two and two are not adding up to four."

As he looked out across the harbor, he saw the tender leave the island. It contained five large green garbage dumpsters. The tender was making its daily trip to empty the filled containers. Moore's attention was drawn to the Secret Service agent, who was guarding the dumpster. It was Kenfield Valero. That's strange, Moore thought to himself. Why would the President's most trusted agent be reassigned to garbage guard duty?

Emerson was determined to find out and a plan quickly formed in his mind. He turned to Hayen and said, "Barry, I need your help."

Hayen didn't say anything. He just stared at Moore.

"Can you help me?" Moore pushed.

Hayen sighed. "Yeah and I'll end up being your accomplice. I'll be spending the rest of my life in jail."

"Not if this works," Moore grinned.

"The operative word here is 'if'," Hayen said stoically. He looked at his friend and made a decision. "Okay, I'll help you. If I'm wrong about you, then I missed this one by a mile."

"You won't be sorry."

"I hope not or both you and I will be facing the wrath of Sybil," he teased. "What do you need?"

Moore quickly outlined his plan.

Miller Ferry's Dock
Downtown Put-in-Bay

The tender bumped against the dock as the dockhand rushed over to secure the lines. Once the tender was completely docked, the dockhand, under the watchful eye of agent Valero, wheeled the first container to a massive dumpster. He connected the container to the dumping apparatus and depressed the switch causing the container to be lifted and its contents to spill into the large dumpster.

Valero leaned against a post and watched as the dockhand lowered the dumpster and returned it to the tender where he began to repeat the process with the second dumpster.

A vehicle, pulling into the parking lot and parking near the large dumpster, distracted Valero's attention. The small van had lettering on the side, identifying it as *"Put-in-Bay Gazette."* Valero watched as the lanky driver emerged and walked to a smaller dumpster next to the large one and threw a box of trash into it. He then slid open the side door of the van and grabbed another box which he also threw in the small dumpster.

The man then turned and approached Valero. "There's sure enough excitement going on around here."

Valero was careful in his response, especially since the man appeared to be with the media. "Yes, there is."

"You guys ever find that Moore fellow?"

"You really need to talk with someone from our media team," Valero said as he avoided the question.

"I thought you might say that."

Valero watched as the dockhand raised the second dumpster and began the dumping process into the large dumpster.

"Kenfield?"

Valero's head whipped around in surprise to look at the man.

"I thought you'd be surprised. I'm Barry Hayen, publisher of the *Put-in-Bay Gazette*. I know your name because someone who admires you and the President told me who you were."

"Emerson Moore?"

"Yes."

"Where is he?" Valero's eyes went straight to the van. "Is he in there?"

"Yes, he's in the van."

Valero began to raise his wrist to his mouth to radio for back up.

"Please don't do that. He wants you to hear him out. If you don't believe what he has to say, then he said that you could turn him in."

Valero began to raise his wrist again.

"Please," Hayen pleaded. "Hear him out first."

Valero paused for a moment as he looked toward the van. "All right. He has two minutes."

As agreed earlier with Moore, Hayen didn't accompany Valero to the van. Moore didn't want to pull his friend into his suspicions any more than necessary.

Walking to the van, Valero looked through the driver's open window and saw Moore lying on the floor in front of the van's middle row of seats.

"You've got yourself into one hell of a fine mess," Valero said as he stared down at Moore.

"Turn around and face the trash containers. I don't want anyone to know that you're talking to someone in the van," Moore instructed.

Reluctantly, Valero spun around and leaned against the van door.

"It's not what you think. I don't know anything about signaling a sniper. Taggart and Benko must be mistaken."

"Oh, I don't need to think about it. We've got a bevy of eyewitnesses stating that you tried to assassinate the President. Taggart and Benko were both there and saw you signal your sniper buddy, whoever he is. Neither of you will get away. This island has been locked down. No one comes or goes without being identified. That was really a stupid idea to try to assassinate the President on an island. How did you think you'd ever get away?"

Moore had been waiting patiently for Valero's outrage to die. Here was his chance. "Kenfield, it's not what you think."

Valero interrupted. "You're right that it's not what I think, it's what I know."

"Would you let me explain?"

A frown crossed Valero's face as he sensed he was just wasting his time. "Be quick about it."

"Something's wrong with the President. He's exhibiting behaviors that he didn't exhibit the day before when we went fishing."

"What do you mean?"

"The first day, I sensed he was going to dump Moran as his running mate. Yesterday, he had decided to keep him."

"And that's an unusual behavior? Come on Emerson, he just made up his mind."

"My sixth sense tells me something's amiss. He seemed a little distant from me."

"Well, sometimes you newspaper guys piss him off. Maybe he was irritated by something you said to him the previous day."

"No, I don't think so. I think somebody got to him. Maybe somebody is threatening him to keep Moran on board or they'll harm a family member. Or, maybe someone's drugged him. Or maybe he's been hypnotized."

Valero interrupted. "Maybe, maybe, maybe. Maybe an asteroid is going to hit this island today. Give it up with these wild hypotheses of yours. You're way off base."

A police boat in the harbor momentarily distracted Valero as he watched two SEALs drop overboard to continue an underwater search for Moore.

"Something's wrong and I need to get to the Castle to find out."

Valero laughed. "That's no problem. I'll just escort you right up there so you can surrender directly to Taggart."

"That's not what I had in mind." Moore thought for a moment and asked, "Can you work with me on this?"

Shaking his head from side to side, Valero responded, "No can do. I've crossed the line far enough by not taking you into custody from the moment I walked over here."

Moore decided to play his trump card. "Kenfield, you're my only hope. You owe me one from eight years ago when I didn't include you in the story I did. I could have ruined your career because of one silly misstep you took."

Valero remembered the incident. He had exercised poor judgment and Moore had let it go. "What do you have in mind? And whatever it is has to include you not leaving my custody because I will need to turn you in."

"Thanks, Kenfield."

"Yeah, yeah."

"I've got to get to the Castle and here's how we can do it. I'll drop into one of those wheeled garbage carts that you've had emptied and ride back over to the island with you. When we get there, you can have the cart towed up the hill to the Castle. Next to the kitchen entrance is the entrance to the wine cellar. You can make sure that the coast is clear and then I can jump out of the cart and enter the Castle through the wine cellar."

"Just like that?"

"Yes, just like that – unless you have a better idea."

"Oh no, I'm not giving you any ideas. I'm becoming enough of an accomplice." A SEAL diver climbing aboard the Police Boat distracted Valero again. When his focus returned to Moore, he asked, "And what are you going to do when you get into the Castle? Just walk into the President's office and ask him what's wrong? He has a ton of people over there working on his renomination acceptance speech."

"I'm not quite sure. My first objective is to get to the Castle. I'll think about the next steps on the way over."

Shaking his head, Valero mumbled, "I know that I'm making a big mistake." He looked over at Hayen, who was waiting patiently. "So, is your buddy the sniper?"

"No way. I don't know anything about the sniper bit. I'm focused on determining what's wrong with the President!"

"Okay, let's get this show on the road." Valero walked over to Hayen. "You need to pull your van over here by this green trash container. Make sure the sliding passenger door is as near to it as possible."

Hayen nodded and walked back to the van. As he opened the door and sat in the driver's seat, he asked his passenger, "Get want you wanted?"

"At least step one is in place."

Hayen started the van and drove it as instructed to where Valero was standing, next to one of the containers with the attached lid held open. "Don't get me into any more trouble than you need to."

"I won't – and thanks, Barry." Moore sat up as the vehicle stopped. He slid open the door and jumped into the waiting container, landing in the bottom with a thud. The lid closed, sealing Moore into his wheeled hideout. It was filled with pungent odors. Moore was thankful that the users of the containers had at least thrown garbage into plastic bags before tossing them into the container. Otherwise, he would have been sitting and leaning against an ooze made up of a variety of decaying vegetables and fruits.

Valero shut the van's sliding door and the van drove away. Valero next firmly gripped the container's handles and pushed it to the waiting boat for the return trip. One of the dockworkers approached Valero and said, "Let me do that for you."

Waving him off, Valero responded, "I'll take care of this one." He wheeled it onto the boat and parked it near the stern, then returned to the dock's edge to supervise the emptying of the remaining containers.

Inside the green plastic container, the heat from the morning sun began to warm up the close confines. Moore wiped a bead a sweat from his brow and tried to make himself as comfortable as possible, which really wasn't saying that much.

In a few minutes, the remaining containers were wheeled onto the boat and the boat left the dock for its return trip to Gibraltar Island.

When they docked, Valero waved off the dockworker. He wheeled the container, in which Moore was hidden, to the edge of the dock and attached it to the rear of a Gator, a motorized cart. Then, Valero joined the dockworker in the Gator and they drove up the hill with the cart in tow. When they reached the Castle, Valero unhooked the cart and wheeled it against the building. He parked it between the door leading to the kitchen and the door leading to the basement wine cellar.

As the dockworker drove the Gator down the hill to the dock, Valero casually leaned against the container and tapped its side. "You still alive?" he asked as he wiped perspiration off his brow.

A tap responded from inside accompanied by a voice saying, "Yeah, but barely."

"Get ready to move when I open the container," Valero said.

"You're going to have to help me," Moore responded.

Looking around quickly to make sure that no one was watching, Valero opened the container's lid. Quickly Moore stood and took in a deep breath of clean air. He gripped the edge of the container as he prepared to pull himself out.

Valero reached for the sweat-covered Moore and helped him over the edge and through the first doorway into the cool wine cellar.

"Let me rest," Moore gasped as the cool air greeted him in the stairway. "I about died in there."

"Just remember, it was your idea," Valero said in a hushed tone as he quietly pulled the door shut behind them. "Now, what's next?"

Moore was leaning against the cold stone wall, trying to get additional relief from his hellish confinement. "I've got to talk to the President," he said in a hushed tone.

"Well, you can't just march up to his bedroom and talk to him. My co-workers would nail you the second they saw you."

"Yeah, you're right," Moore mumbled as he realized the insanity of his idea. He studied the cracks in the wall opposite him as he thought. "There's a way."

"Oh?"

"You bring him to me."

"Just like that?"

"Yeah, just like that."

"You forget that I've been reassigned to garbage detail. If I walk upstairs, there'll be all kinds of questions raised."

"So, you make up some reason for being here."

"I don't know."

"You can come up with something. Think about it. Meanwhile, let's check out the wine cellar and see if we get any ideas."

Moore turned and opened the door at the bottom of the stairwell.

He walked into the wine cellar, closely followed by Valero. Both of them looked quickly around the well-lit cellar, its racks filled with a wide array of island wines.

A groan caught Moore's attention. He looked at Valero, who raised his eyebrows as he heard a second groan. They both looked toward a door to a small enclosed area from which the groans had originated.

Cautiously, they approached the door. Moore released two sliding locks and opened the door.

"What in the world is going on here?" he said as a look of utter disbelief crossed his face.

The Fund Raising Breakfast
Rattlesnake Island

"So once again, I say thank you for your support. And because of your support, I know that we will win by a landslide margin this fall." The President beamed as he looked across the room filled with large donors and saw Taggart standing with two agents and Hertrack inside the exclusive island restaurant's entranceway. "Now, let's finish our hearty breakfast and have a good morning filled with fishing."

The President then stepped from the podium and began to make his way to each table to shake hands and personally thank each donor. Taggart had joined him and followed him closely as he visited each table. His personal attention at each table was designed to ease their disappointment at his announcement that he would not be joining them on the morning's walleye fishing trip. His cancellation, he had told them, was due to an unexpected matter, which demanded his attention that day.

Finished with his obligatory rounds, the President joined Taggart at the door. He looked around to make sure that Hertrack was out of earshot. "How did I do?"

"Perfect, just perfect!" Taggart said. "You knocked them dead."

The President relaxed. "Good. I was a bit nervous to be up there."

"You did fine, just fine."

Hertrack joined them and they walked to the dock where the *Estorel* was waiting to take them back to Gibraltar Island.

The Wine Cellar
Cooke's Castle

Peeling the duct tape off the man's mouth, Moore asked in stunned disbelief, "What is going on here?" He watched as Valero's knife blade cut quickly through the ropes, which bound the captive.

Stretching his arms and slowly and unsteadily standing to his feet as his circulation returned, the captive responded, "I've been thinking about that, Emerson." He looked at Valero as he sat back down on the cot. "Thank you, Kenfield. This is much better."

"Any time, Mr. President," Valero replied. "I thought you had a breakfast speech on Rattlesnake Island this morning."

"I did."

"But, I saw you board this morning and head over there."

"It wasn't me whom you saw board. It's my double?"

It was Moore's turn to comment. "A double? I didn't know that you used a double!"

"I don't. But someone or someones have gone through a lot of planning to pull this off."

"How's that?" Moore asked.

"Taggart is in on this. So is Benko." The President related what had happened since he was awakened early in the morning a little over 24 hours ago.

"So, the palace guard is pulling off a coup?" Moore probed for the President's thoughts.

"I've been thinking about that since I didn't have anything else to do while I was laying here." The President hadn't lost his sense of humor. "I think it's more than that. I think the Vice President knows that I'm going to dump him and he's behind all of this. He gets a double in and then he pulls the strings in the background. He runs the nation for the next four years and then runs for election for two terms. He can actually control the presidency for 12 years."

Nodding his head, Moore added, "Or they assassinate him after a few months in office and the Vice President rides a wave of sympathy into office."

"That could be," the President responded as he looked at Valero leaning in the doorway.

"I'm just stunned by the amount of planning that would have gone into this. You don't just call up Doubles-R-Us and request a presidential double," Moore contemplated.

Benson explained, "They've been doing face transplants for years. First the Chinese and then the French. We've had a couple in the United States."

"You think the Chinese are behind this?" Moore pushed.

"Could be either them or the French or rogues in the U.S. government."

"And I'd wager that the doc doing the transplant and his staff were probably killed afterwards. You wouldn't want someone announcing to the world what they did after the election," Valero suggested.

"You're probably right on that Kenfield. Then there's the coaching and film study of me so that whoever impersonates me could get me down right." The President turned his head and looked at Moore. "I've been so obsessed with my situation that I didn't ask you what you're doing in the wine cellar."

Moore quickly explained his situation over the last 24 hours.

"Sounds like we both have been through one hell of an experience," Benson said as he looked at Moore. "So tell me, what made you suspicious?"

"That was easy."

"Easy?"

"It was the tan lines?"

"The tan lines?"

"Yeah. When we went fishing the first day and we had that healthy discussion..."

"Yes, I remember."

"When it was time to fish, you bent over to reach for your bait and I saw the Presidential plumber's crack."

Laughing for the first time since he had been detained, the President apologized, "Sorry about the view!"

Moore grinned, "No problem. But I did notice your tan line. The next day, the same thing happened, but there was no tan line. Tan lines don't disappear in 24 hours."

"You are observant!"

"That's how I make my living. But it was more than that. When I followed up on our discussion the day before, you, or I should say your double, had changed positions on the Vice President. He felt stronger about keeping the Vice President, but I sensed something was amiss."

"Good sensing."

"It's got me out of and into trouble quite a few times in my career."

"Well, isn't this just the perfect little tea party? Next thing I know you'll be singing kumbaya together!" the voice spoke sinisterly from behind Valero as he was abruptly pushed into the room.

The three men in the small room turned to face the intruder, who was aiming a handgun at them.

"Put the gun away, Benko!" the President ordered.

"Oh, I don't think so."

Benson stared at Benko. "As President of the United States, I'm ordering you to put that weapon down," Benson commanded.

An evil smile crossed Benko's face. "Not this time. I'm done with taking orders from you. You're a has been!" Benko looked at Valero. "Valero, I want you to reach under your jacket very carefully, pull out your weapon and slide it across the floor to me."

When Valero hesitated, Benko spoke firmly, "Do it now or I put a bullet in the President." He then pointed his weapon at Benson.

Reluctantly, Valero complied with the instructions. When Benko bent down to pick up the weapon, Valero edged closer to Benson so he could use his own body as a shield to protect the President.

Moore saw the movement out of the corner of his eye and decided to attract Benko's attention. "What's this all about, Benko?"

"It's none of your business, Mr. Nosy Reporter."

"It's more than Moore's business," Benson interrupted, "it's the nation's business. You tell us what's going on here!"

Snickering, Benko responded, "You'll find out in due time."

"I'll find out right now. I can yell and I'll have the rest of the Secret Service down here in minutes."

Again Benko grinned. "I don't think so. Look around you. We had this room sound-proofed before we arrived," he lied. "You could scream your lungs out and no one would hear you. The same goes if I decide to put a bullet in you. No one would hear." Benko glanced at his weapon and added, "You may have noticed it's equipped with a silencer."

The three captives looked at the weapon and the attached silencer as Benko continued, "This has been carefully planned and for some time."

Deciding to change his approach, Benson asked, "To create my double and prep him to be me is astounding. Did you do it all here in the States?"

Before Benko could answer, Moore chimed in with a follow up question since he anticipated that Benko wouldn't respond to the question. "Sounds like you have a number of people involved, including several members of the Secret Service?"

"Not saying anything about who, what, where or when this double creation and coaching took place, Benson." Turning his head slightly to look at Moore, Benko replied, "You'd be surprised who's involved in this plan."

Before Benko could comment further, a cell phone buzzed in his shirt pocket. He reached in as he watched his captives and answered, "Yes?"

Taggart responded, "Everything under control?"

"For the most part. We have two visitors."

Taggart's face became very serious. "Who?"

"Valero and Moore."

"What in the hell! Any problems?" Taggart snapped.

"Not really. I've got everything under control."

"Okay. We're wrapping up here. I'll see you shortly."

"Okay." Benko ended the call and dropped his phone into his shirt pocket.

"Pretty astute. Not using your radio and using the cell so that no one can overhear you on the radio," Moore observed.

"Like I told you earlier, we're good planners."

"It was Taggart you were talking to, wasn't it?" Benson asked.

Seeing Benko's attention focused on Benson, Moore made an impulsive decision to act. With two powerful strides, Moore covered the distance between Benko and himself. Reaching out with his right arm, his hand grabbed Benko's right hand, which was holding his weapon. It had begun to swing toward Moore in reaction to Moore's charge.

Moore pushed the weapon downward while using his momentum to shove Benko backwards. Benko's head struck the edge of the table as he fell, knocking him unconscious. As he fell, his weapon fell harmlessly to the cold stone floor.

"Way to go, Emerson," Benson said, admiring Moore's action.

"Is he dead?" Moore asked Valero who was crouching over Benko.

"No, but he'll be out for some time."

"We better secure him. Look around for rope and something to gag him," Moore ordered as he stood and began to look around.

"Here's some rope," Benson said as he returned from a corner of the room.

"We can stuff this rag in his mouth," Valero said as he handed a rag to Moore, who was securing Benko with the rope.

"Now what do we do?" Valero asked as he looked at Benson and Moore.

"We're going to march upstairs and expose this charade," Benson stormed and began to walk toward the stairs, which led to the floor above.

"Whoa one second, Mr. President," Moore said quickly.

"What?"

"You don't know who are the bad guys and who are the good guys. We need to flush them out."

"And how do you propose we do that?"

"At the convention."

"The convention?"

"Yes. We'll get you to the convention where you can be seen on public TV. No one would want to take you out in front of all of those witnesses. We can then ferret out who is involved."

"And just how are you going to get me there?" Benson asked, his voice full of doubt.

Moore thought for a couple of minutes and then looked at Benson and Valero. "I know how. First, we're going to create a little diversion to move a significant number of the Secret Service and law enforcement authorities to the south side of the island." Moore looked at Valero. "I think I know how to do this, but I need your cell phone."

"Why?" Valero asked as he handed his cell phone to Moore.

"I'd like to know too," Benson chimed in.

Moore quickly outlined his plan and punched in a number on Valero's cell phone.

"Island Transportation," the voice answered on the other end.

"Dale?" Moore asked.

"Yes, the one and only. You've got the best looking bus driver on the island!" the mischievous Dale McKee responded as he continued to clench his trademark cigar between his lips.

"It's Emerson!"

"Holy crap!" McKee sat straight up in his chair. "What have you gotten yourself into? Trying to kill the President! There's Secret Service all over this place, trying to find you."

"I didn't do it. You've known me long enough that I wouldn't do something like that, right?"

The silvery haired manager of the island's only bus company sat back in his chair and took off his bright blue tinted sunglasses. He looked out the office window and decided not to respond.

"Dale? Are you there?"

Moore heard a long sigh. "I have a bad feeling that if I respond, you're going to get me involved."

"Well, I do need your help."

"I just knew it. And then I'll end up in the slammer with you!"

"Back to my question, you know me well enough that I wouldn't do anything like trying to kill the President, right?"

Another long sigh. "I just know I'll hate myself in the morning! Yes, I know you wouldn't try to kill him. And I'd bet that just about everyone on the island feels the same way."

"Great, now I do need your help."

"Why don't I just go down to the police station and turn myself in now?"

"If my plan works, you'll be featured on the world news tonight," Moore teased his friend.

"Featured?"

"Yep!"

"What if it doesn't work?"

"Then, you will really be featured," Moore smiled.

"Not sure that I like this." McKee groused for a moment. "Alright, what do you need me to do?"

Moore outlined his plan and its timing.

"I can do that!" McKee responded after hearing the plan. "That's something I've wanted to do ever since I began running the bus company!"

"Great. I'll call you when we're ready to go."

"Count on me," McKee said as a grin crossed his face and his cigar dropped to the floor. He disconnected the call and retrieved the cigar, sticking it back into his mouth. Standing he walked out of his office toward a parked bus.

"That was easier than expected," Benson said as he looked at Moore and Valero.

"I knew that I could count on Dale. He's a good guy," Moore said.

"Now, we better get out of here or we won't be getting off these islands." Moore walked to the far side of the wine cellar and began to pull one of the wine racks away from the wall.

"Let me help," Valero said as he joined Moore and began to pull the rack away.

Behind the rack was a four-foot high wooden wall, which ran the length of the room.

"It's here somewhere," Moore said as he ran his hand over the wooden panels, looking for the hidden door. His hand encountered the door's edge. "I think this is it." He bent and examined the paneling and announced, "Yep."

"Good thing you were part of the Castle's restoration team," Benson said as he watched Moore swing the door open to reveal steps. They were chiseled into the limestone tunnel's floor.

"We've got to hurry," Moore said as he waved the President and Valero to step into the old tunnel, which led to the water's edge. Rum runners had used it during prohibition to deliver whiskey to the island's residents.

"Anybody have a flashlight?" Benson asked as he took four steps into the dark tunnel.

"Always prepared, Mr. President," Valero smiled as he produced a small key chain LED light.

"Great," Moore commented. "Can you help me pull this wine rack back against the wall, Kenfield?"

"Sure can," Valero said as he joined Moore.

They tugged at the rack and were able to pull it back in place. Moore then closed the hidden door.

"Mr. President, if you don't mind, I'll lead the way with the flashlight."

"No problem, Emerson. You've been here before," he said as he passed the light to Moore and reached out to touch the tunnel's limestone wall for support.

It took them no more than ten minutes to reach the end of the tunnel.

"Looks like we have a problem," Valero observed, when he saw that the end of the tunnel had been sealed.

Benson looked around Valero to see that Moore's light was directed at the stone wall, which had been constructed to close the tunnel's four-foot high entrance.

"Not really," Moore responded as he pushed at one of the stones at the top of the wall. The stone gave way, falling on the outside. The opening was filled with bright daylight and fresh air began to enter the opening. "There was no strong reason for making this a very secure wall. And, honestly, I had a chance to explore the tunnel during the restoration. So, I knew that it wouldn't present us with a problem."

"Mr. Gorbachev, tear down this wall!" Benson said, mimicking Ronald Reagan's famous quote regarding the destruction of the Berlin Wall.

"We'll have to be careful. We've got Coast Guard and other law enforcement boats guarding the island. We don't want them to see the rocks falling away to reveal the opening," Moore warned.

"But the good thing is that they are trying to keep people from coming on the island. They're looking out and not in. They're not worried about someone leaving the island," Valero offered.

"Well put, Kenfield," Benson commented.

"Kenfield, I need your cell phone. Time for a little diversion," Moore grinned as he punched in the number of the Put-in-Bay police.

Secret Service Command Post
Ohio State Complex

The agent burst through the door into the second floor office where Taggart was reviewing the search results for Moore.

"They've spotted Moore!"

"Where?" Taggart demanded.

"The Put-in-Bay police just got a tip. Moore's hijacked one of the island's buses. Moore's armed and has a weapon pointed at the driver."

"Where are they?" Taggart said as he spun around to look through the large arched window.

"They've crashed through stops signs at Delaware and Toledo. They're heading toward the airport."

"That puts them about here," one of the senior agents said as he pointed to an island map displayed on a large computer screen.

"Shut down the airport. I want agents there, and fast."

"We only have minutes to get them there."

"Do we have anyone at the airport?"

"Yes, we've got two agents there."

"Have them take position to take out Moore if he tries to get to one of the planes. Does anyone know if he's a pilot?"

"Don't think so," one of the agents responded.

"I need to know. Find out. And make sure the bus driver doesn't get killed. Get hostage negotiators out there and have other units respond," Taggart stormed.

Another agent ran into the office. "We just received another report. The bus drove past the airport. It didn't stop!"

"Where's it going?"

"It's the Miller Ferry bus. I bet it's headed there," an agent volunteered.

"Same drill. Run everyone out to the ferry. Pull search teams. Pull patrol boats from security detail around the island and get them to that ferry landing," Taggart fumed.

"If we don't get him at the ferry landing and he gets aboard the ferry, we'll have him trapped. It'll be like shooting fish in a bowl. Stupid idiot!"

"What if he takes hostages on the ferry? The ferry will be full of island visitors returning to the mainland," an agent observed.

Taggart thought a moment. His mind raced for a way to resolve the problem. He didn't want to give Moore an opportunity to tell anyone about his observations regarding the President. "Get a sniper team out there. Take out Moore at the first opportunity. Cover the front and back doors of the bus. Kill him before he steps on the ferry's deck."

"What if the bus driver gets in the way?"

"I'd call it his bad luck. Take out Moore, no ifs, ands or buts!"

Miller Ferry Dock
South Side of South Bass Island

The bus slowed slightly as it turned left at the top of the hill, which led down to the ferry dock where the Miller Ferry *Wm Market* was just beginning to pull away. Its ramp was closing as it began to ease away from the dock.

In the bus, McKee saw the gap between the dock and the ferry widen. With his cigar clenched between his teeth, he depressed the accelerator to the floor and the bus gathered speed as it raced down the hill.

Dockworkers stood frozen as they watched the old bus careen down the hill toward the widening gap between the dock and the ferry. At the ferry's stern, Bill Market changed the ramp's direction and began to lower it in anticipation of what might be happening. He didn't know if there was an emergency, but he knew McKee well enough that there must be something wrong. Besides, he wouldn't let McKee run into the ferry's stern and damage it.

McKee timed it perfect as the ramp dropped. The bus sailed across the fifteen feet of open water and landed on the ferry deck. McKee quickly applied his brakes as the bus crashed into the two center rows of empty cars parked on the ferry. It was as if the bus was a bowling ball scattering pins. As the two rows split and crashed into the two outside rows of cars, McKee gripped the wheel, applied more pressure to the brakes and came to a stop a few feet away from the ferry's front ramp.

He leaned back in his seat and, for the first time, lit his cigar. "I guess this calls for a little celebration! It was a perfect strike," he said to himself as he looked around the deck at the damaged cars on the ferry.

"Freeze!"

Turning his head to the left and looking out the driver's window, McKee found himself looking into the wrong end of a shotgun.

Secret Service Command Post
Ohio State Complex

"What do you mean, he wasn't on the bus?" Taggart screamed into the radio. "I want teams searching along that bus route to the ferry. Divert the choppers to provide overhead surveillance. Moore may have jumped out!"

"Will do," the agent on the other end responded.

"And one more thing."

"Yes?"

"Bring the bus driver here."

"Will do."

Taggart's face had reddened with anger. The agents in the office with him found work to do so that they would not be the next to incur his legendary wrath.

An agent ran into the office. "Excuse me, sir."

"What is it?"

"The Put-in-Bay police just received a bomb threat. It goes off in 15 minutes."

"Where?" Taggart asked as he turned to look out the window toward the island. What he saw astonished him. His view was filled with over 600 boats in some stage of evacuating the numerous docks, which lined the harbor.

"Put-in-Bay's docks, but they didn't say which one. They're notifying all the docks and marinas in the harbor to evacuate the docks. It's going to be a mass exodus!"

"Alert Gibraltar and evacuate the President to the safe house on Middle Bass Island. Recall the Coast Guard and other patrol boats that we sent to the ferry and have them assist with the evacuation. And get a small craft to run me through the cut to Gibraltar Island."

Taggart was referring to the cut, which had been made in Alligator Reef, which runs from Gibraltar Island to Oak Point. It was the short cut from the Ohio State dock to Gibraltar Island's dock.

"Did you want the President's boat to wait for you?"

"No. Get him off Gibraltar and to the safe house on Middle Bass like I told you."

Turning to one of the agents in the office, he said, "I want you to coordinate a bomb sweep of all the docks. Get additional resources if you need them."

"Right!"

Taggart strode out of the office and down the flight of stairs. As he walked briskly to the waiting craft, he saw that the press was converging on Jon Hertrack, peppering him with questions.

The craft pulled away from the dock with Taggart in the bow. He watched as the President was hurried down the steps by a number of agents. He saw him board his boat and join the large number of craft, already departing the harbor. It was mass exodus from the harbor like the Israelites leaving Egypt.

At the Tunnel Entrance
Gibraltar Island

The final rocks were pulled away from the wall blocking the tunnel's entrance and joined the growing pile inside the tunnel. Moore had originally dislodged enough rocks that he could watch the law enforcement boats stationed off shore. When he saw a number of them leave, he knew that the bus ruse had worked.

"Looks like some of them have been ordered to the island's south side," Moore grinned as he imagined Taggart's frustration raging out of control.

"Good idea!" Valero said. "Increases our odds for success."

"Yeah, but I'm worried about the consequences for Dale. I just hope he didn't do any damage," Moore thought aloud.

"What could he have done? Run through a couple of police cars at a roadblock? Once we get through this mess, it'll be taken care of. It was a diversionary tactic to help safeguard me," the President countered.

Listening to the chatter on his earpiece, Valero updated the other two. "It sure is working. They're pulling search teams and redeploying our agents to the ferry dock."

"Time for your call?" Moore asked as he looked at his watch.

"In a second. There's something we have to do first. Can you hold this light, Emerson?"

"Sure. But why?"

"You'll see," Valero replied as he produced a small pocketknife from his pocket. "Mr. President, would you kindly remove your shirt?"

"What?" Benson asked. Then a look of realization crossed his face. "I completely forgot about that," he said as he quickly pulled off his shirt and raised his left arm.

"What are you doing?" Moore asked.

"You'll see. Focus your light here," Valero directed Moore to a spot on the underside of Benson's upper arm. "We've got a little surgery to perform before we take one step out of this tunnel."

Moore peered at the spot on the President's arm and saw a small raised area where Valero began to insert the knife's sharp blade.

"Sorry about this, Mr. President. It should feel like a needle prick and be over in a second."

"Go ahead, Kenfield."

The blade cut through the thin layer of skin and dislodged a small plastic container, which had been implanted there before the President's inauguration three and a half years ago.

Holding it in his hand, Valero said as the President ignored the small trickle of blood and put on his shirt, "Now, we need to get rid of this or they'll know our every move."

"Tracking device?" Moore guessed.

"Bingo! Give the man a prize," Valero teased.

"Didn't know you guys were doing that."

"We've been doing it since Carter took office. But you can't write about this," Valero warned.

"Matter of national security, Emerson," Benson added.

"I see nothing," Moore teased as he looked at the small device, which Valero had handed to him. He dropped it in his pocket and asked, "Now, how about that call?"

Valero looked at the President. "Okay to introduce a little panic on Put-in-Bay?"

"As reluctant as I am about it, it's something we have to do to mask our escape. Go ahead and make the call." Turning to Moore, he added. "Great idea!"

"I just hope it works," Moore said as he turned back to the tunnel entrance and began to remove more stones.

Producing his cell phone, Valero keyed in the number to the Put-in-Bay Police Station.

"Put-in-Bay police," the voice answered.

"You've got a bomb set to explode on B dock in twenty minutes," Valero grunted in the phone and then hung up. Following Moore's instructions, he called the office at DeRivera Park, which had responsibility for most of the dockage in front of the park. Valero repeated his message and hung up.

"Between those two calls, you'll see boats begin to flood out of the harbor. I can see it now as word is yelled from boat to boat and on the radio channels. That harbor will be virtually empty in twenty minutes," Moore said.

"And we'll get lost in the mix," Valero added.

"Provided we get on board a boat."

"That's my department. I'll take care of it."

"Emerson, it's amazing how you come up with these ideas. If you ever get tired of that investigative reporting stuff, you can have a job with me."

Moore continued dislodging rocks from the entrance. "Thanks for the offer, but I love my job. I never know what the next assignment will bring."

Valero joined Moore and in a matter of two minutes, the remaining rocks were strewn on the tunnel floor.

The trio shielded their eyes momentarily as the bright sunlight flooded the tunnel entrance. As their eyes adjusted, Valero stepped out of the entrance and looked to his right toward Put-in-Bay's harbor. He saw the initial wave of departing watercraft leaving the harbor.

"More boats are being pulled from station," he called over his shoulder as a number of the law enforcement boats went against the grain and tried to enter the harbor to help direct the fleeing boats in some orderly fashion.

"I think I see our opportunity," Valero called back to the tunnel entrance where Benson and Moore were secluded. "I know those two agents." Valero was looking at a 32-foot Tiara, which had been rented from Lakeside Marine for offshore patrol duty.

"Hey, Hill!" Valero called to the agent.

"Yeah, What do you want?"

"I need your help. Can you two come over here?" Valero asked as he pointed to the gravel beach.

"What is it?"

"You'll see. Come on. It's important."

Hill turned the craft toward Valero and easily closed the short distance between the craft and the beach. He eased the craft up on the beach and leaned over to look at Valero. "What's wrong?"

"Help me aboard and I'll explain," Valero said as he approached the craft and was lifted aboard by Hill and his partner.

"What is it?" Hill asked again.

"Let's go below and I'll explain." Valero went down the companionway, followed by the two agents. He turned to his right in the main cabin and allowed the two agents to walk past him. When they turned to look at him, their jaws dropped in surprise. "What's this about, Valero?"

Valero's pistol was aimed at the two agents. "Sorry guys, I'll have to explain later. You'll have to bear with me. All I can tell you is that it's a matter of national security. Now very carefully, I need you to use your left hand and withdraw your weapons. Place them on the deck in front of me."

The two agents turned their heads and looked briefly at each other. Hill nodded to the other agent and they both slowly withdrew their weapons and laid them on the deck.

"Now, carefully, kick them across the deck to me."

The agents did as instructed.

"Next, I want your radios and cell phones."

The two agents threw them on the floor.

"Now, I want you to pull your handcuffs and place one set on your wrists so that you're handcuffed together."

The agents complied.

"Now, the other set. Do the same thing with your other wrists."

"Kenfield, you've got to tell us what this is about," Hill said as he followed instructions.

"All I can say is that it involves Benson."

"This had better be good," the other agent groused as the cuffs snapped shut on him.

"Now, both of you, to the forward cabin," Valero prodded and pushed them down the narrow walkway. "Make yourselves comfy and don't come out. We're going to take a little boat ride."

Valero stepped out of the cabin, closing and locking the door as he went. He quickly returned to the main deck and leaned over the edge of the Tiara. "All clear. Come aboard."

With Valero's assistance, Benson and Moore climbed aboard.

"What happened to the agents? Did you harm them?" Benson asked.

"No. Just locked them in the forward cabin. But, you'd better get below, sir. We don't want anyone to see you on board."

"Right you are," Benson said as he turned and went below.

In the meantime, Moore had moved to the controls and began to back the boat off the beach.

"Where to?" Valero asked Moore.

"Lakeside."

"Lakeside?"

"It's not far. It's a resort community of cottages on the Marble-head Peninsula. We'll ditch the boat there and get lost in the crowd."

Moore brought the boat about and began to head across the opening of Put-in-Bay's harbor. As a Sea Ray, flying the University of Michigan colors, began to cross their path, Moore waved them down.

"What are you doing?" Valero quizzed.

"Patience." Moore turned to the slowing boat and drew abreast of it. "What's the ruckus?" he asked as he reached into his pocket.

"Bomb threat on the dock! Everyone's clearing out!" one of the twenty-some-year-olds yelled.

"Don't go in. Everyone's evacuating the dock," one other called over.

"Thanks," Moore said as he leaned toward them. He couldn't resist yelling "O-H!" He didn't expect them to respond with the "I-O" to complete the Ohio State University chant.

Instead, the young men unloosed a string of expletives and turned their backs to them. Smiling, Moore calmly threw the small tracking device into their boat. The Michigan men threw their throttle forward and headed back to Michigan across the lake.

"I saw what you did," Valero chuckled.

Grinning as he pushed the Tiara's throttle forward, Moore said, "They'll be in for a huge surprise when the Secret Service decides to track them down."

"They deserve it. They're from Michigan," Moore, a big Ohio State fan, teased as he pointed the boat toward Lakeside and joined a number of craft exiting Put-in-Bay's harbor toward Lakeside and East Harbor.

Only a few minutes had passed when Valero said, "You have created such havoc today."

Grinning at the wheel, Moore taunted him. "What do you mean me? Like you didn't have a hand in this?"

Looking at Moore, Valero smiled back, "I guess we did create mass confusion."

"Yeah and a perfect cover for our escape. There's no way anyone can track all of these boats."

At the Stone Lab Dock
Gibraltar Island

Bounding from the boat before it was secured, Taggart walked briskly up the hill toward the Castle. Glancing to his right from time to time, he continued to observe the large number of boats fleeing the imminent explosion.

Taggart was mumbling under his breath with consternation about not catching Moore and the bomb threat. He could tell it was not going to be a good day.

As he approached the Castle, he was met by one of the Secret Service agents. "Is the President secure?"

"Yes. He's on Middle Bass Island and we have a chopper on the way to pick him up."

"Taking him to Cleveland, right?"

"Yes. He'll be arriving early for his acceptance speech tonight."

"I'll catch up with him at the Convention Center. I have a couple of matters to attend to."

Taggart resumed his walk toward the Castle and the agent continued on his way to Stone Lab. Brushing past the remaining security guards at the Castle, Taggart made his way down the stairs to the wine cellar.

He pushed open the door and walked into the darkened cellar. "Benko?" He called as an uneasy feeling began to fill him.

There was no response.

"Benko?" he called again.

Hearing nothing, Taggart walked across the room to the smaller anteroom where Benson had been held. He pushed open the door and saw Benko on the floor. He was bound and gagged.

Taggart unleashed a series of expletives as his eyes went from Benko to sweeping around the empty room. He walked out of the room and looked around for Benson. He couldn't find him.

Just then a groan came from the fallen Benko. Taggart quickly returned to his side.

"Benko, you okay?" Taggart asked as he untied Benko and pulled the rag from his mouth.

"Yeah. Just a bit woozy," he said as he rubbed the rather large bump, which had developed on his head.

"What in the hell happened? Where's Benson?"

Taggart fumed as Benko gave him a report. "Valero was in on this?"

"Yep."

"You're sure?"

"Yes, and that nosy reporter, Emerson Moore."

"I don't know what Valero is doing. That little S.O.B. is going to have some serious explaining to do!"

Taggart's lips curled in disgust. He didn't like Moore.

"How did they escape from here?"

"I don't know. I was out."

Taggart knew that he would have heard if the President reappeared. It would have created quite a scene for there to be two Bensons walking around Gibraltar Island. As he quickly processed a variety of scenarios, Taggart concluded that Benson wouldn't know who was loyal to him and who was in on Taggart's plot. Taggart surmised that Benson would do everything he could to expose them on national television that evening at the Convention. The way to prevent that was to find Benson before he showed up at the Convention.

"Come on and help me. We've got to find out where they went. There must be another way out of here," Taggart said as he roughly jerked a groaning Benko to his feet.

"My head hurts," groaned Benko.

"Suck it up, you wuss!" Taggart grumbled as he switched on every light in the wine cellar. He quickly scanned the two small windows, but it didn't appear that the small layer of dust on the sills had been disturbed. He walked over to the door leading to the outside entrance and ran up the steps. Emerging in the bright sunlight, Taggart squinted as he looked around. He saw the large trash container nearby and checked inside to be sure that no one was hiding in it. As he suspected, there wasn't.

He concluded that Benson and company did not escape through this exit since there were too many people around. Hue and cry would have been raised and he would have heard about it. He returned to the basement where he found Benko examining the basement floor.

"What do you have there?" Taggart demanded.

"Scratch marks. I don't recall seeing these before. And they look relatively fresh."

Taggart and Benko's eyes were drawn to the wine rack.

"Let's move it," Taggart said as he moved next to the rack. Benko followed and took a position at the other end. They pulled the rack away from the wall and looked at the wall behind it. Taggart tapped on the wooden wall and then ran his hand along the edges.

"Sounds hollow over here," he said as he produced a pocketknife and began digging around the edges. Suddenly, the hidden door opened as his knife's blade made contact with the release.

Taggart and Benko simultaneously reached for their weapons as Taggart opened the door. "A tunnel," he proclaimed victoriously.

"Yeah."

"You can come out now, Benson! You won't be harmed," Taggart called into the tunnel. They listened for a response. Hearing none, Taggart instructed Benko. "Stay here. I'll run upstairs and grab a couple of flashlights. We'll track them down."

Benko nodded his head affirmatively as Taggart raced up the stairs to the Castle's first floor. Within minutes he returned with the two flashlights and rejoined Benko at the tunnel entrance.

They turned on the lights and directed their bright beams into the tunnel.

"See anything?"

"Nope." Benko responded.

"Let's go. Careful now," Taggart said as he entered the tunnel. He held the light in his left hand and his weapon in his right as he began his descent – closely followed by Benko.

Shortly, they reached the tunnel's exit and they walked onto the small beach.

"They had help." Taggart pointed to the marks left on the beach from the boat, which had been beached during the escape.

"Looks like it," Benko concurred.

A smile crossed Taggart's face as he thought about the tracking implant in Benson's arm. "Let's go. I think I know how we'll find them."

Taggart ran back into the tunnel, followed closely by Benko. They emerged in the wine cellar, ran up the stairs to the outside entrance and walked quickly down the hill to the Stone Lab.

Inside the first floor of the Lab, Taggart produced a key and unlocked the door to a small office where a number of monitors had been set up. He approached one and activated it.

Appearing on the screen before him were two blips. One was coming from Middle Bass Island where Benson's double was waiting for the chopper. The other blip was approaching the West Sister Islands. It would be Benson.

Taggart smiled as he reached for his radio and activated it. "We believe we identified the source of the bomb threat. They're in a boat headed northwest of here, near the West Sister Islands. I want it stopped now!" He gave the coordinates based on his display.

His orders initiated a flurry of activity by the Secret Service agents and the Coast Guard.

"I need a Coast Guard chopper at the Miller Ferry downtown dock now. It'll pick up two passengers. Benko and me. Do not board the craft. We will board the craft and conduct the search."

Not waiting for a reply, Taggart switched off the monitors, grabbed a small portable monitor, and pushed Benko ahead of him and through the office door. "Let's get the lead out!"

They hurried to the Stone Lab dock and boarded a small boat with an outboard, manned by one of the Ohio State staff. The staffer gunned the craft toward the Miller Ferry downtown dock.

Between South Bass Island And Marblehead

Keeping with the pack of boats heading southeast, Moore saw Valero cocking his head to the side as he listened to his radio. "Trouble?" he asked.

"No," Valero responded. "It looks like they may have discovered that the President is missing. They have directed a number of the law enforcement and Coast Guard boats toward the West Sister Islands."

"Good. A little misdirection now and then is a good thing. Especially in this situation. They took the bait!"

"Hook, line, sinker and whole boat!" Valero grinned.

"Any indication that they know that you and I are involved?"

"Nope. Not a word. And they haven't broadcast a word about the President missing."

"And they can't. Makes it a bit messy to have two Presidents running around. It'd screw up their plans, whatever they may be."

Miller Ferry Downtown Dock
Put-in-Bay

Arriving at the dock, they stepped off the boat and waited for the chopper. As they waited, Taggart paced and cast his eyes toward the virtually deserted Put-in-Bay harbor. Only a few boats remained and he guessed they belonged to the islanders.

Within five minutes, the thumping of the rotating blades of the chopper could be heard. It dropped slowly and set down on the dock. It was on the ground no longer than one minute as its two eager passengers boarded.

The chopper lifted off and then flew northwest toward the West Sister Islands.

A Coast Guard cutter and two Homeland Security go-fast boats were the first craft to catch up with a number of the boats headed for the West Sister Islands. The cutter had been en route back from Michigan and had taken up station by the islands. Using its PA system, it was halting boat traffic in the lake. Coast Guardsmen in Zodiacs, which had been launched from the cutter, were herding the boats together. Boats, which decided to ignore the orders to halt, were tracked down by the Homeland Security's go-fast boats and redirected to the herd.

As the chopper approached, Benko exclaimed as he saw the number of boats, which were bobbing together in the lake. "Look how many boats they've got there!"

"Yeah, but our job is easy. We're just looking for one in particular." Taggart looked down at his portable monitor and began making adjustments on it so that he could identify which boat the blips were coming from. When he identified it, he radioed to the cutter. "I need that Sea Ray cut out from the rest of the pack. And I don't want anyone going on board. My man and I are, but cover us."

Following Taggart's instructions, a voice over the cutter's PA system ordered the Sea Ray to slowly ease out of the pack. Two Zodiacs, with Coast Guardsmen manning fifty caliber machine guns, emerged and aimed their weapons at the Sea Ray.

They directed the Sea Ray to a spot 100 feet away from the rest of the pack.

"Hey, what's this all about?" a young man yelled from the Sea Ray.

"Cut your engines," was the only response from one of the Zodiacs.

The chopper flew overhead and lowered first Taggart and then Benko to the boat's deck. Both had their weapons out. The chopper then flew off to await further commands.

"We need to search your craft," Taggart said.

"What's going on? We didn't do anything," the boat's owner said, angrily.

"Benko, check below," Taggart ordered.

The boat's owner approached Taggart. "Listen, if this is all about that chic last night, I didn't know that she was married."

For the first time in the last hour, a smile crossed Taggart's face. "If only that's what this was about!"

Benko reappeared from searching the cabin below. "Nothing. All clear."

The smile disappeared and Taggart produced the portable monitor from his pocket. Switching it on, he used it like a Geiger counter and walked to the stern of the boat. He bent over and picked up the small transmitter.

"Not a good thing," Benko commented as he realized what his boss had found.

Ignoring him, Taggart asked the boat's owner, "Has anyone been on board your boat in the last hour?"

"No, why?"

"We're looking for someone."

"There was that Ohio State dude," one of the other young men volunteered.

"What's that?" Taggart asked as his head snapped around to face the young man.

"Yeah, when we were leaving the harbor some guy waved us down. Wanted to know what the ruckus was about. We told him about the bomb threat. You guys think he did it?"

"What kind of boat was it? How many passengers?"

"We just saw two. It was some sort of police boat."

Reaching for his radio, Taggart called in. "I want a radio check from all law enforcement boats which were assigned to protect the President. Let me know if any don't respond. I need that chopper back here to pick us up. And contact NSA. I want to look at satellite pictures when I arrive at Peach Point. I want pictures of the north side of Gibraltar Island for the last two hours." The orders flew with a fury from Taggart's mouth as he reeled from being outsmarted. "Take them into custody for questioning at Peach Point," Taggart barked at the Coast Guardsmen.

"But, we didn't do anything," the boat owner wailed as Taggart turned his back to them and looked toward the approaching helicopter.

On the horizon, he spotted a second chopper. Taggart's mind sped in a thousand directions as he played out potential scenarios. All of a sudden, a look of concern crossed his face. "Benko, this is getting out of control."

"Yeah. It's not going according to plan now," Benko agreed. He wanted to comment "understatement of the day", but knew when to hold his tongue in front of his explosive boss.

"I want you to take that other chopper to Grosse Ile."

"Grosse Ile?" Benko asked with a shocked look on his face. "Whatever for?"

Taggart leaned toward Benko and lowered his voice as he gave deadly instructions to Benko.

"Will do," Benko said as he watched Taggart being raised into the first chopper where he would radio the second chopper to fly Benko to Gross Ile.

National Satellite Agency (NSA)
McLean, Virginia

The NSA was founded in 1958 by President Eisenhower and after the Soviets launched their first satellite, Sputnik. It builds and operates the nation's reconnaissance satellites. Operating under the oversight of the Department of Defense, Homeland Security and CIA, the agency is staffed by personnel from each of the aforementioned. Their mission is to continue developing and operating a number of innovative overhead intelligence systems for national security.

The windowless room was filled with personnel reviewing images displayed on large monitors from satellites circling the globe. The seven-story building had limited windows and low-lit rooms to facilitate interpretation of sensitive data. There were a variety of rooms dealing with images from different areas of the world.

There was one room set aside for Presidential Activities. In this room, top data analysts worked to review and analyze images of areas of planned worldwide visits by the President. They also were maintaining surveillance from their eyes in the sky on the Lake Erie Islands, paying close attention to boats entering U.S. waters from Canada or any boats heading toward Gibraltar Island. The sophistication level of the Eagle Series satellite allowed the analysts to drill down to view passengers on the boats during day or night.

When the call from the Secret Service came in, the room's activity jumped several notches as they responded quickly to provide the requested data to Taggart. Within minutes, the data was transmitted to Taggart for his review.

Approaching Lakeside
Marblehead Peninsula

"Taggart is erupting like a volcano!" Valero grinned as he turned away from his radio.

"How's that?" Moore asked as he pointed the craft toward Lakeside Marine on the Marblehead Peninsula.

"They just found the tracking device which you dropped into the college kids' boat."

Laughing, Moore said, "That sure did buy us some time."

"It's going to get tougher."

"Oh?"

"They're getting NSA involved."

Moore thought for a moment and commented, "The spy in the sky guys?"

"Yep. They'll probably look at images of Gibraltar."

"Then, they'll see us emerge from the tunnel and identify us?"

"Yeah, and that'll make it interesting because they'll also see the President. How's Taggart going to explain that?"

"Depends on who's with him when he reviews the images. But one thing's for sure."

"What?"

"They'll see that we took the police boat."

"That shouldn't be a problem in a few more minutes. We're going undercover?"

"Undercover?"

"Yes. Tree cover, that is. When we dock the boat, we'll disappear in Lakeside under the trees and get lost in the crowd of residents and tourists."

"I hope there are a lot of trees."

"Oh, there are. It will work nicely."

Grosse Ile Municpal Airport
Grosse Ile Island

The chopper landed east of the large main hangar, located on Groh Road. Benko walked briskly from the chopper to the office to secure a rental car. The chopper's crew was shutting down and settling in to wait for Benko's return as instructed previously by Taggart.

As Benko walked, he spotted a pay phone and headed toward it. Picking it up, he punched in a number, which he pulled from his cell phone directory. His call was answered on the second ring.

"Hello?"

"Code 9," Benko said as he used one of Taggart's prearranged codes. "This is an emergency. I need your help. In fact, I need both of you."

"When?"

"Now."

"This is very unusual. Not a part of the protocol."

"I realize that, but this is an emergency. Can you meet me?"

"I can."

"And what about your partner?"

"I don't know. I'll have to track him down. Where are you?"

"Grosse Ile."

The man on the other end sat straight up. "You're here?"

"Yes. Now get moving. I'll meet you at the boat in 15 minutes. We have a special mission to run."

"What if he can't come?"

"No excuses. I will meet both of you at the boat in fifteen minutes," Benko said as he slammed the phone down. He resumed his walk to the office where he secured his rental. A few minutes later, he drove out of the parking lot, turning right and heading east on Groh Road. He turned right on East Shore Road, following it to the south end and the Grosse Ile Yacht Club.

Benko selected a spot in the parking lot where he could watch new arrivees park their cars and head to the slips. He opened the attachment on the e-mail, which Taggart had sent to his

Blackberry and displayed a photo of the man he was to meet. He then settled back in his seat to wait. He didn't have to wait more than 30 minutes when a white Nissan Altima pulled into the lot and parked. A man emerged from the car. Quickly comparing the photo to the person in front of him, Benko saw they were the same. He shut down his Blackberry and exited his car.

Walking across the lot, the man turned to greet the suited Benko. He looked so out of place that it was easy for the man to guess who he was.

"You called me?" he asked.

"Yes, Hanna. It was me." Benko looked around.

"And you are?"

"Benny Narko," Benko said. It didn't matter what name he gave Hanna. Once their mission was over, names would be meaningless.

Hanna squinted as he assessed Benko. He was suspicious that Benko was giving him a false name. But then again, it didn't matter. Hanna wasn't his real name either. "Just to be safe, give me the code."

"Code 9."

"Where's Taggart?"

"Busy."

"Fishing for walleye in Put-in-Bay?"

Benko raised his eyebrows.

"Yeah, I saw the news reports. Your President went fishing for walleye. Big propaganda show!"

Benko was getting impatient. They had a task at hand. "Where's your buddy?"

"I think he's here. He lives closer than I do." Hanna looked around. "He's probably on the boat, getting it ready."

"Good. Any trouble in getting him here?"

"Initially, yes. I just had to threaten killing his daughter and he came around in two seconds."

"Think he caved in and called the local police?"

"No. He's in too deep."

We all are, Benko thought to himself as he followed Hanna to the boat, a 62-foot Azimut, named *Vengeance.*

On the boat, Carlyle was double-checking his fuel and saw that he had full tanks. He was anxious. The call from Hanna had come unexpectedly. When Carlyle had tried to explain that he had ballet lessons to take his daughter to, Hanna had threatened to kill her. He had thought briefly about going to the police, but he was in over his head.

He wished he had never taken the cash when it was offered to him. He couldn't face the thought of putting his family in the public spotlight. The news about what he had done would create all kinds of emotional hardship for them all.

The sound of approaching footsteps caused Carlyle to look toward the dock. "Al, what's this all about?" Carlyle asked nervously.

"Got a job to do. And we have a helper today." He pointed to Benko as the two men stepped aboard. "This is Benny."

Carlyle extended his hand, but Benko brushed it aside as he started below. "The stuff's down here?"

"Yeah. I'll be right with you." Hanna turned to Carlyle, as he headed below, and said, "Take us out to the lake. I'll be below."

Hanna joined Benko in the main cabin. Benko was surveying the barrels of chemicals, pumps and hoses in front of him. "So, this is how you do it?"

"Yeah, pretty simple. We usually go out at night. Douse the lights. Run out the hoses and turn on the pumps as we cruise. The current spreads it out for us. Then, back to the dock."

Benko peered at the label on the side of one of the barrels as he felt the boat being put in gear and start underway down the channel. "I thought you couldn't procure this in the U.S."

"You can't. We had it shipped to Canada and trucked to the riverbank on the Canadian side. Then, one night, we met my contact along the riverbank and loaded up Carlyle's boat. Very simple."

"Yeah, very simple," Benko repeated.

"It's worked. And no one has caught us. We're too careful. In my business, caution is important."

"In both of our worlds, caution is important," Benko said.

The boat had reached the end of the channel and was heading downstream on the Detroit River to the mouth of Lake Erie.

Hanna walked toward the rear of the cabin. His back was to Benko. "And that's what has me perplexed today."

"How so?" Benko asked.

"All of our runs have been at night. I assumed that Taggart would have told you."

"I was aware of that."

Hanna turned around to face Benko. In his hand was a pistol and it was pointed at Benko. "Why is it such an emergency to run during the day when we are at risk of being picked up by reconnaissance satellite?"

"Put that away. You're being a fool."

"I don't think so. Being a fool, as you say, about matters such as this has kept me alive. Now, why are we running during the day?"

A wave from a passing boat caused their boat to lurch suddenly. Hanna momentarily lost his balance and the pistol wavered from pointing at Benko. Benko saw his opportunity. Quickly closing the gap between Hanna and himself, he grabbed Hanna's gun hand. The two men wrestled for control of the weapon.

As they were wrestling, Carlyle appeared at the entryway. "What's going on here?" he asked wide eyed.

It was the last question he'd ask. Hanna's finger inadvertently closed on the trigger, causing the gun to fire. The main cabin was filled with the explosive sound of the gun firing. The bullet caught Carlyle in the left cheek, just below the left eye. Carlyle tumbled to the deck floor where blood from his lethal wound began to coagulate.

Meanwhile, Hanna and Benko were in the midst of a deadly physical match. Hanna's legs lashed out at Benko as he tried to connect and break a bone to slow Benko's attack. Benko was adept at dodging the kicks and was concentrating on Hanna's neck. He soon was able to position himself so that he suddenly twisted and snapped Hanna's neck, killing him.

Benko rolled off the inert body and lay on the floor, gasping to catch his breath. He suddenly realized that no one was at the controls, guiding the boat on its voyage. Benko stood and rushed to the main deck and quickly assessed the boat's situation. They were fine. No boats were in the immediate area. Benko eased back on the throttle to slow the boat's forward progress and brought it to a stop.

Returning to the main cabin, Benko surveyed the scene. Looking down at Hanna's body, he smiled sardonically and spoke to it. "You're disposable just like a used razor blade. You lost your edge!"

Benko turned to address his next assignment. He needed to destroy all evidence and the easiest way would be to blow up the boat. Benko saw that the barrels containing the chemicals were marked as flammable and decided that the barrels would be his best plan of attack.

He pried the tops off of three barrels. Two were half empty. He walked to Hanna's body and dragged it to the first half empty barrel. He lifted the body up and stuffed it into the barrel. Carefully to avoid staining his clothes with Carlyle's blood, he repeated the process with Carlyle.

Next, Benko began opening drawers as he sought a triggering device to start the fire. He found a small votive candle in the first drawer, which he placed on the counter. He continued looking through the rest of the drawers, but couldn't find anything else, which would fit his need.

Turning to the opened barrel, he slowly tilted it so that some of the chemical contents sloshed out of the barrel and onto the deck. He continued this exercise until there was a thin layer of liquid chemical covering the deck. He then grabbed a pot from the galley and dipped it into the barrel. Next he doused the furniture and cabin walls with the chemical. This will go up like a Roman candle, Benko smiled to himself.

Finding a towel on the counter, Benko soaked it in the barrel and placed the towel on the counter. He opened a drawer and pulled out a large kitchen knife, which he used to cut the votive candle in half. He then placed the votive candle on top of the towel and placed both items on the deck.

Picking up a pack of matches, which he had found earlier during his initial search of the drawers, Benko lit one of the matches. He then knelt down and lit the votive candle. Once the now even smaller candle burned through it would ignite the chemicals in the towel and the fire would spread quickly.

Benko climbed up the companionway to the main deck, and shut the cabin door behind him. In his hurry to leave, he didn't realize that the door hadn't firmly latched shut.

Again, Benko looked around the craft and didn't see any other craft nearby. He went over the stern to the swim deck and climbed aboard the small Zodiac tied to the stern. He started its motor and turned the craft for the journey back to Grosse Ile and the waiting chopper. He was anxious to report back to Taggart that his mission had been accomplished.

A few minutes later as the boat drifted, a brisk breeze opened the door to the main cabin and swirled into the cabin. It was strong enough to blow out the votive candle, ruining Benko's plan for a clean getaway.

Presidential Protection Detail Headquarters Peach Point

The second floor room, which overlooked Put-in-Bay's harbor, had been cleared of all personnel other than Taggart and Benko.

Taggart was hunched over a monitor, scanning the images, which had been sent from NSA.

"See anything interesting?" Benko asked.

"Not yet," Taggart said as he continued scanning the images. He had zoomed in to focus on the area near the tunnel exit. "Whoa, what do we have here?" He stopped and backed up the images. "I think we have it."

Benko leaned over to peer at the monitor.

Displayed in front of them was the image of a man talking to two agents in a boat, which had been beached on Gibraltar Island. Taggart zoomed in for a closer look at the man.

"Valero!" he exclaimed when he recognized the figure. "What's he doing?"

They watched the images and the actions as the two agents disappeared below deck and Valero reappeared by himself. They saw two figures emerge from the tunnel.

"There's Benson and Moore!" Benko said as he recognized the President.

Taggart unleashed a series of expletives. "Why in the hell is Valero helping Moore? He should have taken him into custody or killed him – and not necessarily in that order!"

"There goes the boat," Benko observed as the boat pulled away from the beach.

A few scans later, Taggart said, "And there's our college boys talking to them."

They saw the boats pull away and the police boat round East Point, then the screen went white as the downloaded images ended.

"Now what?"

"For starters, Valero's probably been listening to our radio conversations. Have a signal sent down to his radio unit and deactivate it."

The door burst open and one of the agents appeared. "We've got a police boat not reporting in and Valero is missing."

The timing didn't amuse Taggart. "Yeah, we know. Deactivate Valero's radio. Put out an alert about the missing police boat. I want it stopped, but not boarded. I'll board it."

The agent left the office area, closing the door behind him.

A thin smile appeared on Taggart's face. "There's another way to find Valero and Moore – and the President."

Lakeside Marine
Lakeside, Ohio

The boat had entered the limestone rock-lined harbor of Lakeside Marine. Valero was in the bow and threw a line to one of the dockworkers, who secured it. Valero returned to the stern where Moore had finished tying up. "What's next?"

Before he answered Valero, Moore yelled to the dockworker. "Okay to tie up here for a while?"

"Shouldn't be a problem, Mr. Moore. You piloting police boats these days?"

"They loaned it to me."

"You wouldn't have to borrow one if you bought one of ours."

Moore flashed a smile at the young man. "One of these days. One of these days," he repeated himself.

Valero arched his eyebrows. "He knows you?"

"Some of the folks here do. Friends of mine, Lowell and Elaine Joy, own this marina and boat sales operation. They're ranked as #1 in boat sales in the Great Lakes. This is the place where I come to dream about owning a new Tiara."

"What's going on?" the voice called from the companionway. "Can I come on deck?"

Valero and Moore turned around to see Benson start to emerge on deck.

"Sir, you better remain below. We'll join you. How're your captives been doing?" Valero asked as he and Moore headed down the companionway.

"Been relatively quiet," Benson responded.

"What's next?" Valero asked.

"That's what I was wondering," Benson added.

"First, we need to get you sunglasses and a hat. Can't have you walking around and attracting a crowd."

"But these are potential voters," Benson teased. "I can't go incognito." He took the pair of oversized sunglasses, which Valero found, and placed them on his head.

"Try this for size," Moore said as he handed Benson a black police cap from which he had ripped the emblem."

Benson tried it on and took it off to make a slight adjustment. "Fits now. Looks a bit raggedy."

"What now?" Valero asked.

"We'll leave the boys locked up. It may not take them long to trace us here if they have NSA involved," Moore said.

"What? They have NSA tracking us?" Benson asked.

Moore and Valero quickly updated Benson on what they had overheard on Valero's radio.

"I see," Benson said. "Let's just go public and let everyone know what's going on. That someone has gone to a lot of trouble to create my double."

"I wouldn't suggest we do that," Moore said.

"And why not?"

"Dick, we've talked about this back at the Castle. You've got rogue agents involved and who knows who else is involved. We need to identify who is the mastermind. We'll get you to the convention and interrupt your double's renomination acceptance speech. It will be safer there than trying to do something here, wouldn't you agree Kenfield?"

Valero nodded. "I agree!"

Thinking for a moment, Benson spoke with a firm tone. "I'll go along with your suggestions, but all of the responsible parties for this nasty affair are going to be answerable to the courts."

"Good, then," Moore commented. "Let's get moving. Follow me."

Moore led them up the companionway, across the dock and into a tall, aircraft-hangar-like, metal building. The building was partially filled by boats in some state of repair and others being prepared for customer delivery.

Seeing a truck beginning to pull out of the building, Moore turned to Valero. "You have a cell phone?"

"Yes."

"Give it to me."

"Why? You going to..."

Moore cut him off. "Now. I need your cell phone now."

Valero produced his cell phone from a clip around his waist.

"And you better give me your radio just in case."

"Can't do it. It's privileged."

"Okay, then." Moore ran over to the departing truck and threw the cell phone in the truck's bed.

"Worried about someone tracking the cell phone and us?" Valero asked.

"Yep, and the same holds true for your radio."

"I figure that they're on to us. My radio has been silent for awhile."

"Then, I'd suggest you toss it back on the police boat. Can't have them track us with it."

"Will do." Valero left the building.

"I've got to get us a golf cart," Moore said to Benson.

"A golf cart? We'll never get to Cleveland in time by driving a golf cart, my friend."

"It's so we'll blend in and the roof will help give us cover from the big eye in the sky."

"We can't borrow a vehicle and drive to Cleveland?"

"Nope. If they have us figured out, they'll be throwing up roadblocks on this peninsula. Nothing will get out of here without going through one of the checkpoints."

Valero reappeared and joined them.

"There's a cart over there." Moore pointed to one parked inside of the hanger. "Okay to borrow your golf cart?" Moore shouted to one of the boat workers.

"Sure, Emerson. Just bring it back when you're done."

The three men scrambled aboard with Emerson sitting behind the wheel. He started the cart and they drove out of the building, making a sharp right up the drive and then driving into one of the back entrances to Lakeside.

Lakeside is an alluring, gated Chautauqua community of cottages, restaurants and recreational activities. It was founded in 1873 and hosts many summer training and spiritual educational sessions conducted by the Methodist Church.

Driving past the historic Lakeside Hotel with its massive screened porch overlooking Lake Erie, and, in the distance, South Bass Island, the three felt relatively safe under the canopy provided by the massive trees, which lined the street.

Moore turned left at the Fountain Inn and pulled in a small alley behind Sloopy's. He parked the golf cart behind Joseph Wise Fine Clocks Shop.

"You certainly seem to know your way around here," Benson said as he exited from the front passenger seat.

"I collect clocks, so I'm over here often talking to Joe and Cindy, who own the store," Moore said as he stepped from the cart. "We're going to need their help," he added as he led them to the back door and entered the building.

Walking down a narrow, clock-lined hallway, they emerged into the main showroom, where Moore spied a red-haired, energetic woman wearing red-framed glasses. "Cindy," he called.

She whirled around to face him and a smile crossed her face. "Emerson! Where have you been?"

Moore realized it had been some time since he had stopped in to examine newly arrived clocks. "Been busy. But Cindy, we're in a rush and I need your help. Is Joe around?"

"He sure is. He's out front on the sidewalk, talking with one of the summer residents." She stepped to the front door and called out, "Joe. Joe, can you come here? Emerson's here and needs our help."

Joe nodded his head and ended his conversation. He entered the building and smiled as he greeted Moore. "Emerson, you staying out of trouble?" the dark haired and bearded ornery-looking co-owner asked.

"Funny thing, Joe, that's why I'm here. I'm in trouble and need your help."

Looking at the two men standing behind Moore, Joe asked, "Oh?"

"If I share something with you, can you keep it confidential? Promise not to disclose it to anyone until I let you know you can?"

"You know us, Emerson," Cindy responded as Joe nodded his head. "We wouldn't say anything."

Moore turned and looked at Benson. "Could you remove your sunglasses and cap?"

Benson seemed surprised at the request and stood still.

Moore continued. "They're okay. I trust them."

"Okay, then," Benson said as he removed the items.

"Oh my gosh, Joe. Look at him. It's the President of the United States! And he's standing right here in our shop!" Cindy said in surprise.

Joe nodded his head. "I didn't vote for you," he said stoically.

"I appreciate that, but I hope it won't preclude you from helping us with our dilemma," Benson responded to Joe's comment.

"It won't. It won't stop us. Right, Joe?" Cindy turned and looked into her husband's eyes.

"We'll help because Emerson here asked," Joe explained.

Emerson smiled at his friend. "Thanks, Joe. Does your brother Ray still have the delivery van?"

"Yes"

"Great. Could you call him and ask him to pull out back?"

"No need to. Look there." Joe was pointing outside the front display window to a bright yellow, 1949 Dodge panel truck that had parked in front of the building. The lettering on the side of the truck read "Lake Erie Market." Ray owned the busy market, which was located outside of Lakeside's main gate, less than half a mile away.

Before Benson could replace his impromptu disguise, Ray burst through the door and saw Benson. His eyes widened and his mouth dropped open. "What's he doing here?"

Joe answered his brother before anyone else could. "He stopped by to get the correct time," Joe teased.

Benson responded, "We're here to ask for your help."

"You might want to think about that, Ray. You know I didn't vote for him," Joe commented.

"But I did. What can we do for you, Mr. Benson, I mean, Mr. President?" Ray asked.

"Emerson, would you like to explain to all of us the next step?" Benson asked.

"Sure. Ray, you're all going to have to trust us on this. We can't go into detail at this point..."

"Matter of national security," Benson interrupted.

All three of the Wises nodded their heads in understanding.

"Right. You can't say anything to anyone that you've seen us or helped us until I let you know otherwise. Agreed?"

The three nodded their heads again in response to Moore's question.

"Good. Ray, we'll need you to pull the panel truck around back so we can get in. Then, drive us out through the new gate that's up on the hill."

"I can do that. Then what?"

"I'll let you know as we go."

Ray scooted out the front door to get the truck.

"Thanks, Cindy and Joe, for helping."

"We didn't do anything, Emerson," Cindy said.

"We're going to read about this in *The Washington Post*, Emerson?" Joe asked.

"Joe, you have no idea. This is going to be a blockbuster story and I'm right in the front row on this one."

"Sounds to me like you're more on center stage," Joe retorted.

"He's here," Valero called from the open back door.

"Secret Service?" Joe asked as he looked at Valero.

"Yes," Moore responded.

"Figures. A President can't go anywhere without one. Sort of like a woman going to the bathroom. They have to go in pairs, too," Joe smirked.

"JOE, DON'T SAY THAT!" Cindy admonished her husband as Moore headed for the door trailed by Benson. "Mr. President, could I get your autograph on that sheet of paper?" Cindy asked as the President walked past the sales counter toward the rear of the store.

"Certainly." Benson picked up a pen and with a flourish signed his name on the paper. "Thank you for your help in this matter." He replaced the cap on his head and the sunglasses on his face.

"Thank you," Cindy beamed.

Before he walked out the door, Benson called back to Joe, "And I hope I can count on your vote this November."

"Hope you don't need it to break a tie," the stoic Joe replied as the President closed the door and joined the men in the panel truck.

"Aren't you coming with us?" Benson asked Moore when he saw that Moore was starting to drive off in the golf cart.

"Can't leave it parked here. It'd be a dead giveaway for Joe and Cindy. Ray's going to follow me over close to the campgrounds. I'm going to park it there and cut through the woods to meet you guys," Moore called as he drove off.

Lakeside Marine
Marblehead Peninsula

The muffled voices answered back when Taggart shouted down the companionway of the docked police boat. Taggart, followed closely by Benko, raced below and unlocked the door to the forward compartment.

Opening the door, he saw the two agents handcuffed together and began swearing profusely.

"Did you get Valero?" one agent asked after Taggart's verbal explosion had subsided.

"No," Taggart stormed. "All we found thanks to our great cell phone tracking technology was his cell phone. It was in the back of a Lakeside Marine truck. That's what led us here."

"Valero is pretty clever," the agent continued.

Realizing that the agent had only mentioned Valero, Taggart asked, "Did you see anyone else with him?"

"No. But we heard footsteps. I'd guess there were three of them. Wouldn't you agree, Ralph?"

The second agent concurred, "That's what it sounded like to me, too."

Good, Taggart thought to himself. The two agents didn't know that one of the three was Benson.

"Bill, I found this note on the deck," Hill said as he handed a folded note to Taggart. His name was printed on the outside.

Grabbing the note, Taggart read it. "I don't get it," he grumbled to himself. He refolded the note and placed it in his pocket. "Let's see where Valero and his accomplices have gone," Taggart said as he climbed the companionway and returned to the craft's stern. He then stepped up and onto the dock where a number of agents were waiting for him.

One agent stepped forward. "We obtained some information as to where they might have gone."

"How many were there and did anyone recognize them?"

"There were three. No one had seen them before. One had sunglasses and a black cap."

"Let's have it then. Where are they?"

"I understand that they borrowed a golf cart. We believe they were headed into Lakeside." The agent pointed in the direction of the community filled with summer cottages.

"That's a gated community, isn't it?"

"Yes."

"Shut it down. I want boats offshore. I want the gates covered. Get a description of the golf cart and make sure that it entered through one of the gates and hasn't emerged," Taggart ordered.

"Should be easy to do. It has the Lakeside Marine logo on the side."

"Get moving and someone report back to me. Come on, Benko, we're going for a ride."

They walked over to a waiting Suburban and climbed in. The SUV pulled out and headed in the direction of the entrance to Lakeside. In a few minutes, they were stopped at the entrance by one of the security guards.

"Afternoon, gentlemen," he greeted them.

"Have you seen a Lakeside Marine golf cart enter through this gate? It would have had three men on board." Taggart ignored the pleasantries.

"Why?"

"Just answer my question," Taggart snarled as he flashed his Secret Service identification at the guard.

"Yes, sir, I did see them. They paid their entrance fee and drove down the street here."

"See where they went?"

"Nope, but they bought a four-hour admission pass."

Taggart thought a moment. Were they really planning to leave within four hours or was it a ruse to throw Taggart off track? Did they plan to hunker down in Lakeside? With over 400 cottages, a house-to-house search would take a massive effort. Then, there was the risk of Benson going public.

"Thanks for the help," Taggart said as they drove into the community. Taggart barked orders into his radio as he directed teams of men to conduct a sweep to locate the golf cart. Then, Taggart smiled to himself. *Moore, you're not as clever as you thought you were. You've trapped yourself in a gated community.*

Quarry Pit
Marblehead Peninsula

"Looks like trouble," Ray Wise said as he drove on Route 53 toward downtown Marblehead.

"Sure does," Emerson said as he saw the two police cars blocking the road in front of them.

"What is it?" Benson called from the back of the panel truck.

"Two police cars are blocking the road. Looks like a checkpoint. Looks like they're searching vehicles," Moore responded. "They're having people exit the cars and checking the trunks."

"Sounds like I'll just have to make a public appearance," Benson said in a determined tone.

"Not yet." As the car eased forward in the line of stopped traffic, Moore asked, "Ray, we can't go through that checkpoint. What can we do?"

Ray responded by slowly turning the wheel to the right and entering a small black asphalt parking lot. He drove through the lot and onto a small drive. "It's time for you to do a little praying," he quipped as they entered St. Mary's Cemetery.

"Just as long as the dead being prayed over are not us," Moore teased as the truck kept to the left hand drive and made its way to the rear of the cemetery which was marked by a large, four-foot high limestone rock.

Wise parked the truck in front of the rock. "Okay, everyone out."

The four men emerged from the vehicle and followed Wise to the other side of the rock. From their perch, they looked down on a huge quarry where limestone had been mined for years.

Valero was the first to speak. "Interesting. They excavated all around the cemetery, leaving it as a peninsula of high ground."

The cemetery stood on a promontory of limestone. Its edges were overgrown with briars and trees. The cemetery itself, though, was well maintained.

"Looks like the deserts of Israel," Benson commented as his eyes scanned the bottom of the quarry, which stretched for miles.

"Yeah, it's quite a view," Wise agreed.

"Emerson, what's next?" Benson asked.

Moore had been studying the piles of limestone, which rose a hundred feet in the air, and a number of buildings closer to the village of Marblehead. "Since Ray can't take us any further, I'd suggest we head over to that group of buildings. We need to do it quickly before any choppers start looking for us."

"I think we have time. Leaving that golf cart in Lakeside is going to make them want to search every house there," Valero grinned.

"Still, we don't have time to lose," Moore said as he turned to Wise. "Thanks, Ray."

"Sure, anytime."

"Ray, thank you. I appreciate your help in this matter," Benson said as he shook Wise's hand. "And Ray, I don't want you to say anything about what transpired here or that you even saw me. That's an order from your President."

"Understood, sir," Wise responded as he returned to his truck. Starting his engine and beginning to back up, he called, "Good luck."

The three waved at Wise as they began their descent down the sides of the cemetery to the quarry floor.

Wise slowly drove toward the cemetery entrance. As he drove through the entrance, he depressed his brakes. In front of him were parked three state trooper cars. The troopers were holding their weapons and aiming them at Wise.

"Shut off your engine and step out of the vehicle," one trooper commanded.

Wise did as he was instructed.

"Come around to the front of your vehicle and place both hands on the hood," the trooper ordered. "Anyone else inside the vehicle?" he asked as the troopers began to approach the delivery truck.

"Just me," Wise responded. "What seems to be the problem, officer?"

"You pulled out of the checkpoint line, didn't you?"

"Is that a federal offense?"

Ignoring Wise's comment, the trooper probed, "Why did you pull out of the line? What's down there?" The trooper was looking down the drive from which the panel truck had emerged.

"Graves, just graves. I remembered that I had to visit the grave of an old friend and since I wasn't going anywhere in that line of traffic, I decided to do it now."

"All clear. No one in here." The rear door to the panel truck slammed shut as one of the other troopers finished checking it.

"Then, you wouldn't mind if we brought over one of the dogs over to check your vehicle?" the trooper asked.

"Go right ahead. You won't find any trace of drugs here."

"It's not drugs we're looking for," the trooper responded. "Watch him." The trooper returned to one of the cars and radioed the team in Lakeside, who had already found the abandoned golf cart.

The police dog had sniffed the cushions in the boat on which Benson had been seated and had begun to bark when he recognized Benson's scent on the golf cart seat. The police dog couldn't find the scent in Lakeside and the law enforcement team had become concerned that they might have already escaped from Lakeside.

The trooper finished with his explanation and continued, "Might be nothing to it, but we ought to check it out."

Finishing his conversation, the trooper returned to the other officers who were surrounding Wise and his vehicle. "The canine unit will be here in a few minutes." Pointing to the two troopers, he said, "Why don't you take a stroll through the cemetery and see if you see anything suspicious."

The troopers nodded their heads and entered the cemetery. Ten minutes later, they returned and reported that they didn't see anything. At the same time the canine unit pulled up and parked next to the panel truck.

The dog's handler emerged from the car. He was holding a seat cushion from the police boat, which had been left at Lakeside Marine. He moved to the rear of his vehicle and opened the door. Out jumped a large German shepherd. The dog went immediately to the seat cushion and sniffed. Its handler brought it over to the panel truck and held the door open and the dog jumped into the rear of the panel truck. Within seconds, it began barking.

The trooper looked at Wise. "You want to change your story, now?" he asked as he reached for his radio to report in.

Floor of the Quarry Pit
Marblehead Peninsula

"Hear that?" Valero asked as he cocked his head toward the sound of the barking dog.

"Yeah. And it can't be good news," Moore responded.

"Police dog?" Benson asked.

"That would be my guess. It sounded like it came from the area close to the entrance. Could they have tracked us to the cemetery from Lakeside?" Moore asked.

"I wouldn't think so since we were in the panel truck, but we don't know what happened," Valero replied.

"Think your buddy turned us in after dropping us off?" Benson probed.

"He wouldn't do that. Who knows what happened or what kind of technology they're using to hunt us down. They know we're on the Peninsula. If they're at the cemetery entrance, we still have some time before they pick up our scent and come down into the quarry. We need to get a move on," Moore said in a firm tone.

"Right you are," Valero agreed.

"Follow me," Moore said as he led the trio in a brisk walk to the area with the buildings, conveyor belt and tall piles of limestone.

Within minutes, the men arrived at the building complex. Dust from the limestone being loaded on the conveyor belt filled the air.

"That's our way out," Moore said as he pointed to the moving belt. "The belt takes you out of the quarry, across the highway and onto the ship where the limestone is being loaded."

Benson looked at the stream of limestone shooting onto the belt. "And how do we get on to the belt? And what about getting dumped into a ship's hold at the other end and buried in limestone?"

Moore pointed to the conveyor belt. "We climb up over there on the other side of where it's being deposited on the belt. We'll ride on out. Before we get to the end, we'll swing off the belt and climb down the structure. We'll then board the boat or the tug if a barge is being used for transportation."

"And what about the police dog? Won't he follow our scent?" Benson asked as he looked around the area.

"Don't think so. He'll lose it here with all the dust. They'll spend time searching the buildings before they think about looking on the conveyor belt." Moore cast an anxious eye toward the cemetery on the hill. "We don't have any time to waste. Let's roll."

Moore led the men to the steel structure and began to climb. Within minutes, they were swinging themselves over the sides of the trough like structure at the top and onto the limestone moving along the belt. "Not a very good mattress to rest on," Moore teased from his lumpy position.

From his position at the end of the three men, Valero called, "Hey, they stopped dumping the limestone on the conveyor."

"That's a relief," Moore yelled back. "That means that they're about fully loaded and the ship should be readying to leave the dock."

"Good," Benson commented.

"One other good thing is that the conveyor will shut down. Could buy us some time if they trace us to the buildings. A running conveyor could point them in our direction."

"But, once they figure out that we are on the conveyor and the ship, we'll be sitting ducks."

Grinning, Moore responded, "Not really. I've got a plan."

"Okay, whiz kid," Valero teased.

"I just hope my magic continues to work," Moore smiled as they rode over Main Street in Marblehead and past the quarry operations offices. "See that green building over there?"

Benson saw Moore peering over the edge of the conveyor.

"Yes," he responded as he looked in the same direction.

"Belongs to Ben Richmond."

"The painter?" Benson asked.

"Yes. He specializes in painting lake scenes in this area."

"I believe I met him at a fund raiser. I've got one of his paintings in the White House."

"I didn't realize that. His gallery is on the other side."

Benson rolled over to look toward the buildings in Marblehead and spied the Richmond Gallery. "He's quite an accomplished artist."

"And a good friend," Moore added. He looked as they approached the end of their ride. "Get ready," he said. Then, Moore, keeping a low profile, swung over the edge of the structure and began to climb down. Benson and Valero quickly followed him. In a matter of minutes, they were standing on the ground.

"Now what?" Benson asked as he surveyed the area for a means of escape.

"A little magic," Moore grinned.

"How's that?" Benson asked as Valero chimed in, "You going to pull a rabbit out of a hat?"

"Stealing a boat from the Coast Guard?" Valero asked as he looked toward the Marblehead Coast Guard station where a craft was docked.

"The answer is right in front of us," Moore said as he pointed to the barge full of limestone and the tugboat.

"I'm glad that you're in no hurry to get to Cleveland. That tug will take a week to get there," Valero said sardonically.

"Emerson, don't you think they'll deduce that we're on the tug?" Benson asked.

"I sure do. But it's just another step in our escape route," Moore smiled.

"You mean you have this all planned out?" Valero asked incredulously.

"To be honest with you, I don't. But I am pretty good at coming up with answers on the fly."

"I just hope nobody breaks your wings while you're flying," Benson said in a serious tone. "I'm sure they'll come after the tug."

"That they will and we will be long gone," Moore said with an air of suspense.

Benson and Valero looked skeptically at Moore.

"Bear with me. It's all going to work out." Moore looked at Benson. "I am going to need your help."

"Oh?"

"Yeah. You're going to have to swear some people to secrecy as a matter of national security."

"And who would the people be?"

"Not sure who they all will be, but we can start with the crew on the tug. Come on. We better board before they shove off. And you better take the cap and sunglasses off."

Benson did as he was requested.

As the men approached the tug, Captain Pat Thompson peered through the glass windows of the *Jesse*'s pilothouse. He was a tall, fifty some-year-old with a full gray beard. He had been plying the waters of the Great Lakes for 35 years and had seen a lot of things on the lakes. His eyes bulged as he recognized the President of the United States.

"Tommy," he called down to the engine room as he began to step out of the pilothouse. "You've got to come up here. You won't believe who's coming to talk to us. It's the President of these United States."

"I just knew he'd find me," Tommy called back as he wiped the oil from his greasy hands. "Wendee told me that I'd get in trouble for not voting in the election three years ago," Tommy mumbled to himself as he made his way to the main deck to join Thompson.

"Hi, Pat," Moore called as he recognized his friend. Thompson lived in nearby Sandusky and owned a large collection of military vehicles. Moore had visited with Thompson on several occasions to talk about the history of the Great Lakes and to hear Thompson's stories about his sea adventures. Thompson was also a former U.S. Navy deep-sea diver and a member of the BAD (Bay Area Divers club) and LEWD (Lake Erie Wreck Divers.) Moore also belonged to both dive clubs.

Thompson nodded his head toward Moore and looked right at the President. "Hello, Emerson. And just who do you have in tow with you?"

Before Moore could respond, Benson stepped up and shook hands with Thompson and Tommy. "Good afternoon gentlemen. I'm..."

Thompson interrupted. "Oh, I know who you are. I voted for you in the last election. I'm Pat Thompson. This here is my one and only crewmember, Tommy. He didn't vote in the last election."

A sheepish look crossed Tommy's face as the President shook his hand. "But, I'm planning on voting for you in the next election, Sir."

Benson beamed. "Thank you. I'm counting on it. Emerson, would you like to tell this fine gentlemen why we're here?"

"Sure." Moore turned to face Thompson. "We need your help."

"Anything that I can do, I'll do."

"Are you heading to Cleveland?"

"Yes. We had planned on pushing this barge there. Just about ready to leave."

"The three of us need a ride part of the way there. This is Agent Valero. He's Secret Service."

Thompson nodded at Valero and then peppered Moore with questions, "Why in the world would you want to ride with us? This is the President of these United States. Where's Air Force One? Where's Marine One? Where's his limo?"

Benson responded, "Pat and Tommy, this is a matter of national security. We're not going to be able to answer your questions now, but eventually you will understand. Now, we better get moving."

Thompson shook his head affirmatively. "You're still my commander-in-chief, Sir. Tommy and me will do what you need us to do."

"Then, let's get moving," Benson said as he stepped aboard the tug.

Floor of the Quarry Pit
Marblehead Peninsula

"The dog lost the scent," Taggart stormed as they entered the loading area, which was covered in a light gray limestone dust.

"This limestone dust covers everything," the dog's handler responded to Taggart's comment.

A number of law enforcement vehicles pulled up to the buildings and Taggart began barking orders, "Search all the buildings. And do it thoroughly. Find Emerson Moore, Kenfield Valero and their traveling companion. Bring them all back here. You had photos of Valero and Moore e-mailed to you."

Taggart reached for his radio and issued another directive, "I want this entire quarry searched. Find Moore and Valero."

The Marblehead Chief of Police approached Taggart. "I know of one other place you may want to search."

Taggart looked with disdain at the local law enforcement official. "Shut up, I'm thinking."

The chief shrugged his shoulders and walked back to his vehicle where he placed a call to the quarry operations manager. A few minutes later, he returned to where Taggart was pacing. Taggart's face was filled with fury. The chief, on the other hand, was smiling.

"I think I know where they might be."

"Where?" Taggart snapped.

"See that overhead conveyor belt. It carries limestone down to the dock and dumps it on a barge. Until a little while ago, it was carrying limestone."

"Take me to the barge," Taggart ordered the Chief.

"I can't unless you walk on water."

Taggart didn't respond. He gave the Chief a cold stare. Taggart was getting more desperate and tiring of this game of cat and mouse with the Chief. Sensing this, the Chief continued. "The barge left a while ago. The tug, *Jesse*, is pushing it to Cleveland."

Taggart laughed. He knew that he had the three trapped, if they were on board. He also realized that they would never make it to Cleveland on time by traveling on the slow moving barge.

"We don't know that for sure. I want a complete search of the quarry." Taggart called in an order to the Coast Guard. He told them to find the barge and search it and the tug.

Aboard the Tug
Off Vermilion

"Gentlemen, you understand that I need you to keep my ride with you confidential. No one is to know that you've seen me nor my two companions, no matter what they tell you."

"Yes, I understand," Thompson replied.

"This is the real deal," Moore said. "This is very serious. You may have other Secret Service agents or government representatives telling you anything that they can to try to get you to reveal that you were with the President today. You can't say anything."

Benson added, "We need 24 hours. Everything will be clearer in 24 hours."

"One way or another," Valero commented.

"Mr. President, I've had Top Secret clearance from my Navy days. There are things that I know which will go with me to the grave. I'll treat this in the same vein."

A smile crossed Benson's face. "Thank you, Pat. It won't be necessary this time. Everything will be in the open within 24 hours."

"We better get going," Moore called from his seat at the wheel of the Zodiac, which Thompson was letting them borrow. The 12-foot long craft with the 90 horsepower Mercury outboard was bobbing in the water next to the tug.

"Thanks, Pat," Benson said as he shook hands one last time, placed the sunglasses on his face and then followed Valero into the Zodiac.

"Our mouths are sealed, aren't they, Tommy?" Thompson called back.

"Yep, our mouths are sealed. Yep, they're sealed," Tommy said nervously, repeating himself.

"Thanks, Pat," Moore called as he eased the Zodiac away from the *Jesse* and shoved the throttle forward. He pointed the craft towards the mouth of the Vermilion River.

The Zodiac flew across the lake and in minutes was entering the Vermilion River. Moore guided it past the openings to the numerous canals, running off the river so canal front homeowners could dock their expensive craft in their front yards. He eased the boat past the Quaker Steak and Lube Restaurant, the successor restaurant to Red Clay and the famous McGarvey's fish restaurant.

Vermilion was the name that the Indians had given the lakefront town because of the red clay, which they found there. Moore enjoyed frequenting the town, which previously housed the Great Lakes Maritime Museum, and still housed one of his favorite nautical shops, Lee's Landing.

The boat continued upriver, moving under the Vermilion River drawbridge. After it went under the railroad drawbridge, Moore beached the craft on the river's west bank.

"Now what, Emerson?" Valero asked.

"Follow me." Emerson began to scramble up the embankment.

Bridge Tender's Housing
Vermilion

"I can't do that!" the railroad bridge tender groused. "They'd take away my pension."

"It's just a matter of radioing the trains that the bridge has malfunctioned and is stuck in the up position," Moore explained again.

"I can't do that."

"What if I asked you to do it?" The voice came from the open doorway. The bridge tender swiveled around in his chair to identify the source of the voice. It sounded vaguely familiar. His eyes bulged when he saw Benson standing there.

Smiling at the reaction, Benson asked again, "What if I asked you to do it?"

"What are you doing here? I thought you were in Cleveland to give your acceptance speech."

"I will be. That's why I need your help."

"What about my pension? You going to make sure that there're no repercussions and I don't get fired?"

"Yes, I will."

The bridge tender looked from Benson to Moore and back to Benson. He sighed as he made his decision. "Well, let's get this show on the road," the bridge tender said as he turned to speak into his radio. "Now, what exactly do you need me to do?"

Moore leaned forward. "We need you to raise the bridge before the next eastbound train comes through. You'll need to radio the train that the bridge is stuck and they may have a short wait."

"I can do that." The bridge tender turned to the President. "And I have your promise that I won't get into trouble on this?"

"You have my word," Benson said, nodding his head affirmatively.

"When's the next eastbound train due?" Moore asked as he peered at the control panel in front of the bridge tender.

"Should be within ten minutes."

"Ten minute wait," Moore called out the door to Valero who was keeping watch on the river below. "See anything down there?"

"Nope. All's quiet," Valero replied.

Five minutes later the bridge tender began to raise the bridge and, at the same time, called the eastbound train, which had just passed south of Huron. The locomotive's engineer grumbled when he heard the message and began to slow his freight train. By the time he reached the Vermilion bridge, he was easily able to bring the train to a complete stop.

Picking up the radio, he groused as he called the tender, "How long of a wait will it be?" When he didn't receive a response, he repeated his question as he stared at the upraised bridge. "How long is this going to take?"

The engineer had been so focused on the delay in front of him that he didn't notice three men step from the bushes next to the stopped train. They climbed aboard the rear of the locomotive and one opened the door. It was Benson.

Benson heard the engineer's question and responded. "As long as it takes to lower the bridge."

The engineer's head snapped as it swiveled around to identify the voice behind him. "What in blazes are you doing here?"

"Hitching a ride unless you want me to hop a boxcar," Benson teased. "Look for yourself," Benson pointed toward the bridge. "It's dropping back in place."

Moore and Valero joined Benson in the locomotive as Benson gave his plea again for cooperation and confidentiality. "So, bottom line," he said as he wrapped up his speech, "I need to get to downtown Cleveland. Can you help us out?"

"As long as you make sure I don't get into any type of trouble, we can do it."

"I will. So, let's get rolling."

The engineer eased the throttle forward and the engine slowly began to gather speed and move forward over the bridge.

As they passed in front of the bridge tender's building, Benson waved in acknowledgement of the tender's assistance.

Benson was smiling as he looked at Valero and Moore. "Looks like everything is coming together, Emerson."

"So far. We still need to get you safely into the convention hall. We don't know what these guys will do to try to prevent it."

"I'd expect security to be even tighter now," Valero offered.

"Probably is," Moore agreed. He turned to look out at Lake Erie as the train ran along the shoreline tracks on its way to Lorain and Cleveland.

Aboard the Tug
Off the Port of Lorain

"Here comes trouble," Tommy said nervously.

Thompson looked around and across the stern, "Nothing that we didn't expect," he said as the Coast Guard's 33-foot boat with three super-charged 275-horsepower Verado motors raced toward them. Its blue lights were flashing. Overhead a police helicopter was approaching.

A message from the Coast Guard boat crackled on the *Jesse*'s radio. "Stand by and prepare to be boarded."

"Oh boy," Tommy fretted.

"Relax, we're going to play this game through. You and I gave our word," Thompson said as he began to slow the tug to bring it to a stop. With the barge, it had only been moving at eight knots.

The Coast Guard boat pulled abreast of the tug and stayed alongside until the tug came to a stop. Three crewmembers, brandishing weapons, jumped aboard the tug.

"What seems to be wrong?" Thompson asked.

"Just a routine stop," the Crew Chief responded.

"Helicopter overhead. You guys armed. Looks like everything, but routine to me," Thompson observed.

Ignoring Thompson's comment, the Crew Chief continued, "Anybody else aboard?"

"Just Jennifer Aniston," Thompson quipped.

The Crew Chief's eyes bored through Thompson like a laser beam. "I'm going to ask you one more time. Do you have anyone else aboard?"

"No. But, feel free to search the tug." Thompson anticipated that they would anyhow. "What's all this commotion about?" he asked as he watched two of the men begin to search through the vessel.

The Crew Chief didn't respond as he waited for his men to return.

A few minutes passed and the two returned. "Nothing, Chief," one responded.

The Crew Chief turned to look at Thompson. "We're looking for three men. They were last reported as having been seen at the Lafarge Quarry in Marblehead. That's where you just came from, right?"

Thompson nodded. "Yep. Just filled up the barge. Heading over to Cleveland."

"You didn't see anyone?"

"Nope."

"Did you see anyone suspicious around the end of the conveyor belt? Maybe, dropping off the belt and running off toward town?"

"Nope."

"Okay, then. We're sorry to have bothered you. Have a good trip to Cleveland," the Crew Chief said as he motioned his men to reboard the Coast Guard vessel.

Thompson smiled, "Have a good day, gentlemen." He watched as the helmsmen expertly brought the craft around and pointed it back toward Marblehead. The craft picked up speed as it moved away.

"See how easy that was, Tommy? You just play it nice and cool." Thompson turned back to the controls in the pilothouse. As he prepared to restart their journey, Tommy stepped into the pilothouse doorway.

"They're coming back!" he said with alarm.

"What do you mean they're coming back?" He peered out the doorway and saw that the Coast Guard vessel had turned around and was bearing down on the tug. This time, a crewmember was standing at the mounted machine gun in the bow. It was pointed at the tug. Overhead, the helicopter was also returning.

At the same time, the radio crackled, "Tug *Jesse*, stand by. Prepare to be boarded."

"How do you think they figured things out?" Tommy worried.

"Don't know, but be careful. They might just be bluffing. Don't say anything. We've got to buy the guys time. Remember, you made a promise to the President of the United States. You don't want to do anything that would break that promise, do you?" Thompson asked in a very firm tone.

"I'll keep my promise, Pat."

Within minutes, the Coast Guard boat was alongside and the three crewmembers, looking very serious now, were back on board the tug.

"What seems to be the problem?" Thompson asked.

The Crew Chief looked sternly at Thompson. "Didn't you tell me that you didn't see three men on the dock or by the end of the conveyor belt?"

"Yes."

"Then, you want to explain to me why one of the police dogs picked up their scent from the end of the conveyor belt and across the dock to where your tug was docked?"

"I don't have an explanation. It could have happened before or after we left the dock."

"You think so?"

"Maybe the three men you're looking for met an accomplice and boarded his boat. They could be anywhere on the lake now. Why are you targeting me?" Thompson asked, still playing it cool.

"Nice try. We've been told to bring you in for questioning." He looked at Tommy, standing in a corner of the pilothouse. "Both of you."

Tommy appeared to want to melt into the pilothouse wall.

"And what about my tug and the barge?" Thompson asked.

"These two fine gentlemen will guide it into a safe berth where we'll have the canine unit check it out." The Crew Chief looked directly at Thompson. "You want to change your story now?"

Responding without hesitation, Thompson said, "Nope!"

"Then, let's get aboard my vessel."

Thompson shrugged his shoulders and did as he was instructed.

Approaching Cleveland
Cuyahoga River Bridge

❧

The engineer slowed the train as it crossed the bridge over the mouth of the Cuyahoga River where it emptied into Lake Erie. "Won't be long now," he called to his three passengers.

"Thanks," Moore said as he pointed south. "There's Shooters."

"Shooters?" Benson asked, not comprehending what Moore was saying.

"It's a restaurant and bar on the riverfront. This area is called the Flats. Used to be the hot spot. You couldn't drive a car down the main drag because of the mass of humanity which came here to party on weekends."

"Looks like it's ripe for economic redevelopment," Benson observed as he saw the vacant buildings.

"I wish! Upriver is what used to be my favorite restaurant in town. On the East Bank. It was called The Watermark. I used to dine outside on the deck and chat with boaters. We actually used to run in here from Put-in-Bay for afternoon meals."

The train began to slow.

"Thanks for the lift," Moore called as he exited the cab and worked his way down the ladder.

"Remember not to say anything to anyone for at least 24 hours," Benson said as he quickly shook hands with the engineer and followed Moore. Valero was on his heels.

"You can count on me," the engineer said as the train approached Cleveland Browns Stadium. He turned to look and saw that his once crowded cab was now empty. Boy, do I have a tale to tell one day, he thought to himself. I helped out the President of the United States, he grinned.

Outside, the three men dropped from the slow-moving locomotive and took cover in the sparse brush alongside the tracks.

"Where to?" Benson asked.

"Definitely away from the lakefront. If they determine that we were on the water, they'll have teams watching for us there," Moore said.

They made their way along Front Ave. to West 9th as the train traveled eastward on the tracks next to the cliff. It passed through the station, which took delegates and convention attendees into the Medical Mart Convention Center. It was located on the western end of the Mall on Lakeside Avenue. On the west, it was flanked by the Lakeside Courthouse. Its east side was flanked by City Hall.

The national convention had been in progress for four days with delegates filling every downtown hotel room to the brink. The overflow crowds were also filling hotel rooms in the nearby suburbs. Millions of dollars were flooding the Cleveland economy. It was better than having four nights of Monday Night Football.

There were lines of patrons waiting at such local restaurants as Mallora, Brasa, Blue Point, The Cleveland Chop House, Johnnys, and John Q's Steakhouse. Former Brown's player Bob Golic's Grill was packed nightly as Browns' players mixed with convention delegates. The Grill was on West Lakeside, a few blocks west of the convention center.

Across from Golic's and under the Route 2 overpass, the three fugitives huddled. "What now?" Benson asked. "Are we close to the convention center?"

"Yes. It's a matter of blocks. And I think I know just how we'll get in," Moore said with an air of mystery.

"How's that?" Valero asked. "This town is crawling with security."

"And that's how we're going to do it."

Benson and Valero looked at each other and then back to Moore as Moore reached for the cell phone. He had borrowed it from the train engineer, and punched in a number. The phone at the other end rang and went to voice mail. Moore left the following message, "This is Emerson. It's critical that you call me back right away at this number."

"No answer?" Benson asked pensively.

"No, but I expect a call back quickly," he said cryptically.

"I don't know. Maybe, I should step out publicly now. I need to be at that podium," Benson said as he anxiously looked at his watch.

"Can't do it," Moore responded. "You don't know who the good guys or bad guys are. You step out in front of the wrong person and we all disappear. It sounds like a palace coup to me."

Moore's cell phone began to ring.

Moore depressed the answer key as he picked it up. "It's about time you called back!"

"Well, if it isn't Mr. chaos on legs! E, what have you done? In the last hour, we received pictures of you and agent Valero. We're to stop and hold you two and an unidentified third party. What's going down?" Duncan asked with a serious tone.

"I can't explain over the phone. But, I need your help," Moore said with just as serious a tone in his voice.

"Not sure what I can do. I'm working now."

"That's why I called."

"Because I'm working?"

"Yeah. You're doing the convention, right?"

"Good memory."

"What are you doing?"

"Can't say. I doubt this is a secure line."

"Point made. They using scanners on cell phone calls?"

"E, you know I can't answer that."

"Listen, I need your help and I need it now. You trusted me in Key West and I need that now."

Duncan thought back to their joint adventure during the heist of Mel Fisher's treasure and how the pieces came together at the end. "Okay, what do you need me to do?"

"Leave your team and meet me."

"How did you know I'm on a team?"

Moore smiled. "You guys usually work in teams. Give them some excuse."

"Where do I meet you?"

"My favorite Simon and Garfunkel song. Remember it?"

"Oh yeah," Duncan began to sing, "Hello Mrs. Robinson..."

Moore interrupted him. "Stop it, Sam. Now is not the time for games. Do you remember it?"

"Yes," Duncan answered sheepishly as he recalled the Bridge over Troubled Waters. "But, I need more information. There are a lot of them here." He thought about how many bridges were in Cleveland.

"I'm across from where the team hangs out. I took you to it a few years back."

"Got it," Duncan said as he realized that Moore was under the bridge across from Bob Golic's Grill. "See you in about fifteen minutes."

"Thanks, Sam."

"E, this had better be more important than what I'm doing now."

"Sam, it is."

The two disconnected and Moore turned to Benson.

U.S. Government Electronic Surveillance Center McLean, Virginia

"Sir, I may have something?"

The team supervisor walked to the analyst's workstation. "What do you have?"

"Listen to this?" The analyst replayed the cell phone conversation, which he had just monitored.

"Cryptic," the supervisor said when the message ended.

"Yeah, that's what I thought. Got my attention."

"Can you pinpoint it?"

"I believe so." The analyst began entering several keystrokes as the supervisor observed. Within the last few hours, the Secret Service had requested them to be on full alert for any suspicious phone calls, incoming or outgoing cell calls, at the Cleveland Convention Center. With the President's renomination acceptance speech that evening, everyone was on edge.

"Here we go. One cell phone is in the Convention Center. The other is near the intersection of West 9th and Lakeside Avenue."

"Trace the ownership," the supervisor instructed as he began to nervously clasp and unclasp his hands.

"The one in the Convention Center is classified."

"Must be one of ours then. Who's the other?"

"It's registered to a Steve Rassmussen in Lexington, Ohio."

"Who's he?"

The analyst entered a few keystrokes. "Train engineer."

"Okay. May be nothing, but I'm reporting it." The supervisor returned to his desk and began to send a message to the Secret Service command post at the Convention Center. He also forwarded the message and the data, which they were able to identify. "We'll let them make the call for the next step," the supervisor said to himself as he hit the send key.

Presidential Protection Detail Command Center
Cleveland Convention Center

Taggart was fuming as he reviewed the report from McLean. They had come so far with their plans and he couldn't have it thwarted at the eleventh hour by Moore, who had been so successful in slipping through their security nets. He looked at the report one more time before speaking to his aide. "I want SWAT teams sent to that area. Shut it down and cordon it off! Transmit Moore's and Valero's photos to them. There should be three of them!"

"Do you have a photo for the third?"

"No!" Taggart snapped angrily. "And I want to know who that classified number belongs to. It may be one of our own, but I want to know. I'll get the President's approval if we need it."

Taggart's stress level had been building. This was the fourth report of suspicious activity within the last hour. He was becoming edgier as the time neared for the President to accept his renomination. He wasn't sure what he would do if Benson was able to go public. He had one ace hidden up his sleeve to help prevent that, but it hadn't been played yet. He was concerned that this sticky situation could get stickier.

The aide turned back to his workstation and quickly passed along the instructions.

"I'll be with the President in the Blue Room," Taggart said as he stormed out of the room. "Keep me apprised of what develops."

"Will do," the aide responded.

Across from Bob Golic's Grill
Lakeside Avenue

ぐ∕ふ

The three men watched as a Police SWAT vehicle slowed as it approached Bob Golic's Grill. The driver's window was down and he paused to shout greetings at two young women, who were just walking into its entrance. They laughed and waved back at the uniformed driver whose head then turned to the right.

He looked under the bridge and saw a figure emerge and wave at him, then retreat back under the bridge. Hiding from the eye in the sky, the driver mused to himself. He was well aware of the capabilities of the NSA's Eagle surveillance satellites. He drove under the bridge and parked the vehicle.

Sliding open his door, he jumped out and greeted his friend. "Okay, E. Give me the down and dirty. What kind of mess do you have yourself in?"

"I'd rather talk inside the back of your vehicle. We'd all feel more secure there."

Duncan looked from Moore to Valero to the third man, who was wearing a ball cap and sunglasses. "Okay, if it will ease your anxieties. Follow me."

The three followed Duncan to the rear of the vehicle and climbed in after the door was opened. They settled on the benches along the wall and waited as Duncan climbed in, pulling the doors shut behind him.

"Okay, what's this all about?"

Moore looked at Benson and asked, "Why don't you remove you ball cap and sunglasses?"

Benson did as was requested. Duncan's eyes bulged. "What are you doing here? You're supposed to be in the Blue Room. I heard you arrive." Duncan turned his head to Moore. "Okay, what gives?"

"It's simple. The one at the convention is an imposter. He's a double."

"But, Taggart is there and all the Secret Service guys plus the Vice President. Certainly they would know that they have an imposter."

"Taggart's in on it!"

"What? Taggart?" Duncan's eyes bulged again.

"And the bigger problem is that we don't know who else is involved. Let me give you a quick summary of what's happened over the last couple of days."

When Moore had finished, Benson spoke. "Sam, we need your help to get into the convention. Our plan is to appear when the imposter starts to give his acceptance speech. We need you and some of your SWAT guys, who you trust, to provide me with security until we can determine who the good and bad guys are."

Duncan thought for a moment. "You just can't walk in. They'd stop you and call you the imposter. They could have someone take you out."

Benson nodded his head.

Duncan continued as he looked at his watch. "We don't have much time. There's a little shop over here on West 6th where I can get you the very barest of disguises. But it might work. We can set this up for what people would expect to see and sometimes that works."

"Let's give it a try," Benson said. "Emerson has done a nice job in getting us this far. I'm anxious to get this over with and confront them, especially Taggart!"

"We'll do our best," Duncan said as he opened the rear doors and stepped out.

"Thanks, Sam," Moore said to his friend as the doors were being closed.

"The things you get me into!" Duncan said as he shut the door. In seconds the vehicle was moving.

Five minutes after they left, three police cars parked in front of Bob Golic's Grill. Officers emptied out of the cars and began to search the immediate area. In their hands were pictures of Moore and Valero.

Parking Garage
Cleveland Convention Center

The two police officers watched three costumed convention delegates as they approached the garage entrance. They were wearing white cowboy hats and western style apparel. They waved signs for the Benson/Moran ticket as they walked unevenly. Apparently confused from early bouts of drinking, they were going to try to access the convention by going through the parking deck.

One of the police officers stood and began to approach them to direct them toward the delegate entrance. He hadn't taken two steps when the sound of screeching tires grabbed his attention.

Both officers turned and watched as a SWAT truck turned abruptly into the parking garage entrance and drove through the gated entrance. The two officers withdrew their guns and ran warily towards the vehicle.

Behind them, the back up team, who had been observing the activity from their parked van, called in a quick report. They then began to approach the SWAT truck. Their weapons were also pointed at it.

As the alarm spread, other law enforcement officers began to run towards the area.

With their attention diverted, no one noticed the three delegates walk through the pedestrian entrance to the garage and turn to their right. A Secret Service agent, who had been guarding the elevator entrance, bumped into the lead delegate.

"We made a wrong turn. Which floor is the convention floor?" the lead delegate asked.

"Two," the agent replied as he hurried by after giving the wayward delegate a quick glance.

"Thanks. Re-elect Benson," he chanted three times as he pushed the button at the elevator and the doors opened.

The three men stepped inside.

"Yes. Re-elect me," Benson said as he began to remove his sunglasses.

"I'd keep those on if I were you," Moore said as the elevator began to ascend to the fourth floor where the Blue Room was located.

Meanwhile, the law enforcement official, who had rushed the SWAT truck, was watching as the driver emerged with his hands in the air. "Accelerator stuck," he explained apologetically.

One of the police officers looked over the uniformed SWAT team member in front of him. He saw that he was armed. "I need to see some identification."

"Sure. I'm Sam Duncan," Duncan said as he pointed to the identification tag, which was hanging from a chord around his neck. "I'm on special assignment for the convention."

"Anyone else in the van?"

"Nope. Just me," Duncan replied.

"I'll take over here," the Secret Service agent, who had been guarding the elevator, interrupted. "A couple of you check the van and make sure it's clean." Turning to Duncan, he asked, "And, who are you?"

Three police officers rushed to the van and searched it throughout. "Looks clean," one called back.

Duncan responded to the agent, "Sam Duncan." He removed the lanyard with the attached ID badge from around his neck and handed it to the agent. "The accelerator stuck as I was turning into the garage. I didn't mean to cause any alarm. We've got enough to keep us busy."

"I've got to call this in just the same and get it cleared," the agent said as he radioed the command post at the convention and provided the details. "You're just going to have to hang out here for awhile until you're cleared. It's all protocol."

"Oh, I understand that," Duncan grinned as he looked toward the short hallway, which led to the elevator. Mission accomplished, he thought to himself.

The agent's radio responded with a question and the agent turned to Duncan, "Where were you heading?"

"There's a SWAT team on the top floor of the parking garage. I was joining them," Duncan replied. One advantage, which he did have, was that he knew where all the SWAT teams were stationed.

The agent nodded and radioed in the response.

Presidential Protection Detail Command Center
Cleveland Convention Center

"Better let Taggart know about this," the agent in charge said as he reviewed the reports coming in. "Check all of the monitors from ten minutes before the garage incident to now. I want to know if you see anything suspicious before I see Taggart."

A couple of surveillance technicians rewound to the approximate time and then scanned the monitors. Within a few minutes, one commented, "I've got something."

"What is it?"

"Three cowboy delegates and one's wearing sunglasses."

"Show me," the agent-in-charge said as he leaned over the technician's shoulder. "Why would someone be wearing sunglasses at this time of evening?"

The technician played the video at slow speed.

"Can you zoom in on these other two?" the agent-in-charge asked.

"Sure can." The technician began making adjustments and two faces appeared.

"That's Valero," the agent-in-charge exclaimed as he recognized his teammate. Holding up the photo of Moore, he confirmed his suspicion. "And that's Emerson Moore!" Thinking quickly, he gave instructions to the technician, "Zoom in on the elevator and tell me what floor it stopped at."

While the technician adjusted his controls, the agent-in-charge called Taggart.

The Fourth Floor
Cleveland Convention Center

"And how do we get from the elevator to the Blue Room?" Benson asked as they approached the fourth floor.

"That's where I need our collective thoughts," Moore said. "Maybe, we could have Kenfield take the lead and walk us down to the Blue Room."

"Not sure that I'd get very far with everyone looking for the three of us. They know I'm with you," Valero pushed back.

"Yeah, but they don't know if you are with us willingly or unwillingly."

"That's lame, Emerson," Benson said firmly. "Listen, you've done an outstanding job in getting us this far, but now I'm exercising Presidential privilege." Benson saw the clouded look appear on Moore's face. "Emerson, it's my turn and I'm going balls out down that hallway to the Blue Room and demand explanations."

"But you don't know who you can trust," Moore pleaded.

"No, I don't. But, we are now in the Convention Center for my acceptance speech and I'm taking over all responsibility to finish this." Benson threw his sunglasses to the elevator floor. "I am done hiding and running." The sunglasses were quickly joined on the floor by the cowboy hat. "I'm going to count on there being good people here, who will do what their President requests."

"I'm not sure that this is a good thing, Mr. President," Valero hedged. "You could be whisked away into a side room and detained. The halls will be filled with Secret Service."

A smile crossed Benson's face. "I'm willing to take the risk that many of those good people don't know that I have a double who is going to try to stand in for me tonight. I'm going to take that chance. Being President is never filled with certainty. There are risks and this is a big one."

"It could be your biggest," Moore murmured.

"Yes, it could. And I'm willing to take it!"

Valero and Moore looked at each other. They both realized that it would be futile trying to change Benson's mind. In unison, they both threw their white cowboy hats to the floor to join Benson's.

"Here we go." Moore muttered as the doors opened.

Benson took the lead, stepping confidently from the elevator door where he was greeted by the surprised looks on the faces of two Secret Service agents.

"Mr. President," one greeted him as Benson nodded and began to stride down the hall to the Blue Room. Hearing a scuffle behind him, Benson stopped abruptly and saw the two agents trying to detain Valero and Moore.

"What's the meaning of this?" Benson demanded.

"Sorry, sir. We've been given instructions to take these two gentlemen into protective custody."

"Protective custody, my ass!" Benson stormed. "Release them. That's a directive from your President!"

Releasing Valero and Moore, the agents did as they were ordered.

"And when I turn my back, I don't want you radioing that I'm here or, for that matter, that Moore and Valero are here. Do I make myself clear?"

"Yes," the two agents replied almost in unison.

Benson turned and began to once again stride toward the Blue Room. Moore and Valero walked briskly on Benson's heels.

The Blue Room
Cleveland Convention Center

In the Blue Room were the Presidential double, Benko and Taggart. The double had been practicing his acceptance speech. Taggart was on the radio.

"They're in the building!" he exclaimed in disbelief. His back was to the door and he failed to see it swing open.

"To be more specific, we are not only in the building, we are in the Blue Room," Benson said firmly.

Valero and Moore followed him into the room. As Valero closed the door, Moore produced a .45 automatic, which Duncan had slipped to him in the SWAT van. Duncan had also provided Valero with a weapon. Moore released the safety and pointed the weapon at Taggart, who ended his radio transmission.

"Would somebody like to give me an explanation as to what's going on?" Benson looked from the double to Benko and then to Taggart. "Why don't you start? What is the meaning of all of this subterfuge?"

"I don't need to answer that question."

"You will and I demand an answer right now," Benson fumed.

"I'd answer him if I were you," Moore added.

Taggart had an evil look in his eyes when he turned his head toward Moore. "You know, Emerson, I thought you were a pretty smart guy."

Moore just stared at Taggart.

"But you certainly didn't connect all the dots on this one, did you now?"

Moore didn't respond.

"Moore, have you ever played chess?" Taggart asked.

"Some."

"Then, you know what it's about."

"Strategy."

"Exactly."

"You're going to be our patsy."

"What?"

"That's right. You're going to be our patsy. Go ahead, Valero, tell him."

Moore turned to look at Valero and saw that Valero had pointed his weapon at Moore. "You'd better drop your weapon, Emerson."

"You're in on this?" Moore gasped.

Valero didn't respond.

"I'm stunned, Kenfield." Benson said as he realized that everything was falling apart. His face began turning gray as the blood left it.

"But, you were helping us!" Moore said, perplexed.

"Not so much helping you as going along for the ride to make sure Benson didn't go public."

Moore asked, "I don't get it. Why did you help us by cutting out the tracking device from the President's arm?"

"Couldn't have two Presidents running around, could we?"

"I guess not. But I still don't get it. You could have ended the chase at anytime, but you didn't. Why?" Moore's eyes drilled into Valero as he searched for an answer.

"Taggart knew that I was tagging along with the two of you. I left a note in the boat at Lakeside Marine."

"Kenfield, I am totally shocked by your action, but more importantly by your disloyalty to the President of the United States," Benson interjected.

"These things do happen," Valero said as he shrugged his shoulder.

Moore sensed there was more to it and that Valero was holding back, but he didn't know how to get it out of him.

"I didn't know Valero was in on this!" Benko said angrily as he looked at Taggart.

"I don't tell you everything," Taggart replied stonily.

"Apparently."

Moore asked a question. "Taggart, did you have anything to do with the murder of the two people at the Park Hotel? One was an agent of yours by the name of Sorenson."

One of Taggart's lips curled. "I guess it doesn't matter if I tell you. You've already figured out that your future will be over shortly. It was Benko. Sorenson was too good of an agent and too close to Benson. We couldn't take a chance of him interrupting our plans. He was set up and went for the bait."

Taggart stared at Moore. "Now, I have a question for you."

"Yes?"

"That was pretty clever of you in having a sniper in place to protect you. How did you know to get that set up and who was the sniper?"

"Funny thing about that is that I don't know. I had nothing to do with it and I'd like to know myself. What's the comment about the patsy mean?" Moore asked Taggart.

"Like Valero said. We can't have two presidents running around."

Before Taggart could continue, the door opened and Vice President Jimmy Moran entered. His eyes swept around the room and landed on Benson. "I'm surprised you made it this far."

With a look of shock, Benson stuttered, " JJJJimmy, you're in on this?"

A look of glee filled Moran's face. "Of course, I am. Every good plan needs a mastermind in order to make it succeed," Moran beamed.

"It hasn't succeeded yet because this plan had a master moron driving it!" Moore interjected.

Moran's head shifted quickly toward Moore as he exploded with a string of expletives. Calming, he continued, "You're such a smart ass, Moore. Think you're cute coming up with the tag Vice President Moron. Picked up by all the media and it's been dogging me since. Let me tell you one thing, Mr. Know-it-all reporter. If there's a moron in the room, it's Mr. Emerson Mooreon!"

Moore shook his head from side to side at the asinine comments from the Vice President. Deciding to redirect the conversation, Moore asked, "So, you put this whole thing together? The double, the switch, getting rogue Secret Service agents to help you?"

"It took months of planning and figuring out who I could trust."

"And the double? Any connection to the murder of the plastic surgeons in France?"

"I am impressed. You knew about that?" Moran asked.

"I was aware, but didn't tie it in until just now." Moore looked at the double. "How did you find this guy?"

Moran was relishing his moment of glory. "He's a Hollywood impersonator. I saw him at one of the smaller clubs in Vegas and had him approached. Then it was off to France for surgery to make him look more like Benson and then lots of coaching and practice on how to act like the President."

The look-a-like President chimed in. "Yeah, they're going to announce tomorrow that this was a huge hoax pulled on the American people and government agencies so that they can see how loose our security is."

"Is that what they told you?" Moore asked with a raised right eyebrow.

"Yes."

"You, sir, are very naïve. Doesn't it make you think for one minute that there's more to this? They've already killed two doctors. You've already jeopardized our nomination process by naming Moran as the running mate for the second term. Who authorized you to do that?"

"The real President. Mr. Benson." The double looked at Benson.

Moore turned and looked at Benson. "Did you authorize him to act on your behalf?"

Benson's lower jaw protruded as he responded. "I didn't authorize any part of this charade. I have no idea what would make you think you were acting on my behalf."

Moore looked at the double. "Care to comment?"

"Taggart delivered all of the messages for Benson."

"And you believed him?"

"Maybe not so much now after hearing all of this."

"You are naïve!" Moore looked at Taggart and Moran as his mind raced through scenarios, which may have been part of the plot. "This is a plan to keep Moran as the running mate."

"Very good," Moran beamed. "I was confident that Benson was going to drop me from the ticket."

"I was," Benson agreed.

"I knew it! That's why we had to be sure that I was renominated on the ticket with you."

Moore continued with his hypothesis. "Once you were renominated, there would be no need for the President to remain alive, right?"

"You're getting ahead of yourself, Moore," Moran said, surprised by how quickly Moore was putting two and two together.

"But why would you want to run the risk of the double doing something stupid in the re-election process or during the debates? Especially during the debates where he could never be ready to impersonate Benson to the full extent he would need to."

"Very astute, Moore," Moran said in amazement.

"So, what were you going to do? Assassinate the Presidential double? You were already going to have to kill the real President."

Moran looked at the double whose face was now filled with fear as he realized what had been in store for him. A sinister look filled Moran's face. "Again, very astute. And I guess, I can tell you since our plans are now going to have to change. Yes, the double would have been assassinated. We expected that the grief and hysteria would help overcome some of this nasty organized crime link junk I've been fighting. The assassination would have been timed to take place before the first of the Presidential debates."

Glancing at the double, Moran continued, "There's no way he'd ever be prepared to handle the debate. Good catch on your part, Moore. I'll give you that."

Moore didn't respond.

Continuing, Moran said, "I would have moved up to President and selected my own running mate. We would have ridden re-election in on the coattails of a nation's grief."

"So now, you're going to have to kill Benson and the double," Moore pushed.

Both Moran and Taggart had evil looks on their faces.

"And, to make sure nothing happens, you're going to have to kill them both tonight!" Moore said as he pushed his conclusion.

"Not quite right," Taggart grinned.

Everyone in the room looked at Taggart.

"Slight change in plans. You're going to kill them both tonight. You're our patsy, remember? And like Oswald, we'll take you out, too. You'll be the lone assassin," Taggart smirked.

"Good idea," Moran concurred. "We'll play on the convention's sympathy right away. I'll become President now!"

"And what about the double's body?" Moore asked.

Taggart just nodded to a large chest on wheels in the corner. "Like Valero said earlier, we can't have two presidents running around."

"And how do you feel about all of this?" Moore asked the double.

Shaking his head from side to side, the double answered, "This isn't what I signed on for. I've made a mistake." He took a step toward the door. "I've made a big mistake." With that he sprinted toward the door.

Taggart produced his weapon and shot the double through the chest. At the same time, Benko pointed his weapon at Benson and began to pull the trigger. To everyone's surprise, Valero instinctively threw his body in front of Benson and took a bullet in his left lung. Simultaneously, Valero fired. His weapon sent a round into Benko's forehead, killing him instantly.

As Taggart's weapon began to swing around to point at Benson, Moore, who had retrieved his weapon from the floor, began firing. Several rounds caught Taggart squarely in the chest, knocking him to the floor and killing him as Taggart's weapon discharged harmlessly.

As the din in the small room subsided, Moran surveyed the results. Four bodies were on the floor. Benson and Moore were now kneeling over Valero. Moran walked over to Benko's body and picked up his weapon. When he looked toward Benson and Moore, he saw that Moore had his weapon aimed at Moran.

"Drop it, Moron," Moore yelled.

"Do as he says," Benson added.

"Not this time, Mr. President," Moran said as he inserted the gun barrel into his mouth and pulled the trigger. Moran's body dropped to the floor, joining the others.

The locked door to the room burst open as an army of Secret Service agents and Sam Duncan burst into the room.

Standing and speaking authoritatively to the agents, Benson instructed, "Everything's under control. Give us a moment and we'll explain. And get a doctor in here for Valero. He saved my life!"

Benson knelt back on the floor where Moore was talking to Valero. "I don't get it. Why did you do that?"

"I'm curious too as to why you went along with this. You could have stopped this before we escaped from the Castle." Benson added.

"Or when you helped me return to Gibraltar Island in that trash container," Moore chipped in.

With drops of blood gurgling from his lips, Valero responded, "I wasn't 100% sold on Taggart's plan. I guess that's why I helped you escape. And I didn't know all the details until tonight. Then, it came down to what I've been trained to do and that's to protect the President. I did it without thinking for one millisecond." Valero paused as he groaned. "There's one more thing."

"What's that?" Moore asked.

"Neither you nor the President gave up. You were determined to get here. That determination and the way you improvised on the fly, as you tried to do the right thing, probably influenced me more than anything else to help me make my decision. It was all affecting me subconsciously and I didn't realize it until Benko tried to take out the President. I'm sorry I wavered and let you down, Mr. President."

Benson patted Valero's head, "What's important Kenfield is that you made the right decision at the end. I thank you and the nation thanks you for doing the right thing!"

"Let us through," the EMT's yelled as they pushed aside Benson and Moore to examine Valero. A doctor entered the room and joined them.

"Is there a room here where we can talk?" Benson asked.

"Yes, across the hall. We've got a meeting room."

"Let's go there," Benson said as he exited the room. "Where's Jon Hertrack?"

"Right here, Mr. President."

"Good. We're really going to need your help on this," Benson said as they walked into the room and he stood at the end of the table. "Now, I'm going to give a two minute update as to what has transpired here and then we're going to talk about what we're doing with tonight's convention."

"Hertrack?"

"Yes?"

"Have someone get a message to the convention floor that everything is under control and that I will be appearing shortly."

Hertrack's fingers flew across his laptop as he e-mailed a message to one of his associates near the convention podium. He hit the send key and directed his attention to the President, who was appreciatively sipping a cup of black coffee, which had appeared magically.

"Tonight, this needs a shot of whiskey in it." Benson set the cup on the table and looked at the room, which was now filled with senior agents, advisors and other staff members.

"Is Sam Duncan in the room?"

"Back here," Duncan yelled.

"I'd like you to join me here and bring a few of your SWAT team buddies with you."

Duncan and several of his team members made their way to the front of the room. "This will come as a surprise to many of you and, especially, to Sam, whom I just met earlier tonight. Folks, I'm putting Sam in charge of the Presidential Protection Detail on a temporary basis." Benson looked at Duncan. "You okay with that?"

"Whatever you need me to do, Mr. President," Duncan responded in a shocked tone. Out of the corner of his eye Duncan saw Moore grinning at Duncan's new assignment.

"Good. Folks, the reason I just took that action is that the Secret Service, which we have taken so much pride in, appears to have several rogue agents in it. These rogue agents were involved along with Vice President Moran to wrestle the Presidency away from its legitimate holder. They were going to accomplish this by assassinating my double and me.

"You'll note that the Blue Room is littered with bodies. They are Vice President Moran, who took his own life, Agents Taggart and Benko, who were part of this plot, and my double, who they killed when he attempted to flee. Agent Kenfield Valero took a bullet for me and saved my life. It appears that he may have been involved on the fringes with the plot, but had a change of heart when it counted. He was wounded and is receiving medical attention. We should keep him in our thoughts and prayers for a speedy recovery. I'm sure that he will bring quite a bit to light.

"The reason I've appointed Mr. Duncan here to his new role is to provide me with protection. I'm going to ask the Justice Department and the FBI to conduct an investigation of this take-over plot and to identify any other rogue agents who may have been involved. I know the service is filled with many fine and dedicated agents, but we must get to the bottom of this. If you have any suspicions, I want them turned in to the FBI. Do we have in the room the agent-in-charge of the FBI's Cleveland office?"

"Here, sir."

Benson saw an uplifted hand. "And your name is?"

"Ricker."

"All right then, Mr. Ricker. We're going to need your team on site immediately to start with the Secret Service agents, who are here. Mr. Duncan and his SWAT team will monitor all agents at the convention.

"Now folks, I'd like to clear the room. I need to prepare my remarks for the convention. I need the following folks to stay. Duncan, Moore, Hertrack..." Benson rattled off the names of several political advisors and those not named filed out of the room.

After the room emptied, Benson looked around at the small team in front of him. "Folks, we have some serious work to do in a limited amount of time. I need to address the convention."

The Main Podium
The Convention Center

A figure emerged from the curtains and approached the podium. It was Jon Hertrack. He looked over the crowd before he began to speak. There was a strong sense of uneasiness on the convention floor. The conventioneers were rattled by the rumors, which had been sweeping the floor over the last hour. Reports of gunshots and an attempted assassination of the President had filtered down to the attendees.

"Ladies and Gentlemen. There have been a series of unexpected events, which are going to have us do things a bit differently. To further explain what all of this means, I'd like to introduce to you our President, Richard Benson."

Benson, still wearing his western style cowboy suit, walked briskly to the podium as pandemonium broke out on the convention floor. It was a mixture of relief at seeing the President unharmed and excitement to hear his upcoming acceptance speech. The bedlam from each of the state delegations mixed in with the frenzied discussions by the media when they saw that Vice President Moran had not appeared to introduce the President. They also noted that a number of armed SWAT team members had taken positions below the podium and along the wall of the area behind the podium.

"Thank you. Thank you very much," Benson said in acknowledgement. But the crowd continued their rally.

Benson tried on several more occasions to speak, but the crowd would not stop. Finally the crowd stopped and settled in to hear Benson's acceptance speech.

"Thank you all for your graciousness and support. I am very pleased to be here tonight. In fact, most of you have no idea how appreciative I am to be here tonight. What started out a few days ago as a trip to Gibraltar Island to get an update on this massive fish kill issue has taken so many twists and turns that it could be fodder for a good novel.

"Never in the history of party politics and national conventions have there been events like those which have transpired over the last several days. These unprecedented events rattle the core of our nation and the fabric of what it was built upon. Folks, there has been a plot to seize control of our government by assassinating me."

The already quiet convention floor became even quieter.

"There were a number of factions involved with this and I have ordered the Justice Department and the FBI to start an immediate investigation. We will identify each and every wrongdoer who was a part of this plot to assassinate me. Rogue agents from my Protection Detail were involved in this plot."

A gasp filled the convention floor as Benson revealed the assassination plot.

"We've identified several of them and are running an investigation on others as we speak. You'll notice that we have a few SWAT team members evident." He paused as he looked over his shoulder at the uniformed personnel and chuckled. "But then again, it would have been hard for you to have missed them."

Nervous laughter greeted Benson from the convention floor.

"For the interim, I've appointed this team as my personal protection team. Sam Duncan, who served this country well as a NAVY SEAL and was working with the Protection Detail team in Cleveland for this event, will lead the team for now."

Benson spoke slowly as he prepared to make his next announcement. "I am sorry to say that it appears that the lead plotter was Vice President Moran."

An audible gasp filled the convention floor at the shocking news.

"When we tried to take him into custody, he committed suicide," Benson said slowly as the crowd once again gasped. "We are hoping that the investigation will reveal the plotters' motives although we know that one was to conduct a palace coup and wrestle away the Presidency from me and to place Moran in control. I do want everyone to know, and that goes for all foreign nations who are watching this broadcast, that we do not feel there was any foreign involvement in this plot. Neither do we feel that organized crime was involved. But, let's let the investigators do their job and announce their findings."

From the doorway to the podium area, Moore had been standing with Hertrack and observing the convention's reaction to Benson's address.

"Before I proceed with my dialog, I'd like to bring one person out to stand with me." Benson turned and looked toward Moore. "Emerson, would you join me?"

Moore cringed. He didn't like being in the limelight. He was just as happy blending into the crowd. When it was necessary for him to step up, he would, but it wasn't his preference to stand in the spotlight.

Benson called a second time to the reluctant Moore. "Emerson, come join me." He turned his back as he expected his request to be honored.

Moore slowly walked to the podium as Benson continued. "Folks, this is Emerson Moore from *The Washington Post*. Emerson and I go back a few years."

Benson placed his hand on Moore's shoulder. "I wanted to recognize Emerson and Kenfield Valero, one of my Secret Service agents. The two of them helped me escape from the plotters and creatively found a way to get me here tonight. Mr. Valero couldn't be here at the podium with us right now. You see, he did his duty tonight and in an act of bravery just as he was trained, he sacrificed himself when one of the plotters fired at me."

Another gasp rippled through the convention floor.

"I am pleased to say that Mr. Valero is receiving medical care at the Cleveland Clinic. I spoke with Doctor Michael Rollins and he assured me that Mr. Valero will recover from his wound. Folks, would you join me in giving a round of applause to Emerson Moore and Kenfield Valero?"

The convention hall was filled with the thunderous applause as Benson shook Moore's hand. Moore waved to the crowd and turned to walk away. As he did, Benson commented as he played to the convention, "We need to see if Mr. Moore is interested in a position with my administration."

Moore immediately shook his head from side to side as he walked to the doorway to rejoin Hertrack. He had a couple of experiences with local politics and those experiences convinced him that he'd better stick to reporting.

Once the noise from the convention floor settled, Benson continued, "Now the first order of business for us to address tonight is the now open position of Vice President and my running mate for this fall. I've talked briefly this evening with the Attorney General Linda Deline and conferred with our noble party chairman, David Smail, to make a decision. It's actually the decision, which I had planned to announce before I was kidnapped and the imposter chose Moran last night as my running mate. My selection is Ken Coughlin, Governor of this great state of Ohio."

Pandemonium broke loose on the floor as Coughlin and his family walked through the doorway to join Benson at the podium. As Coughlin walked by Moore, Moore congratulated him. "I was for you from the get go, Ken. Congratulations!"

Coughlin nodded his head. "Thanks, Emerson," be beamed as he walked by, still dazed by the developments of the last hour. When it was announced yesterday that Moran would still be Benson's running mate, Coughlin had resigned himself to delaying his move into national politics. But, all that had changed tonight.

Moore and Hertrack watched as Coughlin went through a brief acceptance speech and Benson followed with his own acceptance speech. The night was going to be filled with relief and serious partying.

"Where you heading?" Hertrack asked as Moore began to walk down the hallway.

"Need to find a cell phone, lap top and a place to sequester myself. I've got a story to write."

"No partying?"

"Work comes first," Moore replied as he felt a surge of energy burst through him. In his mind, he was already beginning to write the opening paragraphs. "Got to go and call in."

Moore disappeared into one of the media rooms. He was on a mission.

Two Days Later
Approaching Gibraltar Island

The Zodiac was sprinting across the water between East Point and the dock in front of Gibraltar Island's Stone Lab. It didn't take more than a few minutes for Moore to rush to meet with Dr. Jeff Reutter at the Lab after he received Reutter's urgent phone call.

Moore tied up the speedy craft at the dock and stepped onto the dock. He paused for a moment to look around the dock and replay the events from a few days ago. This was the first time he had returned to Gibraltar Island since his adventure. He walked past the patch of undergrowth, which was still rustling from the movements of the Lake Erie water snakes. He chuckled to himself as he thought how the snakes had helped him with his escape.

"Emerson!"

Moore looked up and saw Barry Hayen, the publisher of the *Put-in-Bay Gazette*, approaching. "You look a lot more relaxed than the last time I saw you," Hayen beamed as he ran his hand through his thinning gray hair. "And you're clothed," he teased.

"As I should be," Moore replied. "What's up? I got a call from Jeff to get over here as quickly as I could. Think it's about the fish kill?"

"That would be my guess. He sounded pretty excited when I talked with him."

The two men began walking toward the Lab as Moore asked, "Did you hear about Dale McKee?"

"Nothing other than I expect he's up to his eyeballs in lawsuits and insurance claims for crashing that bus into those parked vehicles on the ferry. Good thing those vehicles were empty and no one was hurt."

Nodding his head in agreement, Moore said, "He's getting a Presidential pardon."

"What?"

"Yeah, he's getting a Presidential pardon. Benson felt that he played a pivotal role in distracting law enforcement authorities so that we could make our escape. Benson has the Justice Department working things out with the insurance carriers." Moore didn't tell Hayen that Benson was also pardoning the tug crew for misleading the Secret Service. Lying to federal authorities was a felony.

"Dale will be relieved."

"I bet. I heard that he had doubled his blood pressure medicine since the ferry jump."

Hayen stopped with his hand on the door to the first floor entrance to the lab. "Tell me. The sniper, was it your buddy, Duncan? That's still an unsolved mystery. No one seems to know."

"I don't know. I asked Sam when I saw him if he had anything to do with it and he swore that it wasn't him. He said he was in Cleveland at the time and working with convention security."

"That sure is strange. You get in trouble and someone just happens to be in the right spot to help you out."

"Yeah, but that's how my life goes. I'm very fortunate."

"That, my friend, is an understatement. Somebody up there," Hayen pointed to the heavens, "is watching over you."

"Must be my guardian angel," Moore grinned.

"Seriously, you don't have any idea who the sniper was?" Hayen probed.

"Honestly, I don't. I'm going to walk over to the Park Hotel and scope it out for myself. I'll see what I can uncover."

"Good luck," Hayen said as he opened the door and the two walked into the building. They hadn't taken more than five steps when Reutter's voice boomed at them.

"Good news, gentlemen!" Reutter said as he hurried to greet them.

"You've found the source of the fish kill problem?" Moore asked.

"It's better than that. Here, come with me." He ushered them into the first floor lab room. "Look here. Tell me what you see."

Hayen and Moore looked around the room, which was filled with technical instruments, testing equipment and two dozen large aquariums.

Moore was the first to respond. "Huh, I see perch swimming in about 75% of the tanks."

"Exactly. These fish were gathered from various points around the mouth of the Detroit River. You may recall that the satellite imagery was showing a swath of death which started in that general area."

"Yes," Moore responded as he recalled their earlier meeting.

"They're surviving. The last test, which we took in that area, showed the water contamination level dropping."

"That's great!" Moore said.

"I'll say," Hayen added.

The radio cackled in the hallway outside of the lab door.

"*BIOLab* to Stone Lab. Come in."

"That's John Hageman. He's in the *BIOLab*, taking water samples and netting specimens." Reutter walked to the radio and responded.

"Stone Lab to *BIOLab*. How's it going, John?"

"Jeff, we've had to call the Coast Guard."

"What?"

Moore and Hayen crowded around Reutter.

"Yeah, we made an interesting discovery this morning."

"What did you find? More fish kill?" Reutter asked.

"You're close, at least on the kill part. We found a boat adrift. It's from Grosse Ile. We hailed it, but didn't get a response. So we came along side and boarded her."

"Did you find anyone on board?" Reutter asked.

"Yes, I was just coming to that. We found six open fifty-five gallon barrels in the main cabin. Based on the labels on the drums, it looks like we found our source of contamination."

"What was it?" Reutter queried.

"It read VHS-D1," Hageman replied. "And we found pumps and hoses so that it could be pumped into the lake."

"That explains the fish kill."

"We found two more surprises."

"Oh?" Reutter asked.

"We found two bodies. One looks to be of Arabic descent. The other was a white male. I'm kinda thinking it might be the boat's owner, but that's for the Coast Guard to figure out." Hageman caught movement out of the corner of his eye and turned to look. "And here they come. I'll radio back when we have more info. Over and out."

"Roger." Reutter placed the mike on the radio and turned to Moore and Hayen. "Looks like we may have found our source."

Moore was the first to speak. "So, what does that chemical do?"

"It's actually a virus which kills fish," Reutter responded. "It's probably a derivative of VHS. The D1 on the label is the first clue. Certainly it would be possible to genetically engineer the virus to be more effective against yellow perch. It's primarily a cold water virus and perch are primarily a cool water species. The genetic engineers may have worked to make VHS more virulent in warmer water in addition to trying to make it target perch. And it looks like it worked."

"This bioterrorism stuff is nuts!" Hayen fumed under his breath.

"It's amazing how people are pressured into doing stuff like this," Emerson observed.

"Or, it could have been done in a terrorist-run lab where they work on bioterrorism initiatives." Reutter continued, "I've got to contact Jon Hertrack at the White House. They'll want to stay advised. He sure got a nice promotion out of all this. White House Press Secretary."

"He did and he deserved it," Moore said. "We'll let you make your call and I'll check back with you and the Coast Guard about this news. I'll need to file a story on it."

"Why don't you check back with me in about thirty minutes?" Reutter asked as he started to walk to a nearby office.

"Wonder who killed the people on the boat and who they were working for," Hayen said aloud.

"Me, too." Moore added as he looked across the harbor. "I wouldn't be surprised it if was all linked to Taggart."

Aunt Anne's House
East Point
The Next Day

Moore ended his cell phone call and grinned. Jon Hertrack had called to invite him to a dinner at the White House in three days. It was an appreciation dinner to honor those who had participated in the President's rescue. Hertrack was placing calls to Sam Duncan, the tug captain and his first mate, the bridge tender, the train engineer, Dale McKee the bus driver and the three Wises from the Joseph Wise Fine Clocks in Lakeside. Moore grinned at the thought of the President trying to win over the stoic Joe Wise. Hertrack had also said that they were going to invite Kenfield Valero, if he was ready to leave the hospital.

"Emerson, here's your mail."

Moore took the large envelope from his aunt. As he did, he heard something rattle inside. He looked at the handwriting and didn't recognize it. There was no return address and it was postmarked from Langley, Virginia.

Carefully, Moore opened the envelope. As he did, a spent shell-casing fell out of the envelope and tumbled to the dock's deck. Moore bent over and picked it up before it could roll between the planks and into the water below. It was a casing for a .416 round. He set it on the table next to him and opened the sheet of paper, which had also been inside the envelope.

Moore settled back in his chair and read the brief laser-printed note.

Emerson,

Thanks for believing in me and helping me out of the mess with the PIB police. I returned the favor. I know you've figured out how I did.

Good luck.

There was no signature, but Moore knew who had sent him the letter. And now he knew who the sniper was. It had been Cody Eastwood, but he was going to keep that information to himself. He tossed the shell casing into the bay and tore the letter and envelope into small pieces, which he then threw into the water.

He watched as the water soaked through the paper and took the pieces to a watery grave.

A smile crossed Moore's face as he looked at Gibraltar Island and thought about the events of the last week.

"Oh, Lord have mercy."

Moore spun around to see his aunt returning to the dock. She was waving another envelope in the air as she approached him.

"Emerson, I've got one more letter for you. I dropped it on the way out here."

She handed him the second piece of mail and smiled as she looked at the tranquil harbor, "It's so peaceful out here."

Moore put his arms around his aunt's waist. "There are days though."

Her head cocked to the side as her blue eyes drilled into him. "And don't you do anything to disturb the peace! You caused enough ruckus last week," she admonished him good-naturedly.

"Can't help it, Aunt Anne. Trouble just has a way of finding me."

"Oh, I give up!" she said in mock indignation as she began walking back to the house.

"There's a good Japanese sea monster movie on in about an hour if you want to watch it with me," he teased.

"You're incorrigible!" she yelled as she kept walking to the house.

Moore sat down on the edge of the dock and allowed his legs to dangle above the water as he looked at the front of the envelope. It looked like the envelope had been through the wringer.

It was soiled and had water stains on it. The postmark read Steinbach, Germany. The return address was also from Steinbach and the name shown was Andreas Kalkert, an unfamiliar name to Moore.

Moore opened the envelope and began to read the letter. His eyes widened as he digested its stunning contents. Finished with reading the letter, Moore quickly stood and walked briskly toward the house. He had three items on his mind. First he had to Google Andreas Kalkert. Second, he was going to Google the items referenced in the letter. Third, he was going to contact Kalkert and make travel arrangements to Steinbach to meet with him.

Moore took the stairs two at a time as he raced to his upstairs office and his waiting laptop.

Coming Soon
The Next Emerson Moore Adventure

Sanduste